I0682190

TART VS. SHORTCAKE

A TARTALICIOUS ROMANCE

ROWENA MAY O'SULLIVAN

ROWENA O'SULLIVAN BOOKS

1

**To:** theeditor@drivemenwild
**From:** Madam Delicious
**Subject:** Recipe for your next issue

**Shortcake for your Honey-Pie**
1 basic shortcake mix
1 tray of washed sliced strawberries
1 bowl of freshly whipped crème
1 honey pie (aka girlfriend or significant other)

**Method:**
Place shortcake mix in the cupboard.
Get honey pie naked and horizontal.
Arrange sliced strawberries on honey pie.
Smother with cream and nibble your way to heaven.
No forks required.

GEORGE HURLEY WHISTLED TUNELESSLY, PLUCKED A DEAD pansy off a parched plant, tossed it into the garden, and gave himself a stern talking to while he waited for Charlotte Meyer to open the door.

Get over yourself. Move on.

But his resolve was short-lived when the door opened and there she was. His traitor of a heart thumped in his chest and he wondered whether he would need to call for a medic, because damn it, she glared at him, her eyes filled with recrimination when he'd been, somewhat foolishly, hoping she'd finally come to her senses.

Apparently not.

She wore an apron with a semi-naked cover model on the front and a *Do Not Disturb* sign over the model's penis, but it was the smear of cream with a hint of strawberry parked in the corner of her mouth that revealed everything he needed to know. She had been baking and was eating one of her signature short-cakes. The oh-so-mouth-watering Strawberry Delicious Short-cake. Without him.

"What do you want?" Her eyes were stormy emeralds. "I told you not to visit me at home any more."

She stepped back ready to shove the door closed but he leaned in, using his body weight against the timber. Beating cream and sugar by hand had made her strong and it took all his strength to stop her from locking him out before he'd said what he'd come to say.

Still, knowing he was asking for trouble he swiped at the taunting strawberry, placed his finger in his mouth and sucked it clean. Big mistake. The taste caused him to remember just how delectable, Charlotte, and her baking was. Damn it! He'd missed her like crazy. "You haven't lost your touch."

"Maybe not. But you have." She stepped back into the hall and tried her utmost once more to shove the door closed. She failed. "No touching the goods allowed."

Her cheeks were pink with delectable temper. "You need to learn self-control," she huffed, her wistful tone making him just the slightest bit hopeful. "It's sadly lacking when it comes to touching people you oughtn't."

His vision clouded as he recalled the unique talent she possessed when armed with a few simple ingredients – a talent he had appreciated to its fullest on many occasions.

"Let me in. We have business to discuss?"

"No way," she said. "Cupcake is the lord and master of my domain these days."

Cupcake? His heart sank. Jealousy twisted his gut into a tight, painful knot. "Who the hell is Cupcake?"

Charlotte's lips pursed into a satisfied pout. "He's loyal and dangerous. So watch your words or you'll find a certain part of your anatomy separated by razor-sharp fangs."

She had a new boyfriend called Cupcake and he had fangs? "Who are you dating? A vampire?"

"Cupcake." She glanced over her shoulder and snapped out an order. "Come."

"Subservient as well," he muttered, more to himself than to Charlotte.

Her new love woofed and George heard the scrabble of something scratching her precious polished floorboards. Another woof preceded an enormous, ungainly puppy bounding down the hall to the front door. An out of control avalanche of fur and limbs slid to a halt next to his mistress, his tongue lolling, his jaw drooping in a dopey adoring grin as he leaned his body against her leg.

George hid his relief behind sarcasm. "Give me a break."

Charlotte shot him her *I'll get you* look, and pointed at his nether region. "Attack. Bad man."

George's nether region shriveled a fraction. To his relief the large ball of fluff continued to lean against Charlotte's thigh and peer dotingly up at his mistress.

"Cupcake? He's an Old English Sheepdog! If you want a guard dog, you need to name him something manly like Buster or Fang." He had to admit to himself, the bundle of fur pretending to be a dog was nearly as adorable as his owner.

"Your opinions no longer matter. Tell me why you're here, then get lost."

"It's Sally." He cursed his inability to be subtle. Cupcake growled, sensing his mistress's renewed tension at the mention of Sally's name, and George thought, uh-oh, maybe the dog wasn't so gentle after all.

He took two steps backward. "She wants you to appear as her star guest on Tempting Tarts."

Charlotte gave voice to her obvious horror. "You've got to be joking. That two-timing tart steals my man and now she wants me to... to..."

"Look." George took another step backward when Cupcake's mouth curled back to reveal sharp incisors. "I told her it was a crazy notion and that you'd say no." Damn it. "Need I tell you, yet once again that you've got the wrong idea about Sally and me. She's a sweet girl." He winced at his careless use of words. "Ah... she's...." Damn it.

"Sweeter than me?"

Okay, careful wasn't going to work, and he was fed up tiptoeing around Charlotte's feelings. "Right now you'd turn even the sweetest dessert sour. There is nothing going on between Sally and me. There never was and there never will be."

She snorted her derision, but he'd seen the flash of doubt in her eyes before she pointed at George and issued an instruction to Cupcake. "Attack. Bite off his balls."

His balls instinctively shriveled. "So. I'll take that as a no to Sally's show?"

"Correct." And then she slammed the door in his face.

Better a flat nose than no balls.

2

"BUT I'M SUCH A NICE PERSON." EVERYONE LIKES ME. WHY doesn't she like me?"

From anyone other than Sally, the media-coined Queen of Tarts, their statement would have labeled them with an over-the-top ego. Sally, on the other hand, stated the absolute truth. She was as sweet off screen as the tarts she conjured up on screen each week. Sweeter even, if that was at all possible.

"I never said she didn't like you. She declined your generous offer," George sidestepped. "It's not the end of the world. You're the darling of daytime cooking shows in Seattle. You don't need guests to raise your profile when you're getting enough media attention of your own."

"I'm ecstatic you think so," Sally said. "But Charlotte makes the best shortcakes this side of the universe. Her book *Shortcakes To Live For* is still top of the bestseller lists. That makes six months at number one. Six. She's my heroine. We must have her on the show."

"Regretfully, her answer is a definite no."

Only his business partners, Myrtle and Viggo, knew the reasons behind his breakup with Charlotte. He knew Sally would be horrified to learn Charlotte was convinced she was the reason.

Yes, Sally was talented and gorgeous, but he didn't fancy her in the slightest. Which made for an excellent working relationship. It was fair to say he socialized with Sally outside of work, but that was all it ever amounted to. A meal here, a publicity stunt there. It is true that such acts could be misconstrued as being unfaithful if you believed everything you read. Or lacked trust in your partner. And that seemed to be where Charlotte's issues arose.

Three months ago, a steady stream of articles and photos of Sally with him on her arm had been flashed all over the internet, in society pages of newspapers and gossip columns, with partner-destroying headlines such as "Sally Tempts George" and "Sally's Tarts Are Far Sweeter than Charlotte's."

"If I'm so darned popular," Sally insisted, "I'd have thought she'd jump at the opportunity to promote her book. And what about her cooking schools? Surely a plug for those would benefit her as well."

"She doesn't need plugs of any sort. She's booked solid for the next year with a waiting list that could fill another three." A slight exaggeration, but Sally didn't need to know that. "Besides, she's media shy. She does publicity interviews, book signings and demonstrations under duress. She never wanted to be famous. She only wants to bake."

"Maybe I could issue the invitation personally," Sally mused almost to herself. She picked up Snuggles, her Chihuahua, and cuddled him under her chin. "I'll take Snuggles with me. No one can resist my little darling honey-bun."

He felt the blood drain from his cheeks. "No. Not a good idea." He had visions of Cupcake devouring Snuggles in one bite. He had plans for Sally's career, and sabotage by Charlotte – he was pretty sure that's what would ensue – wasn't included on the menu...ah, list. Sally was set to become America's next best sweetheart. There was interest from more than one major network in taking her show nationwide, and he didn't want Charlotte destroying Sally's promising future over a case of mistaken jealousy.

Sally batted the false eyelashes she wore for her show at him. He could see the cogs in her brain whirling at a thousand miles an hour. "Try again for me, George. I won't take no for an answer."

———————

This time Charlotte's apron sported the image of a big apple positioned dead center of her chest, with a bite out of it. Under the picture in big bold letters were the words, *BITE ME!*

Life could be so cruel.

"What the hell is wrong with you?".

"I'm doing my job." George secured his briefcase in front of his groin in case Cupcake had morphed into a man-eating tiger since this earlier visit.

"And that would be...?" One of her shapely eyebrows arched upward.

A dab of sugar sparkled in the afternoon sunlight on one cheek. He fought the impulse to lick the sweetness off. "Securing you a spot on Sally's show."

"What I really want is to grab Sally's blonde locks and dunk them in one of her tarts," she declared. "But we can't always have what we want. You go tell *sickly sweet Sally* to stick her head in the oven and gas herself."

He cringed. That was low, even by Charlotte's standards. He was gratified to see a flicker of discomfort in her eyes... momentarily.

"She has no idea you dislike her so much." He was in groundhog hell. His deep frustration deepening his voice to a soft growl as he sought to convince her of his innocence. "Damn it, Charlotte. Read my lips." He emphasized the negative just to make sure she got the message this time. "Sally and I have *never*

ever had an affair, and we are *never ever* going to. She also has *no* idea you hate her."

The lure of her cinnamon-encrusted lips was so enticing. A flicker of a thought that maybe, skin on skin would aid the absorption of truth into her mouth and filter through to her addled brain cells. Where the hell was a recipe for trust when you needed one?

Then... eureka. There it was. The doubt in her eyes she couldn't cover up in time. "She doesn't know?"

Exasperation colored his words to an even deeper growl. "Not a clue."

If anything, the confusion in her green eyes, made her appear even more delicious than ever. "How is that possible?"

But George was so over explaining himself. He relaxed his grip on his briefcase, and flexed his cramped fingers. It looked as if Cupcake wasn't going to be called upon to do his duty today.

Charlotte's eyes brimmed with moisture. Jeez. Don't cry. He hated the idea he could make her cry. A gust of wind blew through the narrow corridor between their bodies. Some of the cinnamon and sugar lifted from her cheek and danced in the afternoon light like magic dust before wafting up his nose, whereupon he began to sneeze repeatedly.

While he sneezed away, Charlotte worked up a good batch of indignation. "Three months. Are you so afraid of me you couldn't front up and tell me the truth?"

My God, she was wonderful when riled. The only way to silence her when she got like this was to tug that wild, golden-haired-sugar-coated woman into his arms and kiss her until she was breathless.

His fingers loosened a little more on his briefcase, but a snarl from Cupcake reminded him of how precarious his position was. "You seem to forget I tried. Repeatedly. You've been unreasonable, irrational and insanely jealous of a woman who is as sweet as the tarts she bakes. I'm sorry," he held a palm up when it looked as if she would object, "but that's the truth. You should be baking me one of your shortcakes as an apology."

She looked guilty for all of two seconds. "You didn't care enough to fight for me."

"I've been hoping you'd see reason all by yourself once you'd calmed down." He softened his response by reaching out to her, smoothing a hand over the bare skin of her forearm. Cinnamon and sugar transferred itself to his skin. He resisted the urge to lick it all off. "And yet, here I am, once again, enduring your wrath."

"Because Sally sent you."

She palmed the skin he'd just caressed. Would she do the same if he cupped her cheek? "I'll take any excuse to see you. Even if it means having my balls ripped off by your guard-dog."

He could sense her mind whirling, reaching for more reasons to hold him at arm's length and having trouble finding any.

But then she discombobulated him with her next comment. "I don't believe you should visit me anymore." Her lips trembled and her eyes shimmered with unshed tears.

"You can't avoid me all the time. We have business to discuss."

"Not anymore. You're fired."

He hadn't seen that one coming. "You can't fire me. I'm your agent. We have a contract." Panic rushed like a sharp dart into his heart and wedged itself there. He tensed, waiting for the verbal punch. She looked him squarely in the eye, and he could see she meant every word.

"I have a contract with GVM Media. Viggo can look after me instead."

"Viggo!" God forbid. "He's a number cruncher and a silent partner. He knows nothing about media or publicity. Very few of our clients even know he's my partner, and that's how he likes it. Silent. In the background where no-one can see him."

She leaned down and gripped Cupcake's collar and tugged

him backward into the house. "Well, he's about to get a crash course in agenting."

And the door slammed in George's face for the second time that day.

At least he still had his balls.

3

CHARLOTTE EYED THE DECADENT CHOCOLATE SHORTCAKE IN the large Tupperware container strapped into the passenger seat. She'd baked it especially for Viggo and instructed herself not to eat it or any more sweet things for an entire week. Which was a pity as this meant pretty much everything in the food chain as far as she was concerned.

Viggo tended to come into work when everyone else was about to go home so she'd chosen to visit close to GVM's closing hours. Mentally, she catalogued each day as she made her way through heavy work traffic.

- **Friday (today)**: *Bribe Viggo with shortcake to act as her agent.*
- **Saturday/Sunday**: *Invent new recipe and reply to fan mail.*
- **Monday**: *Cooking School. Teach bunch of people how to bake Peach Delight Shortcake.*
- **Tuesday**: *Concoct raunchy recipe for next month's Drive Men Wild. Something with cherries in it. Attend local bookseller cocktail function.*

- **Wednesday:** *Vet visit. Make meaty treat as apology for vet sticking nasty needles into Cupcake.*
- **Thursday:** *Demonstration at city hotel to leading pastry chefs.*
- **Friday:** *Judge local play center bake-off.*
- **Saturday/Sunday:** *Nothing. Bliss. Heaven. Forty-eight hours to lose seven pounds.*

Having applied her time usefully, she managed to snag a visitor park right outside the front door of GVM. Two minutes later she made her way into reception, placed the shortcake on the counter and checked out her reflection in the stainless steel panels sectioning the wall behind the reception desk.

She liked these panels. They made her look slimmer.

"Is that for me?" Myrtle, the 'M' in GVM who did everything George and Viggo didn't, including reception, vibrated with excitement as she lifted the lid on the box and peeked inside. She groaned, licked her lips and waggled her fingers as willing the tart to magically levitate toward her. "Oh, sweet heaven. Come to mama."

Charlotte tapped Myrtle's hands away. "Oh no you don't. This is for Viggo."

Disappointment flared in Myrtle's hazel eyes. "What for? Why? All of it?"

"Yes, all of it."

"He can't eat that much by himself."

"Big shortcake, big bribe."

Myrtle's eyes lit with interest. "Bribery works. But he still won't need all of this. Come on, Charlotte. I'm hungry."

Charlotte huffed. "Yeah. Right."

"I am. I haven't eaten for hours. I've been slaving away at this desk since early this morning without a break. Just a small piece. He'll hardly notice."

It was a large shortcake. A little bit wouldn't hurt, she

figured. Especially as none of it was going in her own mouth. "Got a knife?"

"Funny you should ask." Myrtle slid open her second drawer and pulled out an enormously large and lethal-looking knife with a bone handle.

Unable to contain her curiosity, Charlotte had to ask, "What else have you got in there?"

"Can't tell you, else I'd have to kill you."

"Go right ahead," Charlotte flung her arms wide then gestured to her heart. "Right here would be the best place."

Myrtle took her eyes off the shortcake long enough to ask, "What's George done now?"

"It's what he hasn't done." Charlotte's eyes narrowed. "He let me believe he had a thing going with Sally all these long months and now I find it never happened."

Myrtle cut herself an enormous slice. Enough for two people in fact. "You need to apportion some of the blame to yourself."

Charlotte was affronted. She thought Myrtle was on her side. "How can you say that?"

"It's the truth. It was you who dumped him for something he didn't do."

Charlotte's backbone crumpled and she felt as if she'd shrunk several inches. "He could have tried harder to explain." But her protest was weak. Myrtle was right of course. The blame was hers.

Myrtle dug into her drawer again and pulled out a plate. "I've got a gun in here too," she said with a wink. "Want me to shoot him for you?"

"You would do that for me?" Charlotte grinned. "Thanks Myrtle. You're a brick. But who would pay your wages?"

"I've got it covered. Viggo's the moneyman around here. I might even get a bonus for a job well done. Plus, if GVM goes bust I could be your media secretary. Solution solved."

She slapped at Myrtle's hand as she went for another slice. "No more. The rest is Viggo's. I intend to sweeten him up and ask him to represent me instead of George. It's obvious affairs of the heart and work don't mix."

Myrtle stared at her as if she'd lost every one of her marbles. "Girl, you've got to be loco. Viggo is a man of the night. Sometimes I wonder if he has a secret life as a vampire. I swear that long black coat he wears has wings."

"You've been reading those books again, haven't you?"

Myrtle tugged open another drawer to reveal several paranormal romance novels. "When I've polished this lot off I'll lend them to you."

Myrtle knew Charlotte's secrets. Including her anonymous identity as the author Madam Delicious, who penned saucy recipes for the men's monthly magazine Drive Men Wild.

"I'm serious," Myrtle insisted. "Viggo doesn't possess a single particle of marketing nous in his remarkable celestial body. He comes in late, goes home even later and the bills are paid on time. That's it. George does the schmoozing. I do everything else."

It was just as well Charlotte had been repped by GVM for three years now. She knew the score and could advise Viggo on the hop, as it were. "He'll want to represent me when he's tasted my Decadent Chocolate Shortcake."

"Shortcake bribery will work with most people." Myrtle waved her empty fork at Charlotte. "But I'm not so sure it will work on Viggo. He's impervious to female charms." Myrtle leaned forward, her ample breasts resting like stranded balloons on her desk. "Believe me, I've tried a few moves on him without success."

Charlotte spluttered out a laugh. "Possibly because he's your foster brother and he knows you're not serious. No one could miss your... ah... ample charms."

"That's likely to be it. God knows I've wiggled these beauties at him many a time and he's barely registered their presence." Myrtle shimmied her shoulders and her breasts quivered like cupcakes with too much baking powder in them. "These here are lethal weapons."

Charlotte took a step back as if expecting them to burst forth from Myrtle's far too deeply cut top. "I don't doubt it for a second."

Myrtle cut herself another slice of shortcake. "You need a lethal weapon too." She shoveled oozing chocolate into her mouth.

"I have one," Charlotte said sadly. God, she was pathetic. "Or at least I had one once."

"Oooh." Myrtle paused mid-munch. "Tell me everything."

"My shortcakes are my weapons. Especially when he used to eat them while ..." She paused as she pondered on whether she should reveal a bedroom secret to the woman who had been known to tell a tale or two to anyone who would listen.

"Lying down," Myrtle finished for her, giving her an out. She practically inhaled the rest of her slice before speaking again. "Come on girl. I know these things. I read your suggestions in Drive Men Wild every month." She licked her fingers clean, one at a time, while continuing to speak. "It's no surprise to a woman of the world like me. Plus, there's much to be gleaned from the other articles as well. Can't feed them the same sweet thing all the time. Experimentation is key."

Myrtle leaned down and pulled out the last drawer at her desk. Charlotte leaned over the counter and her mouth gaped as she realized just what kind of experimenting Myrtle was talking of.

"I have no desire to handcuff myself to anything or anyone. Even if pink fluff is attached."

"Think of it as candy floss. Variety is the spice of life," Myrtle expounded. "It's a cliché I know, but it's still a fact."

"I do variety," Charlotte protested weakly. "Or... I did. Now I wallow in shortcake alone."

"Well, allow me to wallow in it while you take a moment to drag yourself up out of the doldrums. Where's your backbone? Where's the Charlotte I knew before you started doing the horizontal rumba with George?"

"I lost her somewhere," Charlotte admitted. "But my back-bone is returning."

"Anytime soon would be good." Myrtle helped herself to a third piece.

Charlotte asserted some of her backbone and slapped Myrtle's hand. "Put that back. It's for Viggo."

"I've touched it." The tip broke off and fell onto the desk. Myrtle stuck her finger in the chocolate filling then licked it clean. "Oh, look. I touched it again." She scooped up a portion with her fork and it was gone in seconds. She grinned, a devilish sparkle in her dark eyes. "Wouldn't want to spread germs."

Charlotte rolled her eyes and a chuckle escaped her lips. "You're incorrigible."

"Damn right." The rest of the slice disappeared into Myrtle's mouth.

Charlotte grabbed what was left of the shortcake off the counter. "So, where is he then?"

Myrtle's cheeks bulged like a squirrel storing nuts for winter. She chewed until she could swallow. "He came in early, did something resembling work and then took off."

"You ate half the shortcake and now you tell me he isn't here. You've got some cheek."

Charlotte refused to let her new backbone slump. She'd been all fired up to cajole Viggo into representing her. She stared at the remaining shortcake, knowing she would have to make a new one and come back another time. "Will he be back later tonight?"

Myrtle shook her head. "He mentioned something about heading out for a spot of stargazing. If the sky remains clear, I imagine he'll be out all night."

"What about tomorrow?" Myrtle relieved her of what remained of the shortcake, and she didn't protest.

"Who knows." Myrtle shrugged. "He's a master of now you see him, now you don't."

"You have the same talent when it comes to eating short-cake." Charlotte slung her bag over her shoulder. "I know where he lives. I'll hunt him down if I have to." She wagged a finger at Myrtle. "And as for you, my friend. Be warned. You won't be getting any more shortcake anytime soon."

Myrtle merely laughed and said, "Go on believing that if it makes you happy."

4

VIGGO SAT OPPOSITE GEORGE AT THEIR LOCAL WATERING hole, O'Flanagan's, reading a text from Myrtle. He looked up. "Charlotte was in the office with a big fat bribe. She wants me to represent her. Myrtle's eaten the bribe."

George's spirits sank along with his whiskey to the pit of his stomach, and soured. He tilted his head back to ease the discomfort in his shoulders... but how did one ease the broken heart in his chest?

"You need to be more like me. I'm immune to women in all shapes and forms," Viggo declared. "They're nothing but trouble. Numbers are easier to decipher, and far more predictable."

George slugged back another gulp of throat-burning liquid. "No matter how hard I try, I'm not immune to Charlotte. I adore her."

One of Viggo's caterpillar eyebrows arched. "And thereby making all our lives miserable."

George glared at his foster brother who was also his best mate. If only his silent partner at GVM Media would shut up. "Maybe you *should* rep her."

Shock flared briefly in Viggo's dark eyes. Not even George

and their immediate family knew what went on in that quiet, intense brain of his. George's mother, Alice, used to quote the old cliché *still waters run deep* to George as an explanation for Viggo's preference for a more solitary existence.

Viggo took an appreciative sip of his expensive, top shelf, single malt whiskey. "Charlotte's correct. You're afraid of commitment. Otherwise you'd have been kicking her front door down months ago and protesting your innocence."

George shot Viggo his best fed-up glare and considered accusing him of the exact same problem. "Have you got liquid jelly for brains. I damn-well tried to. Charlotte slammed her blasted door in my face every time." The tip of his nose tingled and he resisted the urge to rub it. "I'm sure my nose is flatter than it used to be."

Viggo laughed. "Here's to flat noses." He tossed back the rest of the liquid in his glass.

"How the hell does anyone understand a woman's mind?"

"The thing is," Viggo lectured in a lazy, measured tone, "women never mean what they say. All the magazines tell us so."

Viggo had worse luck than him when it came to women, so George guessed his view was skewed. All the same he continued to listen.

"Read Drive Men Wild, the one Charlotte writes for," Viggo elaborated. "Not Charlotte's article. I mean the section called Ask Steve. I read it last month. It focuses on how to understand women. It's all there. The upshot is, few men are successful in navigating a woman's mind. They're from another planet. The jury's out on which planet that is. Most say Venus, but I believe it's more likely to be Pluto. It's no longer classed as a planet and it's distant, dark and completely unreachable."

George almost wasted his expensive whiskey down his front. "You read that crap."

Viggo wafted a hand in the air. "I'd finished the monthly accounts and was filling in time while waiting to see if the weather would clear before heading out to the observatory. I spotted the word Venus on the cover and thought it was an article on astronomy."

George just about laughed himself silly, and he ended up having a coughing fit and drawing the attention of those nearby. Eventually, he uttered, "I'm feeling happier already."

"Just stating facts as I know them to be. I won't waste my time with them. Women, that is. Although, Myrtle's hoping I'll learn something and that I'll become more sociable."

It was George's turn to scoff. "She wants you. She's been trying it on since you started sprouting tufts of hair in places other than your head."

Viggo jerked back in mock horror. "She has not. She's at least ten years older than me."

"Two years, mate. Two years, and you know it. She's been waggling those womanly assets at you since she developed them. Just after you came to live with us around your thirteenth birth-day, I seem to recall."

Viggo shot George a warning glare. George knew his friend avoided talking about his life prior to his adoption into their family. "What assets would they be?"

George rolled his eyes in resignation. How could he be so obtuse? "You need to see a specialist."

It was Viggo's turn to roll his eyes. "I'll bite. What kind?"

"One who deals with impotence. There's definitely something wrong with your testosterone if you haven't noticed Myrtle's assets. No one would miss them in a million years."

"She's our foster sister. We might not be blood related, but dating her would be like committing incest. Try imagining dating her yourself and you'll understand where I'm coming from."

George paused for a second, but couldn't bring himself to picture it either. "I get you. But one day you're going to have to set Myrtle straight. What's worse is you don't date at all. There's something definitely wrong with you."

"Just because I choose not to date doesn't mean there's anything wrong with me."

"It's only one piece of your anatomy I'm worried about. It's an appendage that dangles..."

"All right, all right..." Viggo erupted into a deep, chesty laugh. "It's you who's side-stepping the real issue here."

"And that is...?"

"Charlotte."

"I'd prefer to talk about you."

"I don't want a larger profile at GVM," Viggo protested. "I only joined you in this venture on the proviso I remain in the back room and look after the accounts. You do the schmoozing."

"Help me out for a few weeks. Charlotte's career pretty much runs itself," George justified his argument. "She'll soon see how little you know and beg me to take her back on."

"Your confidence in me defies belief."

George got the feeling Viggo wanted to plant a not-so-friendly fist in his face. He grinned. "That's what family does. Back's each other even if they don't completely agree."

"She could defect to another agency," Viggo continued, and George's smile morphed into a scowl. "If news gets out she's fired you, they'll be making moves to poach her soon enough. *Short-cakes To Live For* has had a dream run."

"That's why you must take her on. She's too valuable to lose." Except George wasn't referring to her dollar value and Viggo knew it. No, she was more valuable to him on an emotional level, and he wasn't ready to part with her, but he also knew appealing to the monetary aspect of their business would definitely interest Viggo.

"I know nothing about contracts."

Years of friendship armed George with the knowledge Viggo was weakening. It was all there in his tone, even if his eyes remained guarded. "I'll do the initial leg-work and you can do the rest."

"And the rest consists of...?"

"Setting up and escorting her to book signings, radio interviews, that kind of thing."

Viggo stared glumly into the dregs of his whiskey. He signaled to the waitress for another. "One proviso."

George mentally cheered. "What's that?"

"I'll do it for a week only, if you agree to woo Charlotte back into your arms for all you are worth. The two of you are made for each other."

George's eyebrows arched at the huge admission from Viggo. His brother was a romantic after all. "Charlotte's no pushover. One month and you've got a deal."

"Two weeks and not a day more."

"Make it three. I can't possibly woo her in such a short a period."

"It only took days the first time."

"We didn't have emotional history then. Two weeks is too short a time. Three."

Viggo took another whiskey from the waitress. "Two and a half weeks. Eighteen days."

"What kind of deal is that?"

"The best you're going to get. I've got an astronomy conference in New York at the end of the month and I'm not missing it, even for you."

5

Eighteen days. How the hell was he going to mend his relationship with Charlotte in less than three weeks? George was crazy about her. Always had been, but he hadn't truly realized just how much she meant to him until she'd kicked him out of her house with a sugar-encrusted footprint on his behind all those months ago.

She was bohemian, curvy, unpredictable, and totally delicious in every possible way. How could she imagine he was the slightest bit interested in Sally? The notion to him was unfathomable.

Charlotte was a wooden spoon gal. She creamed butter and sugar like no one else. A memory of her breasts jiggling as she worked industriously in her kitchen filled his head, clouded his brain and turned his thoughts to mush. She gauged everything by smell, taste, and touch. He'd never known baking to be so sexy until she'd served him one of her signature shortcakes in the style of her Drive Men Wild alter ego, Madam Delicious.

George didn't want to lose her, but he was beginning to realize that getting fired wasn't the worst thing in the world to happen. He'd actually considered firing himself more than once, but Viggo's lack of interest in the business other than the red line had always stopped him from asking for help. Viggo was the dark and mysterious type. The brains behind GVM's financial success. Surely nothing would go wrong with him at the helm?

George checked his watch. It was eight in the morning. He held a steaming double shot espresso in one hand for him and a cappuccino for Myrtle in the other – their regular morning order. Putting his back to GVM's front door, he nudged it open, only to discover there was an extra person at work.

Myrtle immediately bellowed at him, "I hope those are for us. Viggo's head is about to explode from lack of caffeine and I'm feeling the need for some myself. My brain is scrambled from his incessant questions."

George gaped as he handed Myrtle her coffee. "What the hell?"

Viggo's arm shot out and plucked the remaining coffee from George before he could protest. "Thanks. I needed this."

"I needed it too," George protested, and attempted to snatch it back, but Viggo's arms were far longer than his.

"I'm teaching Viggo the basics." Myrtle sipped her hot drink, a gleam of mischief in her dark as chocolate eyes. "Don't be such a sad-sack, George. I'll get you another drink in a few minutes." She inclined her head at Viggo. "Believe me, this one needs it far more than you do. Just look at those eyes. They're bloodshot and square behind those glasses."

George had to agree. Viggo looked as if he needed to sleep for a week. "It's Charlotte you're looking after, not the entire business."

"If I do something, I do it well."

"I applaud your keenness, but it isn't necessary."

"He was here when I arrived," Myrtle said, shuffling paper into small piles. "I had to take him under my... uh... wing, and teach him the basics. He didn't even know how to switch the phones from night to day."

George looked at the two of them huddled together like co-

conspirators behind the reception counter. He should have listened to his advisors. Never go into business with family.

Myrtle was stirring the pot and making mischief. "You can have the day off," she declared to George. "I've got things covered."

"We have more than one client," George exclaimed in a burst of peevishness. He turned to Viggo, hardly believing it was true. "How long have you been here?"

Viggo grinned. "Since four this morning. There was a star party up Tiger Mountain. It morphed into a get-together at someone's house afterward. I was pumped and wide-awake so instead of heading home, I came here." He yawned and stretched his arms above his head. "I'll head home for some Z shortly."

"And when might shortly be?" George knew Viggo's version of a get-together was a discussion on celestial bodies… not the ones shaped like women. Plus, he didn't particularly like the feeling of being superfluous to Myrtle or Viggo's requirements.

Viggo stood up, a contract in his hands. He waved it at George. "I'm out of here as soon as this gobbledygook makes sense to me."

George grabbed the sheets of paper and tugged. "This so-called gobbledygook is Charlotte's contract for her next book. I'll take care of it."

"You can't. You've been fired."

"Like I said last night, I'll guide you." George headed toward his office. "Come with me. I'll give you a brief rundown on her current schedule and then you need to go home to sleep and shower. Lesson 101 in agenting. No falling asleep in front of a client and no smelling like you haven't showered in a week either."

Viggo stood and followed George down the hallway toward their office. Myrtle leaned over the reception counter and called out, "I'm perfectly capable of teaching Viggo everything he needs to know. And he doesn't smell."

Both men turned back. Viggo hiked up one arm, and sniffed

and then gave her the thumbs up signal. Then he winked at her. "You've done a fantastic job, Myrtle. Thanks for taking the time to show me the basics."

Myrtle rewarded Viggo with her warmest come-hither smile. Her assets vibrated as she placed a hand over her heart. "Anytime."

"Myrtle," George interrupted and waited until he had their foster-sister's attention.

Myrtle gave him an irritated glance. "Yes, George?"

"Coffee, Myrtle. Get me coffee. Please."

Myrtle's nose lifted a fraction in her version of a snub and said a very rude word before adding, "Get it yourself. I'm on a break."

6

AT ANY TIME OF THE DAY, GREENSPAN STUDIOS BUZZED WITH a frenetic over-the-top energy George thrived on. If he was quick he'd catch Sally before she headed home with Snuggles. The receptionist acknowledged him as he walked through the revolving doors. "Afternoon George."

"Afternoon." He kept walking instead of stopping for a chat as he often did when visiting the studios. One of his very first jobs had been as a man-Friday of sorts for Greenspan. He knew many of the staff well and the rabbit-warren of a building like the back of his hand.

Sally had her own dressing room, signifying to him as well as everyone else, she was *someone*. Other less important personalities shared dressing rooms, but Sally had progressed to one of her own within six months of Tempting Tarts going to air. Two years later, she was the toast of Seattle, garnering attention from many of the bigger networks across the country. If he had his way, she would be the toast of the world as well. It was what Sally wanted and it was why he worked his butt off schmoozing with everyone and anyone, attending events he often didn't want to go to, and networking with people he had no real desire to speak with.

A series of high-pitched barks practically pierced his eardrums seconds before he knocked on Sally's door. A scrabble of paws on the floor and Sally's soft tone gently reprimanding Snuggles confirmed George wasn't wrong in assuming she was still at work.

Snuggles, thank God, was tucked securely under Sally's arm when the door opened. Given the opportunity, the fluff ball, as he preferred to call the dog, had been known to scurry into the bowels of the building, refusing to be found for hours at a time. Hide and seek appeared to be his favorite pastime. On one memorable occasion, he'd, somehow, trotted onto a live set, jumped on the couch, curled up next to a well-known personality, and proceeded to clean his private parts mid-interview.

Snuggles was almost as famous as Sally.

"George. You just caught me but I'm in a hurry. I've somewhere to be."

"No problem. This won't take long and I can walk out with you. Just wanted to provide an update on Charlotte." He redirected Snuggles' nose from sniffing his underarm. That little thing loved dark suspicious places. One day he would knock himself out smelling something particularly odorous.

"Ooooh, Snuggles," Sally cooed. "Does George smell yummy?"

George shot her a withering glance.

"What?" Sally grinned at him, laughter lacing her melodious voice. "He loves it."

"All that cooing to that fluff ball is unseemly."

She let out a short bark of raucous laughter. So unlike the immaculate persona she presented for her fans. "Snuggles loves it." She held the fluff ball's small jaw and cooed, "Who's my little honey-bun, my little snookums?" Snuggles morphed into an excited wiggling dynamo and attempted to lick Sally's face off.

She sent George an all-too-sharp glance. "So what is it that's brought you to see me so late in the day, when a phone call or text would do?"

"Charlotte refused your second offer." He attempted to soften the blow when he saw a flicker of disappointment in her eyes. "She's not keen on appearing on television." This much he knew to be true. She had an aversion to anything making her look ten pounds heavier, and, as she'd told him often enough, television wasn't her friend.

Sally paused, giving him a considered look. "This has upset you more than it has me."

His despair on how his life had turned to shit must be showing. He wasn't going to admit this side of the century, especially to Sally, the reasons behind his breakup with Charlotte, so he said nothing.

But, Sally wasn't going to let him off easily. "I thought you were over her." Her expression softened, the laughter dimming to concern. "But you're not. Are you? You're still in love with her."

"I'm not talking about my past relationship with Charlotte with you." He looked for an escape. "I thought you had somewhere to be?"

She checked her watch. "I do need to get going." She passed Snuggles into his unwilling arms and turned away to pick up a large box George knew she transported tarts in. It looked heavy and he wondered where she was off to. As far as he knew, she didn't have much of a private life outside of work.

"Let me carry that for you." They swapped their so-called parcels.

"You should have told me seeing Charlotte would be painful." A crease appeared between her eyebrows. "Maybe she turned my invitation down because I sent you."

She was too sharp for her own good. "I thought you'd be more upset about Charlotte refusing your offer."

She shrugged, and Snuggles took the action as an invitation to wriggle and lick whatever was within reach. Her head jerked back from his wayward tongue. "If she doesn't want to appear on my show we can't twist her arm."

Damn it! George was immediately suspicious of her swift acceptance. She might have a heart of gold, but this pint-sized woman never gave up anything this easily. He wanted to ask why, but they'd reached the elevator and the door slid open. It was jammed with workers leaving for the day. They both squeezed in and Snuggles licked the bare arm of the closest person before Charlotte muzzled his mouth and softly apologized.

A murmur of "isn't he adorable" and coos filled the confines of the elevator. George rolled his eyes and Sally beamed. Everyone, it seemed, was in love with Sally, and therefore in love with Snuggles by default.

By the time they poured out into the basement parking lot, the opportunity for George to question her about her swift acceptance of Charlotte's rejection had passed.

7

SALLY PULLED INTO A PARK RIGHT OUTSIDE THE FRONT
entrance of GVM. George's unexpected arrival at the studios had
prompted her to take a detour on the way home. She wanted
Charlotte's address and her best bet was Myrtle.

It was sheer luck she had made another test chocolate tart
that afternoon because now she intended using it to loosen
Myrtle's tongue instead of giving it to her neighbor. She'd bake
the old guy another one when she got home because it was his
birthday and he'd been unwell of late. What was a birthday
without cake or tart or something to sweeten the day?

Sally knew Myrtle was a pushover when it came to sweet
anything, and she intended to sweet anything Charlotte's address
out of her.

Her high heels clicked on the concrete as she walked around
to the passenger door and leaned in to pick up her creation. One
leg swung out, and her short lemon mini-skirt slid up to reveal
what she knew was a perfectly proportioned leg. Take advantage
of your assets was a motto she lived by, and she knew her assets
well enough to know she wasn't revealing anything other
than leg.

Hefting the container holding the tart in both hands, she tapped the car door closed with the sole of one shoe and made her way to the front entrance of GVM, before putting her butt to the glass-paneled door and pushing her way in.

Reception was empty. She took a moment to check her reflection in the mirrored paneling. Pretty darn good. She winked, blew herself a kiss and laughed at her own idiocy before heading around to the other side of the reception desk to see if Myrtle's purse was there. Nope. Gone. Darn it.

It was after five, so she accepted the woman had every right to a life outside of work. Just because she, Sally, worked every hour of every day didn't mean everyone else did as well.

But the front door was unlocked. George had mentioned he was on his way home. A door clicked shut. She stood unmoving and listened. Did she just hear a cat meow? Snuggles, his little paws perched at the mouth of her bag slung over her shoulder, emitted a low growl. Sally's eyebrows rose a notch, noting his ears flattening against his head. There was someone here, and it wasn't Myrtle.

If she'd had hair on the back of her neck, it would have stood on end right this second. *Don't be a coward*. It has to be Myrtle.

Placing her bag and the tart on the reception counter, she set Snuggles on the floor. Whoever was here, he would seek them out. Retrieving her bag and the tart, she pursued Snuggles down the hall, his tiny bark loud, his tail, what there was of it, wagging like a metronome, before he disappeared round the corner and out of her line of sight.

She heard a loud screech and a whimper of protest. Rounding the corner, she was confronted by the weirdest looking cat she'd ever seen. It lashed out at Snuggles with what looked like razor claws, in an attempt to scratch out his eyes. Her tiny dog's tail was firmly tucked between his legs, his ears flattened backward and upon seeing her he backed up, retreating behind Sally's legs.

The cat bounded onto a desk and positioned itself atop a pile of paper, its fur frazzled, an expression of what Sally could only surmise as irritation on its face. The cat looked as if it had received a jolt of electricity. It glared down at Snuggles with superiority and Sally laughed out loud. It was the funniest looking feline she had ever seen.

Viggo hadn't heard anyone come in. Apparently he'd forgotten to lock the front door. Clouds had moved in, so he'd decided work would best fill the hours while he waited to see if they would clear enough for him to venture out to do a spot of stargazing.

"Who are you?" Sally frowned, her knuckles white from gripping her bag as if she were about to use it on him as a weapon.

Viggo quickly figured out she didn't know who he was. He was a silent partner after all. "This is my company? If you're going to set your dog on me I should warn you, my cat is fierce and his claws are lethal weapons."

He had never had an occasion to meet Sally in person. Cuter and more sassy than any woman had a right to be, she was a tiny bunch of perfection in a short tight skirt and killer stilettos. The container she carried was almost as big as she was. He sure as heck hoped there was a tart inside it. He licked his lips. His stomach was hollow and the saliva in his mouth increased. He should have eaten something before heading back in to the office. But darn it, he had this unexpected craving to taste not only the tart, but Sally as well.

"This is George's company," Sally protested. "This is his office."

Viggo pointed to the door and the sign on it. "I'm the V in GVM."

Sally stared at the sign for several long seconds before turning back to regard him with what appeared to be narrow-eyed suspicion. "I've never seen you here before."

"Keenly observed." He stood and leaned over the desk, and held out his hand. "Viggo Freedlander. George and Myrtle's silent business partner."

Something resembling a dog snarled from behind Sally's ankles. She didn't rush to shake his hand, so he lowered it, sat back in the swivel chair and waited for her to digest the news.

She looked pissed. "George never mentioned a partner."

"Which is how I like it."

"Well, isn't this an unexpected kink in my universe. I guess you're telling me the truth. You don't look like a criminal. There's no bag of loot slung over one shoulder and you don't appear to be carrying a gun."

He saw one of her eyes twitch. Was she nervous? "I'm going for a more laid-back invisible look myself."

She blinked. "Invisible is one thing you're not, although I can't believe my eyes right this minute." She shoved the container toward him on the desk. "This is for Myrtle. I thought she'd still be here."

He pulled the container toward him so he could prise off the lid. "I watch your show every day." He inclined his head toward the flat screen on the wall, but his focus remained on her. "Occasionally I watch with George, but mostly I'm here in the evenings only."

He witnessed a flush of heat rise up her sternum to her neck and spread to her cheeks.

"So Myrtle's gone then?"

"She has." He eyed the concoction layered with chocolate and raspberries. "She left early. So did George. He did mention going to see you at the studios. You must have missed him." He wondered if the tart had a solid layer of chocolate underneath. He could resist almost everything except chocolate. Especially the rich, velvet smooth, dark, sinful kind. He was sure there was a whole packet of sin in there. "Can I have a piece?"

She shrugged. "If you want. I saw George earlier. It's Myrtle I want." She slipped her enormous bag off her shoulder, dug out a long rectangle case, and placed it next to the tart. Inside was the largest, sharpest knife he'd ever seen.

His eyebrows rose. The tart was bribe material, he surmised. But why the hell did she have a humungous knife in her bag?

As if reading his mind, she said, "I'm a former girl-guide. I'm prepared for every eventuality."

"I'm eternally grateful." He cut himself an enormous slice. "Ah, sweet mercy," he declared seconds later. "Chocolate and berries. A match made in the stars."

There were advantages to being George's silent partner after all. Man, if this tart was anything to go by she deserved every accolade ever made. His eyelids rolled shut and his taste buds soared halfway to heaven. "Delicious," he mumbled, and devoured the rest before speaking again. "AMAZING."

He found himself wondering why he had remained a silent partner for so long. He'd never met Sally. He'd never tasted her tarts. He glanced up at the television. Even her show didn't reveal her true talent, and he admitted to himself he was halfway to being seduced by the larger-than-life personality inside that pint-sized body. She was something else and more and strangely, he wanted a slice of her as well.

He growled a warning when Osiris padded across the desk to sniff the tart. "You won't like it. Chocolate is bad for you."

He broke off a piece of biscuit crust into his palm and held it out to his little companion, who sniffed, let out a distinctive meow before lapping it up and then spitting it back out.

"What kind of cat is that?" Sally inquired. "I've never seen one like it before."

"My guess is Osiris is an Abyssinian crossed with a Persian. I don't really know." He stared pointedly at Snuggles. "What kind of cat is yours?"

She erupted into laughter. "You're joking, right?"

"He's smaller than Osiris, so I figure he's either pretending to be one or experiencing an identity crisis."

"Snuggles is pedigree Chihuahua." She picked him up and

placed him at the other end of the desk. The two animals eyed each other warily from their vantage points.

"Anything that small would have to be. Otherwise what's the point?"

Sally blocked Snuggles' ears. "Don't listen to the bad man."

"Snuggles is lucky no-one has squashed him flat before now."

She released a shocked gasp. "That's nasty."

"Well, look at him. He's so tiny he's practically invisible."

"You could say the same about your cat."

"Osiris has fur, claws and agility."

"Snuggles has a bark and a fierce bite."

"Osiris is loyal beyond belief."

Sally snorted. "Don't you know anything? Cats are the masters of their own lives. Dogs are loyal companions to the very end."

He considered her comment as Osiris licked himself into sensual oblivion. Then he rocked back in his chair and slammed his hand down on his desk. Osiris and Snuggles jolted at the sudden noise. "Damn it. You win."

But the look on her face told him she wasn't finished asking questions. "Why are you a silent partner?"

He shrugged and helped himself to another slice of tart. "George is the one with the schmooze skills. I'm the figures man. I'm more interested in keeping GVM above the red line."

Alarm flared to life in her eyes. "I didn't know GVM was in financial difficulty?"

He belted out another laugh. "Far from it. And all down to my accounting skills and the talent on our books, namely yourself and a handful of others, including Charlotte Meyer of course."

"Speaking of which, that's why I'm here. Charlotte's address. Can you give it to me? I'll let you keep the entire tart if you hand it over."

He studied her until she squirmed and tapped the pointed toe of her stiletto on the tiled floor with, was it guilt, or impatience? "Well?" she finally looked up and asked.

"We don't give out client details. You of all people should know that."

"I want to issue her a personal invitation to appear on my show."

"George has already asked her twice. She said no both times."

"I thought if the invitation came from me she might change her mind."

"I'm not so sure she will. You know the history with her and George. She sees you as the *enemy*."

Sally frowned. "Me? The enemy? What are you talking about?"

Damn it. He'd wandered into sticky territory. All that sugar in the tart must be destroying his brain cells. "That's something you need to ask George."

"I'm asking you. You brought it up."

God help him. It was time George sorted his personal life out. "You stole her man."

Sally's eye's flared in surprise and her mouth opened and closed like a guppy out of water. "I did no such thing."

"I know it. You know it. George knows it. But Charlotte...?" He shrugged, not bothering to finish his sentence.

"Why would she think that? It's ridiculous. Surely George has explained."

"He tried and failed."

"He didn't try hard enough then."

The color in her cheeks bloomed to an adorable pink. Clearly, she was shocked, and was baking herself into a batch of sheer annoyance. "I'm going to fire that useless agent of mine."

Uh-oh. He stood up and came round to where she stood. My God, she was tiny. He attempted to soothe her ruffled feathers. "Not a good idea. George is the best agent in Seattle."

"In that case, you must be too."

"I don't do agent. I do accounts."

"You must have learned a few tricks over the years. How long have you been his partner?"

"Since GVM's inception. But that doesn't mean I know anything about schmoozing."

"Well, you'd better start learning. As of tonight, you're my new manager."

One moment Viggo was nothing but a figures man, and the next he was representing their top two clients. How the hell had that happened? Within hours he'd gone from silent, invisible and uncommitted to vocal, visible and committed, and he wasn't liking it. He barked out a laugh but felt no humor or satisfaction. This was going to play havoc with the way he preferred to live his life. Quiet, ordered, uncomplicated.

He eyed the remaining crumbs on the plate and flicked them onto a napkin, screwed it up and tossed it into the trash. He smoothed his hand down the length of Osiris's back. A purr started deep within the feline and his little friend looked up and released a loud satisfied meow of pleasure.

No longer able to concentrate, Viggo turned off the computer and wandered over to the window and peered outside. Even the weather seemed to be against him. Heavy clouds now obscured a sky beginning to darken as night approached. He'd planned to head to a local park to try out his new telescope, but visibility would be patchy at best. There would be no star gazing tonight.

He glanced at the backpack wedged under his desk, containing a thermos of coffee and sandwiches for his night's vigil. The rich tart Sally had given him had filled his stomach, but it was her delicious self that filled his mind. There was no room left for much else except a dollop of incredulity. He must be drunk on the alcohol he suspected was in the tart. It was the only reason he could come up with for feeling as if he'd been blindsided.

"Come on." He leaned down and hefted his backpack over his shoulder and called for Osiris, who had wandered off somewhere.

Osiris came bounding round the corner, tail upraised, twitching expectantly. The cat had wandered into Viggo's life just under four years ago, and had not left his side since. The feline had conned him with her bedraggled, and sad eyes. Viggo had fed it some cheese from a bread roll and that was all it had taken. He'd gone from an indifferent pet person to a cat lover overnight.

"We're outta here. The weather is against us and George needs to hear the bad news from me. Plus, I'm going to need pointers on how the hell I'm going to manage these two women without shooting myself or the company in the foot."

8

THE NEXT MORNING SALLY USED HER POWERS OF PERSUASION, in the form of a warm custard tart sprinkled with a light dusting of nutmeg, on Myrtle. When Myrtle went to the kitchen to grab plates without locking her screen first, Sally wheedled the details out of the computer in seconds and thanked her mother for insisting she study technology as a backup plan in case she couldn't realise her dream of being a star failed.

Less than an hour later Sally stood in Charlotte's driveway surveying a cottage with picture postcard windows and an old-fashioned front porch.

Smoothing her hands down her best and extremely expensive skirt, she cleared her throat and squared her shoulders. She was about to meet her idol, and wanted to make the best impression possible.

"I doubt she remembers me," she murmured softly to herself as she made her way to the front door.

Knocking four times with her knuckles on the wooden door, she waited. A dog barked and then yelped. Snuggles' head popped out of the doggy bag slung over her shoulder, his little ears alert with interest. Next there was the sound of something breaking and a very loud unfeminine curse coming from within the house.

"Uh-oh." Sally looked down at Snuggles who'd begun to growl. "Maybe we've come at a bad time?"

But it was too late to turn around and leave. The door opened and there she was, Charlotte Meyer, Sally's former idol from school, looking less idol-like than she could have imagined, due mostly in part to the large dollop of pink meringue atop Charlotte's head. It wobbled crazily like a cute hat. Sally stifled a giggle, figuring Charlotte didn't know it was there.

A large dog, also festooned in pink meringue, squeezed past Charlotte, leaving a large smear over her apron. His tongue lolled in a happy, curious manner. He halted a mere inch in front of Sally and looked up hungrily at Snuggles, who peered down at him with interest.

My God, Charlotte's puppy – she thought it was a puppy – was enormous. Sally clutched the doggy bag securely to her side, thinking it was possible he could eat Snuggles for breakfast and not issue a single burp afterward.

Sally looked for dislike, jealousy, any of those feelings one might have when faced with the woman who had supposedly stolen her man. The only thing she could see reflected in her expression was one of astonishment.

Ignoring the pounding in her heart, Sally held out her hand. "I'm Sally Forbes." She tamped down the growing desire to jump up and down and squeal like a groupie. "You may not remember me, but we went to the same high school. I was a few years behind you but you were my idol in Home Economics. Actually, you're still my idol."

Charlotte stared at Sally, her mind all a-jumble. Sally had looked up to her at school. Who knew? Not her, for sure. She also hadn't known Sally was going to turn up at her door looking perfectly bright and shiny and just a tad nervous. She wouldn't have thought Sally was the nervous type.

Charlotte swiped at a blob of meringue on her cheek. She suspected there was more on her head because Sally's eyes flickered upward a few times before pasting on a star quality, shiny-bright smile before looking her square in the eyes.

More importantly, Charlotte had a disaster to deal with. Namely the one in her kitchen. And the not-so-tiny fact she, Charlotte, resembled something Cupcake had dug up out of the garden.

"Can't talk now," she blurted before Sally could say anything else. "Disaster." She spun on the balls of her feet and raced back into the house.

She skidded to a halt at the kitchen door to survey the mess. Cupcake followed. What she didn't expect was for Sally to follow as well.

Sally immediately gave voice to the disaster in Charlotte's kitchen. "How the hell did this happen?"

"Cupcake," Charlotte grunted. "My dog," she elaborated. "I didn't see him behind me, and I fell backward over him. My Strawberry Marshmallow Shortcake flew out of my hands." She looked upward. "How it managed to hit the ceiling defies belief."

"It's lucky neither you nor Cupcake were hit by the dish as it descended." Sally pointed to the pink sugary concoction still stuck to the ceiling and laughed. "It could have been death by meringue."

The image of her lying on the floor, dead, surrounded by her own creation made Charlotte laugh too. She wanted to hate Sally and yet..., she didn't.

"Your meringue must have been lighter than air," Sally added. "I'm very impressed."

Charlotte didn't know how she felt about Sally turning up unexpectedly at her house, let alone inviting herself into the kitchen.

"Without doubt, it was the best marshmallow ever. It separated mid-flight from my supposedly unbreakable Pyrex dish and floated up in a display Willy Wonka would have been proud of." Cupcake wiggled and she her lost grip on his collar. "Stop." Charlotte cried as he waded into the kitchen to lick up the mess littering the floor. He stopped. A miracle. "Stay."

Shards of glass littered the floor. Charlotte tiptoed in and bent down to inspect Cupcake's mouth and paws, looking for cuts. Nothing. Thank God. Her racing heart slowed a fraction.

"I'll mind him," Sally offered. "You clear away the broken glass."

Charlotte twisted round, lost her balance and landed on the floor on her bottom. If she had been feeling charitable she could have acknowledged it was a small mercy she hadn't landed on anything sharp.

Glancing over her shoulder she shot the perky Sally her best evil eye. But it did nothing to faze the pint-sized queen of tarts.

Sally was peering at the disaster that used to be Charlotte's sparkling 1950s style test kitchen. Her pride and joy. Could today get any worse? The entire room looked as if a bomb had exploded. A meringue bomb. The room was an open invitation to ant colonies within a hundred-mile radius, and it was going to need intensive cleaning to return it to its normal pristine condition.

She picked herself up off the floor and dusted her backside, knowing her cheeks were as pink as the sticky meringue all over her. She was horribly embarrassed. Bet Sally didn't see her as her idol anymore.

She was in shortcake hell, so she figured Sally should join her on the journey. An evil imp residing in the dark recesses of her brain took control of her mouth. "I'll lock Cupcake in the living room and we'll tackle the clean-up together. Then you can tell me why you're here."

"No problem," Sally said without hesitation, her voice annoyingly cheerful. "But where will I put Snuggles?" She looked at Cupcake, her meaning clear.

Charlotte was astonished by her immediate acceptance. Cupcake, a mere puppy, was almost impossible to keep in check, so she understood Sally's reservation at leaving her tiny dog in the same room. Right now he was visibly vibrating with excitement under her hand. "Cupcake won't hurt him. He's practically a vegetarian."

"One lick of Cupcake's enormous tongue and Snuggles could end up wedged like a bone in his throat."

Unable to help it, Charlotte laughed. She didn't want to like Sally, so she kept her amusement brief. She nodded toward the bag slung over Sally's shoulder. "Will he stay in that bag? If so, put it on the table over in the corner."

Sally eyed the purpose-built Formica dining table that accommodated at least eight to ten people at the far end of the room and said, with what seemed to be a reluctant nod, "That will work."

Charlotte hesitated. She couldn't believe Sally had agreed to help her. "You do that then. I'll de-meringue Cupcake and lock him in the living room first and then we'll get started."

Sally tip-toed in her Manolo Blahniks between splodges of goo and glass on the tiled floor. One small slip and she would go splat on her backside just like Charlotte had. She placed the doggy bag on the table, and when Snuggles would have climbed out, she pointed her finger at him and sternly instructed, "Stay." For once, he stayed. Maybe because he was in a different environment and there was a big Chihuahua-eating dog in the room next door. "Do not move," she added, in case he was planning an escape when she wasn't looking. "Or no treats tonight."

Snuggles looked lovingly at her, and Sally fought the urge to pick him up and tell him she didn't mean it. Instead she surveyed the mess. How on earth was she going to clean this and not turn herself into a greasy ruin? The diamonds on her watch sparkled at her. Unclipping the strap, she placed it in the side pocket of the bag. She considered her shoes. Her very *expensive* shoes. She unzipped a compartment in her bag and pulled out a pair of pink ballet slippers. "I knew you would come in handy one day," she said to them with a self-satisfied smirk. "And today is the day." Slippers on her feet and shoes safely stowed away, she delved into another pocket and withdrew a pair of thin rubber gloves.

While waiting for Charlotte, she worried at her bottom lip and considered how she could save her suit, which had cost more than a month's salary, from becoming tomorrow's trash.

9

CHARLOTTE FROZE AND GAPED, FEELING AS IF SHE'D JUST gone from a frumpish size 14 to a bloated 20 in five seconds flat. Not so much from Sally having already begun to clean her kitchen floor, but because, well, she was pretty much, naked.

Sally looked up, her smile as bright as a sunbeam and without an ounce of embarrassment in her eyes. "Hope you don't mind I started. If the meringue dries, it's going to be harder to clean up. It's fortunate I arrived when I did, otherwise you'd be cleaning forever."

Sally was a perfectly proportioned size 06, possibly smaller than that, and looked amazing even if she was, right now, on her hands and knees picking up pieces of glass and placing them on a large envelope she must have snagged from the countertop.

Charlotte blinked and took a mental photo for when she was old and needed a laugh. "Why did you take off your clothes?"

"You would too if you knew what they cost."

"Well, I'm not taking mine off." Charlotte peered down at her apron which hid, she hoped, some of the additional pounds she'd put on since breaking up with George. Her dress was a baggy, gypsy, multi-colored number that should have been tossed out years ago, but it reminded her of her mother, who had unexpectedly passed on to the next life way too soon, and Charlotte couldn't bear to part with it. Not yet anyhow. But right this second, she felt huge and downright dull compared to the bright vivacious woman on the floor.

Shaking her head, she turned away to regain her composure and instead dug around in one of her cupboards, before emerging with her arms full of products, most of them natural, organic, and unlabeled and plonked them on the bench.

Sally pointed at the bottles. "What are those for?"

"Watch and learn." Charlotte collected a bucket, filled it with hot water, unscrewed a bottle of white vinegar and poured a goodly portion into the bucket along with a few measures of baking soda. She picked up a bottle of eucalyptus oil and shook a few drops into the mix. "There. Not only does this oil smell wonderful, it's a natural sanitizer as well."

She passed the bucket to Sally. "Baking soda and white vinegar will clean most surfaces. The eucalyptus makes it smell nice. I don't like chemicals in the kitchen – far too toxic – so I make most of my cleaning products myself. The rest I get from an eco-store."

Sally peered into the bucket and inhaled the aroma. "I'm impressed. You could market this under your own name."

"George said the same thing," Charlotte admitted. "It's something I might do in the future. Right now, all I want is to de-goo the kitchen." *And get you out of my house before I embarrass myself further.*

She got down on her knees and revealed to Sally the wonders of cleaning naturally. Working in silence from separate ends of the room, they made their way to the center of the floor. That done, they turned their attention to the cupboards and walls, and finally the ceiling with the aid of brooms with stockings tied around the brushes.

"We work well together." Sally turned to the counter, the

final surface left to wipe down. She sprayed the surface with Charlotte's concoction. "And this cleaner smells wonderful."

"We worked well together because we were at opposite ends of the kitchen." Charlotte couldn't help admire Sally's willingness to lend a hand. "Two cooks in the same room is asking for disaster." It had taken them nearly an hour to de-goo the room, and not one word of complaint had emerged from Sally's mouth. She'd worked diligently, thoroughly and seemed, weirdly, to be enjoying herself.

Sally quirked her head as she pondered Charlotte's statement. "Why would you say that?"

"I like things my way in the kitchen." She was still digesting Sally's earlier declaration that she, Charlotte Meyer, was Sally's idol. Incredible. "You were at school with me? I'm sorry, but I don't remember you."

"I was a couple of years behind you. Your name was on the honor role in your final year. You excelled in home economics and that's what I wanted. I've followed your career ever since."

Charlotte didn't know what to say. "So you're a patisserie chef because of me?"

Sally nodded. "Kind of. I loved to bake. You excelled in all things cooking and I wanted to be you."

Moisture threatened to fill Charlotte's eyes. She was feeling so horribly guilty for thinking such bad thoughts about Sally. "I don't know what to say. I think that might be the nicest thing anyone's ever said to me. Thank you."

Sally sat down on the chair by the dining table and petted Snuggles, who had been sleeping in the bag for most of the past hour but was now awake. "Thank *you*."

Charlotte leaned her elbows on the counter and clasped her hands together, and finally looked Sally in the eye. "You still haven't said why you're here." Although she had a pretty good inkling.

"To appeal to your better nature to come on my show. And to apologize for George, the imbecile, in continuing to let you believe we were having an affair. He was a good agent. It's such a pity."

Charlotte wanted to defend George, and only just stopped herself from uttering that he wasn't an imbecile. "What do you mean he *was* a good agent?"

Sally grinned. "I fired him."

Charlotte gaped. "You what?"

She shrugged and pulled off her rubber gloves and stuffed them back into her bag. "I've hired Viggo." She turned and fixed Charlotte with an intense stare, as if she was trying to read her mind. "You *do* know about Viggo?"

"What kind of question is that? Has he finally grown wings and flown off into the night?"

"That he's the V in GVM." Sally plucked Snuggles out of the bag and gave him a cuddle and allowed him to lick the rest of her makeup off her face.

"Of course I do." What an odd question. "The jury is out on whether he's alive or dead. because he only comes out at night." Charlotte chatted as she stored her cleaning equipment away and tossed the rags into the laundry basket. "He a loner and keeps to himself most of the time. But I'm much more interested in knowing why you've fired George."

"Two things. First, until yesterday I had no idea you thought George and I were having an affair. That our supposed *affair* was what caused you to break up with him. I can't believe he hid something so important from me. Second, I also can't believe he never mentioned Viggo before or that I was stupid enough not to ask what the V represented in GVM. Until last night I had no idea Viggo even existed. Of course, it's not all his fault. I should have been more observant. I ventured into GVM last night with the intention of bribing your address out of Myrtle, and found Viggo and that unusual cat instead."

Charlotte was inordinately pleased to discover Sally wasn't perfect after all. "Thanks for helping me clean up and all, but I'm going to have to speak to Viggo. He's not supposed to give out personal client information."

"Oh, he didn't. He refused. So this morning, I swung by the agency and I it's entirely possible that I may have used Myrtle's computer to look you up when she wasn't watching."

Charlotte nearly laughed but she managed to keep a straight face. "And why was it so important you visit me in person?"

"As I said, I wanted to apologize for that no good ex-agent of mine for not clarifying he and I have never had an affair. Mostly, I wanted you on my show."

Before Charlotte had a chance to respond Cupcake began to whine and scratch at the living room door. Snuggles barked in response. Sally spotted a smattering of meringue still on the floor, put Snuggles back in the bag and got back down on her knees to clean it away.

Charlotte frowned. "Did you hear something?"

Sally looked up. "Just Cupcake and Snuggles."

But then, both women froze, Sally dressed in a bra and thong and still on her knees, and Charlotte, her apron and behind greasy with marshmallow, sugar, strawberries and meringue, when Viggo walked into the kitchen with George two steps behind.

Charlotte didn't know who was more shocked, and she took a moment to feel something – a smidgen of compassion for Sally who was practically naked and looking very, very embarrassed as she got up from off the floor. All four of them stood and nobody said anything. Charlotte swore she could hear the tick tock in George and Viggo's minds as everyone registered astonishment at what they were witnessing.

Then Cupcake barged between George and Viggo, breaking the awkward silence as he barked and headed straight for Snuggles like a homing pigeon. Snuggles got extremely agitated or excited, Charlotte couldn't tell, and wiggled like crazy until the doggy bag tipped over and he toppled out and tumbled to the edge of the table. Cupcake's tongue lolled and swiped a long lick over Snuggles, and the small dog sort of flew off the table and landed in a scrabble of paws on Charlotte's now extremely clean floor.

Sally screamed. Charlotte screamed. George and Viggo swore up a blue storm. Snuggles took off across the kitchen, out the door and down the hallway with Cupcake on his tail.

"Cupcake," Charlotte yelled. "Get back here right now."

"My poor baby," Sally yelled louder and ran through the gap between George and Viggo in all her nearly naked glory and down the hall behind the two dogs. "Are you hurt?"

"Of course it's not hurt." Charlotte couldn't hide her sudden irritation as she followed. "Cupcake only licked it."

"The it you're talking about is my baby boy. And he's precious to me. He could have broken something falling from the table."

Practical Sally had evaporated, Charlotte noted. The woman had become Manic Sally, and how could she imagine her nearly invisible puppy had fallen from the table when everyone could see he'd jumped.

"What kind of person keeps their dog on a table anyhow?"

"You told me to put him there. You said he'd be safe."

"Women." Viggo boomed from behind them. "Stop arguing and get those critters."

Both women turned to stare at him. "Critters," Charlotte mouthed to Sally.

"Old-fashioned word for an animal," Sally explained to Charlotte unnecessarily.

George piped up. "Charlotte loves old-fashioned things."

"Pity you don't." Charlotte tossed the snarky comment over her shoulder and followed the dogs as they tore down her hallway and into her bedroom.

Cupcake's nose was plastered to the floor and his derriere waggled in the air as he squeezed the top half of his ungainly body under the bed. She guessed Snuggles had taken refuge under her bed. *Oh cupcakes and sausage rolls!* She couldn't remember when she'd last vacuumed under there!

All four adults hunkered down and peered under the bed. Sally sprawled herself on the floor and slid half way under. Charlotte hid a giggle. She'd never expected to see Sally's behind at such close range and hoped to never again. She hazarded a guess George and Viggo hadn't either.

"Come here my little snuggly-wuggly," Sally crooned. "Did the big doggie give you a fright?"

Charlotte shot Viggo and George a disbelieving glance from the opposite side.

Cupcake continued to bark repeatedly. Snuggles snapped his less shrill bark back. Charlotte snapped out instructions. "George. Grab Cupcake and take him outside. He's frightening Snuggles."

"Cupcake doesn't like me," George muttered, but he dug his heels into the floor, cuffed his hand beneath the ungainly puppy's collar and tugged. "Come. Outside."

Cupcake didn't budge an inch. George tugged again. Nothing.

"Put some muscle into it, George," Charlotte suggested and smothered back her amusement.

George shot her a *do you want me to do this or not?* glare.

"Cupcake." Charlotte raised her voice to be heard over the cacophony of barking. "Go with George. He has biscuits."

George growled. "Where are they?"

Her mouth twitched. "Right-hand side of the pantry in a big blue bucket on the floor."

Just in case the big hairy monster had changed his mind about eating Snuggles as an afternoon snack, George gripped the collar hard and pulled. Cupcake fish-tailed and slid sideways under the bed. Any second the end of the bed was going to lift off the floor.

Charlotte and Sally let out a unified cry and George decided it was time to bring the goodies to the dog.

He let go of Cupcake and charged from the room and down the hall, calling, "Goodies, Cupcake. Goodies." He rushed into the kitchen, located the bucket, tugged off the lid and pulled out a handful of tough-looking bow tie cookies knotted at the center.

"These better work," he grunted as the decibel level of barking increased, causing his ears to ring.

Racing back down the hall, he slid under the bed alongside Cupcake, and waved the cookies under the dog's nose. "Yum, yum."

Viggo sniggered.

Cupcake ignored him. Snuggles whimpered, caught sight of Cupcake's treat and forgot he was scared. He took a couple of steps toward George.

"No" Sally screeched, and reached out to him. "Come to mama." Snuggles sat, lighting in his dark brown eyes to a warm glow. He tilted his head this way and that. Cupcake stopped barking and sniffed the air. His backside quivered and his tail whacked George's thigh with a loud thump, thump, thump. Then he spun toward George and made a lunge for the biscuits.

The bed rose off the floor. Sally snatched Snuggles before it nearly took off across the room. George hit his head on the base in his urgency to remove himself from danger and swore the air blue once more.

"Cupcake," Charlotte cried out. "George. Save my baby boy."

"Don't just stand there," the almost naked Sally yelled at Viggo. "Help George with Cupcake."

Viggo exploded into raucous laughter. He indicated to one corner of the bed and George got the message and went to the other corner.

"On three," Viggo instructed and counted, "One, two, three." They lifted the bed. Cupcake thrust his nose into George's crotch and looked up, his tail thumping against the underside of the bed.

"Get him out of the way." George had stuffed the goodies into his mouth to free his hands.

Charlotte snatched the goodies from his mouth and wisely kept any comments to herself for all of two seconds. "Don't you know anything about dogs. His tail's wagging. He's thanking you for saving him."

George glared at Charlotte. She waggled the treats precariously close to George's crotch. "Come to mama."

George chuckled on the inside but stepped backwards just in case Cupcake thought his crotch was a goodie.

10

THE DOGS NOW CONTAINED, SALLY DETOURED INTO THE bathroom and back into her suit, retouched her foundation, lipstick and slipped on her shoes. When she emerged she looked as if she'd sprung fresh from the pages of Vogue.

Charlotte nearly threw up from a bout of jealousy. How did she do it? Clearly it was an art in which Charlotte lacked talent. She had, in the past, attempted to emulate style and always failed. She was buxom. Rubenesque, even. There was nothing svelte or stylish about her. She was more…, Mother Earth.

Sighing heavily, she gave up thinking about herself and focused on George and Viggo's untimely arrival instead.

"Can you explain why you let yourself into my house without knocking? And let Cupcake out of the lounge?"

"He was whining," George said. "Cupcake that is."

"You could have knocked."

"The front door was open." George looked to Viggo.

Viggo added his two cents' worth. "Cupcake was making so much noise we thought something must have happened to you."

"Do you think he locked himself in the living room by himself? Sorry, but he hasn't learned that particular trick yet."

Viggo's eyebrow arched and his mouth twitched into an almost-smile. "But you could have been lying unconscious in the same room as him. Or worse, savaged by a rabid dog."

Charlotte snorted. "Cupcake is not rabid."

George cleared his throat. "He was five minutes ago."

"He could have wolfed down Snuggles in one mouthful," Sally added. Apparently she was still upset about Snuggles almost becoming a snack. "Cupcake needs to learn self-control."

George actually snorted. "Snuggles is the least obedient dog I've ever met."

Viggo failed to stifle his half horrified, half amused bark of laughter. Apparently, he also held no qualms in broaching the subject of Sally's near nakedness earlier. "Never mind the dogs. Why were you, Sally, barely decent and on your hands and knees in Charlotte's kitchen. As your new manager, I have to tell you kinky cleaning won't win you any points with the viewers or further our plans to make you a wholesome household name across America."

"Unless that's the kind of attention you're aiming for," George added. "It could be interesting but we'd have to switch your show from day to late-night to reach the right people."

The startled expression on Sally's face was priceless. "You think I'm into kink?"

"Oh for goodness sake," Charlotte threw up her hands. "Give up the innuendo and tell us why the two of you are here instead?"

Viggo winked. "George is teaching me aspects of the business, including showing me your kitchen. And I have to tell you, this visit is turning out to be far more entertaining than I ever expected."

Charlotte stood in front of the television later that afternoon, watching Sally whip up a modern, no-fuss, minimum effort version of a lemon drizzle tart. How did she do it? Not a hair out of place as she smoothly explained each step of the process. The end result, a masterpiece.

Every mouth in Seattle would be drooling. She knew hers was. The woman was a witch and her magic was white, bright and goody-goody.

Sally was everything Charlotte wanted to be and wasn't. Smart, sassy and titillatingly beautiful. And a natural blonde as well. She heaved a sigh. The harbored resentment of the past few months had evaporated into a big blob of globby disappointment. She'd wasted so much time and energy hating someone who clearly didn't house a devious bone in her tiny little body. The darned woman was so nice it nearly curdled the contents of Charlotte's stomach.

She felt hot, sticky, and fat. Her reflection in the mirror after everyone had gone revealed the undeniable truth. As she'd thought, there had been meringue in her hair. She suspected there had been more until she'd crawled under the bed. She'd had to clean under there as well.

A small glimmer of amusement tweaked the corner of her lips upward. No wonder George had had such a hungry look in his eye. It wasn't for her earthly delights, the bounty of her body, her sparkling personality or witty repartee. No. It was for the concoction on her head. And all three unexpected visitors to her home had zipped their lips and not said a word.

11

THE NEXT DAY CHARLOTTE ENTERED GVM ARMED WITH A
freshly baked Strawberry Marshmallow Shortcake. Her stomach
churned like a confused ice cream machine. One minute she was
hot, the next cold. She couldn't believe she was about to do this.

Myrtle looked up from her computer screen and her eyes
widened in appreciation when she saw the large dish in Charlotte's hands. "Here comes the most amazing thing I've seen in a
very long time."

"I take it you're not talking about me." Charlotte had to
admit her this Strawberry Marshmallow Shortcake was looking
particularly scrumptious. The memory of her previous disaster
lingered. She fought the urge to pat her hair for signs of
meringue as she surreptitiously checked herself out in the
paneling behind Myrtle. "Sorry. This isn't for you. It's for my
new agent."

Myrtle let out a sound of pure disgust. "Agent, schmagent.
George is an idiot. I'll be out of a job before the year is over if he
lets this go on much longer."

"It was my decision. Not his."

"Viggo doesn't know diddly-squat."

"He's your partner. You've been in business together for years. Some of it must have rubbed off on him."

Myrtle's eyes twinkled. "I've been trying to rub myself off onto him for years but nothing sticks. It's never going to happen. You know how it is with him and promotion. Have you ever seen Viggo at a PR event, book signing, television studio, or anywhere other than behind an accounts book or a computer screen?"

Charlotte attempted to recall any of these particular events. George had been her agent for, what, three years now and she'd never witnessed Viggo showing interest in anything other than dollar signs and the stars in the sky. She didn't even know if he had a girlfriend.

What had she done? Her career was about to nosedive and it was all her fault. "He must have learned something over the years. I need to give him a chance."

"We do not. I'm pretty sure we've already had this conversation, but just in case you've forgotten, he keeps the books. Yes, he's a smart so and so, but the two of them work best with Viggo doing the books and George doing the schmoozing. They're the yin and yang of this business."

Charlotte placed the shortcake on the reception desk. It was getting heavy and her arm ached almost as much as her heart. George had a way with people. He'd certainly had his way with her on more occasions than she could count, and she'd loved it each and every minute. She sighed as a wave of despondence washed over her. "I don't mean to be fatalistic, but what's done is done."

"Well, undo it, girl."

"How?"

"Take George back."

"I'm thinking about it."

"Think fast before the company turns into an upside-down cake."

"Don't speak of cakes that way. It's sacrilegious. My syndicated columns and cook books make more than enough to keep this business ticking over without me having to write another recipe."

"You mark my words." Myrtle was intent in getting her point across. "Impending doom is all I can see if this farce continues."

Charlotte shook off the far too heavy wave of despondence weighing her shoulders down. "Get over it. I'll have you know I'm serious when I say I'm considering taking George back. If he'll have me. I'd call that character growth on my part. Wouldn't you?" She didn't wait for an answer. "I was ready to never speak to him again." She only hoped he would be receptive to the apology she planned to make. After all the evil, barbed comments she'd uttered over the past few months, she had serious doubts it would go well.

"Hurry up. The sooner the world of GVM rights itself can't be soon enough for me."

The doomed look in Myrtle's eyes was Charlotte's undoing. She pushed the tart toward her. "Have a slice." Food always lifted Myrtle's mood.

"You said it was for Viggo."

"Is he here?"

"I shouldn't really tell you this, but, he's in the office trying to make sense of a new contract for Sally. She's set to go nationwide if all goes according to plan."

This was big. Very big. "Nationwide." Charlotte paused for a second and looked for an ounce of envy. Nope. Nothing. "How wonderful."

"It sure is. Except with Viggo at the helm it may spell disaster for Sally's career."

"Is George with him?"

"Nah-uh." Myrtle was sizing up the tart before slicing an enormous wedge. "He's gone for the day. God knows where. Check O'Flanagan's. He practically lives there these days." She placed the wedge on a paper napkin from a stash in one of her drawers and dug around for a fork. "Never say I'm unprepared," she informed Charlotte once she'd found the item and filled her mouth with shortcake.

A moment of silence ensued. Charlotte smirked as she watched Myrtle's eyes roll back in sensory heaven. She knew how to shut her up. "Thanks Myrtle. Let me know if the short-cake is a one or two thumbs up treat later."

Charlotte picked up the rest of the tart before Myrtle could eat another slice, and went in search of her new agent. Myrtle was right. Something had to be done.

12

Viggo's head hurt from staring at all the convoluted words in Sally's contract. It was a jumble of letters and legalese although he understood the basics.

"Gobbledygook," he told Osiris, perched on the pad next to him, licking a paw. Osiris stretched and ambled over to sit on the contract and lick his private parts.

"I knew you'd understand." He ran a hand down Osiris's back. "My time is precious. All this reading is eating into the time I should be writing my presentation for the astronomy conference."

"Try eating this instead," Charlotte suggested from the doorway. "It'll give those tired brain-cells some extra energy."

Viggo jumped and Osiris, startled by his master's sudden movement, sprung onto all fours, hackles raised, and hissed at her.

She took a step backward. "Sheesh. A fine welcome."

"Maybe if you'd knocked. You frightened Osiris."

She gave him a disbelieving stare. "I frightened *you* more than your cat."

"Startled. You startled me." He paused and took stock of the situation. She wanted something. She had a sweet treat in her hand and a determined glint in her eyes. It didn't bode well for him. He tended to cave when she came bearing gifts. "What do you want?"

"I want you." She winked at him, placed the plate on the table and wagged a stern finger at Osiris. "Do not touch."

Viggo felt himself grow pale. "You want me?" This was a complication he hadn't envisaged.

Her voice grew sultry, her eyes twinkled and her lips twitched. "More than you can imagine."

Then it dawned, she was teasing him. "What do you really want?"

"I've decided to accept Sally's offer. You know. To appear on Tempting Tarts. I need to know what the show's content will be, how much air time I'll have, yada, yada, yada."

He gulped. "Air time?"

"Yes. I expect you'll want to draw up a contract outlining the details."

"Contract?" His stomach sank and he lost his appetite. "Offer? Speak to George. He understands these things far better than I do." He checked his watch. "I'm sure if you head down to O'Flanagan's and explain he'll agree to take you back on."

"I'm sure you mean I'll agree to take *him* back on. But, until such time, you're my manager." She gave him a considered look. "Tell him I'm willing to negotiate."

Wisely, Viggo kept his mouth shut. Osiris, on the other hand, took the opportunity to stick out his tongue and got stuck into the creamy marshmallow topping. Cream frosted his whiskers like snow on twigs, and when the furry creature looked up with his almond shaped eyes, Viggo couldn't help but chuckle.

Charlotte placed her fists on her hips. "Bad cat." She reached out to snatch the plate away, but Osiris hissed and bared his frosted teeth. Her hand snapped back to her hips like elastic. "Stop him," she instructed Viggo, the inflection in her voice rising as Osiris plunged in for more.

"Must be good." Viggo sat back with his arms folded over his chest. There was no way he wanted those feline fangs piercing his skin. There was one thing he knew about his mysterious cat, and that was to never interfere when he was eating.

Charlotte was indignant in her reply. "Of course it's good. I'm the best there is."

"Nothing wrong with your confidence," Viggo retorted. "You're full of it. Get down to O'Flanagan's and whip your man into a frenzy. He's crazy about you. Can you imagine how it must feel to be in love with someone who doesn't love you back?"

A dreamy expression filled her eyes. "He loves me?"

"As if you didn't know."

Charlotte sighed. "But will he forgive me?"

Viggo shrugged. "That, I can't answer."

"It would be better if he and I keep our personal and working relationship separate."

"Believe me, if you keep me on as your manager, the misunderstandings will be many and you could see an end to your career as you know it." He picked up Sally's contract and waved it at her. "These suckers are not my forte."

"The good news is I can help you with mine, so that's one less thing you have to worry about. You're going to need George's help with Sally's though. I've never had a television series."

Viggo pushed his chair away from the desk, alarm in his eyes as Osiris began to make choking noises. "What about helping with puking cats?"

"Not my area of expertise." She backed off further.

He leaned forward, grabbed Osiris, and tried to find somewhere to put him. As he twirled in a circle, marshmallow exploded from Osiris's mouth and sprayed all over his desk. Two seconds later the most enormous fur ball he had ever seen landed plop in the middle of Sally's contract.

Charlotte had the effrontery to laugh so hard she had to cross her legs. "I nearly wet myself."

Viggo didn't want puddles of any kind on his carpet. "This is where you leave."

She uncrossed her legs and shot out the door. Seconds later he heard Myrtle's explosion of mirth as Charlotte divulged the juicy details on her way past reception.

And to think he'd thought the day couldn't get any worse.

13

CHARLOTTE FOUND GEORGE HOLED UP IN THE SNUG NEAR THE back of O'Flanagan's, nursing a whiskey and looking glum and lonely. Guilt slammed her heart into an erratic beat. The bar was filled with locals and chatter and laughter and the steady thump, thump, thump of music coming from speakers behind the bar. She could hardly assemble her thoughts for the noise, let alone hear or comprehend what anyone was saying.

She flung herself down in the snug seat opposite him and shouted above the din. "Just how many of those have you had?"

George muttered, "What's it to you?"

"You're my agent. I want you sober."

"You must have amnesia. You fired me."

"So one little thing goes wrong and you decide to drown yourself in alcohol."

"I've had one whiskey. I do not call that excessive."

She changed tack. "So, do you want me back? As a girl-friend." Nothing like being direct even if she felt as if she might barf up a fur ball just like Osiris had earlier.

George said nothing. Just glared at her as if she'd grown two heads. A little hope in his eyes would have been nice. Anything, to give her a glimpse of hope.

The lack of anything shook her confidence somewhat. "A few days ago you were begging at my door. You still love me. I know you do."

"Today is a new day. I'm no longer your lover or your agent."

Had she misunderstood the light in his eyes when Cupcake was trapped under her bed? Granted, her manner over the past few months had been anything but friendly, but still, she'd thought the tension between them had eased.

"Viggo is reading Sally's new contract?"

Alarm flared in his eyes. He leaned forward in his chair. "What new contract?"

"Surely you knew about it?"

"I've been working on something with one of the major networks. I've not seen anything in writing."

"Well, Viggo has."

"Fuck me." He slugged down the rest of his whiskey in one gulp and then took to coughing madly.

"If you can't get Sally to take you back, you're going to be in deep doggie do-do."

Between coughs, he managed to say, "When did you become Sally's champion? What happened to the jealous harridan I've been dealing with for the past three months? Didn't you threaten to set Cupcake on me only the other day? Tell me why you're really here."

This was proving to be so much harder than she'd antici-pated. Charlotte sighed, signaled to a waitress, and ordered a Tequila Sunrise. "You want another whiskey?" she asked George, but before he could respond she pointed to his drink and shouted her order to the waitress, "Give him another one of those."

"When did I become such a wimp?" he muttered.

"Darling, you are not a wimp."

"I'm no longer your darling."

"I'm trying hard to be nice."

"You'll have to do better."

"I have a suggestion you're going to love."

"And that is...?"

"We get back together as a couple while you're no longer employed as my agent."

He coughed into his whiskey. "Get serious, will you."

Unnerved, she was suddenly not so sure of herself. "I *am* serious."

"I'd rather you took me back as your agent. Less pain that way."

She should have been hurt by his comment, but she knew him well enough to hear a spark of interest in his voice. "I'd prefer for you to be my lover."

"Don't I get a choice?"

"I just gave you one."

"It worked fine when I was both agent and lover, until your crazy jealousy got in the way.

This wasn't how the conversation was supposed to go. She knew he still cared for her despite his being evasive right now. But then she deserved it. Hadn't she been just as evasive and twice as difficult over the past three months? "I was entirely mistaken."

"Yes, you *were*. It's my word I wanted you to believe, not Sally's."

Apprehension was giving her an acid stomach. "So what do I have to do to prove I'm serious?"

"You froze me out and shut the door on my face too many times to count. Tell me, how would a relationship between us be different this time?"

She swallowed her pride. "For a start, take Sally back on. Myrtle says Viggo will ruin everything if he's left in charge. Or at least check her contract, make sure she's not going to lose out because of my bad behavior. I can handle Viggo. I've been doing this long enough to know what's involved as far as my bookings and appearances go. That way you can promote Sally and have me in your life at the same time."

"What happens when I attend events with Sally and you can't be there? Am I going to have to pacify you, constantly insist nothing is happening between Sally and me, no matter the media conjecture? I don't know if I care to go through all that again."

"It won't happen."

"How can you be so sure?"

"I know you. I know Sally."

"It could be another client, a woman, I'm escorting to an event. What then?"

"I've always believed I wasn't good enough," she blurted, only realizing the truth of her statement when the words fell from her lips. "I couldn't understand why you wanted to be with me when you could have petite and beautiful. The one thing I've recently discovered is that you make me feel better about myself."

"You don't need me or anyone to do that for you. You need to feel better about yourself all on your own."

Tears formed in the corner of her eyes. This wasn't going well at all. "How do I do that?"

He shrugged. "I don't know."

She sank back in her chair, averted her face and tried not to let tears spill onto her cheeks. She tilted her head from side to side to drain the fluid away before she turned back to face him. "So your answer is no."

"No." He paused and her stomach sank clear through to the floor. "That's not my answer.

Hope blossomed briefly. It wasn't an outright no and that was encouraging. "Then what is?"

"I don't know. You're need to be patient while I think this through."

Patience, as George well knew, wasn't her strong suit. But, she wasn't about to roll over and give up. He knew she was determined, feisty, tricky and plain old-fashioned in a whole lot of ways.

She was also a hippy with attitude at heart, but her attitude was born from insecurity. "Don't think too long. I might change my mind."

George glared at her, and she felt herself color. "Okay. Take your time. How long will you need? One hour? Two? Maybe overnight? How about twenty-four hours?"

He snorted. "I might need longer."

There was a hint of amusement in his eyes that made her hope. "How long do you need? It's either yes or no."

"I'm not making a serious decision lightly. You need to prove to me you've changed."

"I *have* changed."

"Pardon me if I have trouble believing you."

"Pardon me for opening up to you." An image formed in her mind of another time and place where she'd opened up to him. She so wanted to do that again.

"You can open up further tomorrow. I'll pick you up at eight o'clock."

"What kind of opening up are we talking here?"

"Not the kind you're imagining. We will embark on a series of dates."

"Dates." she literally squeaked, hardly recognizing her own voice as excitement fizzed like sparking bubbles through her veins.

"You're going to have to prove to me you've changed."

Just what that entailed she didn't know.

14

VIGGO MADE HIS WAY TO GREENSPAN STUDIOS RECEPTION, secured a pass, and endured an exhausting magical, mystical discovery tour through the rabbit warren of corridors and rooms until he finally located the studio where Tempting Tarts was filmed.

Sally was going to be ecstatic Charlotte wanted to be on her show. He wasn't so sure it was a great idea himself, even if they had seemed particularly chummy the other day. Unfortunately, he couldn't get the image of Sally semi-naked on Charlotte's kitchen floor out of his head or, rid the unexpected and instant attraction he'd felt that first time she'd sauntered into the office and sparred verbally with him over Osiris and Snuggles.

This wasn't good. He didn't do relationships. Especially where the woman was a client. He'd seen what had happened between Charlotte and George and he wasn't about to start something that could end badly. Plus he didn't do permanent and his instincts told him Sally was a *permanent* woman who didn't play fast and loose with anyone.

Standing at the back of the room, Viggo watched with a mild sense of awe as Sally prepared a mouth-watering concoction for that day's recording. Some sections of the show were pre-recorded and now it was nearly time for her to go live. He told himself he'd come to the studios to learn more about the business, to get a better feel of how she worked her work magic in front of the camera. In truth, he found he wanted to see her again.

He was about to make Sally's day. Her year even. He hoped he knew enough not to screw-up her chance of taking her show national. He tapped where his inside jacket pocket was, ensuring the contract was still tucked safely in there. Certainly, this contract burning a hole in his pocket was heading in the right direction and even he, with his lack of legal experience, recognized Sally was on track to become a star.

And that was why he was going to make a concerted effort to persuade her to take George back on. It really was in her best interest.

When the message came through from the control room that there would be a thirty-minute break before the show went to air, Viggo emerged from the shadows and headed into the show kitchen.

"Hi," he said as he came up behind Sally, who was just shy of pressing her nose against the glass door of the hot oven as she peered in at a tart she'd prepared earlier.

Startled, she spun round and looked up at him. Heat flushed her cheeks to a delicate pink and his libido kicked into overdrive. Damn it.

She smiled with genuine warmth which only served to fuel his interest in her. "This is a nice surprise. Are you here to..." she smoothed her hands down over her hips and shot him a flirty grin, "manage me?"

Oh man. "I'm here to persuade you to un-manage me by showing you this." He reached into his jacket and pulled out the contract. "It arrived early this morning."

Sally continued to look into his eyes. "What is it?"

"A contract."

"I have one. With GVM."

"This contract will allow us to share you across America. You're about to become a national sensation."

She gasped and whisked her future from his fingertips. She unfolded the document and scanned the pages, whipping from one page to the next in quick succession before hugging the paperwork to her chest and grinning madly.

His heart went kerplunk. He was in deep-deep trouble. "This is serious," he told her. "You need George to explain what all this legal mumbo-jumbo entails. I understand the basics, but there are clauses in here I have no understanding of."

She batted her lashes, her cheeks flushed with excitement. "I have every confidence in your abilities."

"You need George for this."

A flash of irritation flickered in her eyes. "I want you. Not George."

"Come on, Sally. Be reasonable. I know diddly-squat about this kind of deal. It's got clauses and conditions requiring expert analysis. These pieces of paper could make or break your career. George is the one with the contract law degree. He's the best in the industry. And, I for one, do not want to be the cause of it all going wrong because I misunderstood one of the clauses or tied you to something entirely unacceptable."

"I am never unreasonable," she responded indignantly. "I'm the most reasonable person I know." She filled her cheeks with air then puffed it all out on a huge sigh. "I'll tell you what." She fanned the contract under her chin. "I'll take a look at it myself. If it's as difficult to understand as you say it is, I'll let George take a look."

Relief. He fought back a grin of success. He had a double degree in applied mathematics and astronomy. If he couldn't understand it, he'd bet all the stars in the universe she wouldn't either.

Sally was determined to keep him in the studio. She liked this tall enigma before her. "Is this your first visit to the studios?"

There was something yummy about him, even if he seemed a little prickly. She was good at seeing beneath prickles though. There was a reason why she'd never met him before, and she was determined to find out why he hid himself behind Myrtle and George.

He nodded and surveyed the room filled with lights, taking in the power cords wending like snakes across the floor. The area was way smaller than it appeared on screen. "Hopefully it will be my last."

"I'll try not to take that comment personally." He was clearly a man of few words. He had been far chattier when he'd had a tart in front of him. "So what's your favorite?"

"Pardon?" he said, as if he had trouble keeping up with her sudden shift in conversation.

"Your favorite tart. What is it? I'll make you one as a thank you for bringing me such wonderful news."

She laughed at the mix of conflicting emotions flickering in his eyes and the tongue unconsciously licking at the corner of his mouth. Surprise. Hunger. Determination not to be blackmailed by food.

When he didn't speak she rattled off the names of several tarts she thought might possibly tempt him. "Raspberry Delight? Lemon Delicious? Pecan Berry? Chocolate Decadence?"

He cleared his throat. "Ah... it's not necessary to make me anything. It's George you should be aiming to impress. He's the one who got you this offer."

"I like to think my talent got me this offer." She'd witnessed the hungry look in his eyes when she mentioned chocolate. She pressed her index finger against her lips as they tilted upwards into a huge beam of happiness she couldn't contain. All her dreams were coming true. Every night since she was a little girl, she'd dreamed of making tarts and writing cookery books and having her own television show. Most people read stories. She devoured magazines and cookbooks, attended courses, watched cooking shows and baked the same thing over and over again until it was near to perfect in her eyes.

In her wildest dreams she was not only a national success but an international one as well. Like Charlotte with her cookbooks. Sally didn't crave fame for the sake of it. She truly loved what she did. Oh, okay. For the fame too, but not to be adored. Just to be recognized as the best. Oh, all right then. She didn't mind a little adoration too.

Her hopes for the future were all coming true. Viggo was the man she'd always dreamed of. Only he didn't know it yet. But she did. She'd taken one look and fallen hard. She looked up dreamily and her eyes brimmed with tears. She was going to cry with the sheer happiness of it all.

Alarm flared in Viggo's deep brown eyes. "I thought you'd be happy about the contract?"

"I am happy," she insisted as tears streaked down her cheeks. "I'm overflowing with joy."

"It doesn't look like it to me." He fished around in his pockets and produced a scrunched-up napkin.

She took it and beamed at him. "Thanks." She patted her cheeks dry, only to have fresh tears glisten in her eyes. She patted the moisture away again. "I cry when happy *and* sad. These are happy tears."

"Oh, I see," he said, but she could tell he didn't. Not really.

"I'm so happy," she told him. "I just have to give you a hug." She lunged forward and wrapped her arms around him and rested her head on his chest. Gosh, he was so tall. He felt wonderful and warm and smelled delicious. Almost like cookie dough. She burrowed in as much as decency allowed on a first hug.

He went stiff and awkward and tried to pat her on the back, but his arms were trapped by hers as she embraced what she could of him. She would have to go slow. If she came on too fast, she just knew he would run in the opposite direction. She inhaled. Oh my, he really did smell delicious. One of her legs left the floor and her knee bent in ecstasy.

A loud whistle from a cameraman echoed through the studio. Viggo stepped back, and she had to let go or look like a clinging limpet. Pity. He was all warm and toasty and he was giving her very tartilicious ideas. She hugged the contract once again to her chest, missing the loss of his warmth.

Viggo looked down at her, a guarded look in his eyes, that made her take a tiny step back to give him a little more space. "I do have more good news for you."

Sally grinned. "Let me guess. Charlotte's agreed to be on the show."

"How did you know?"

She squealed her delight and jumped up and down her arms raised in the air, like an Olympic runner claiming victory, the contract flapping wildly. "Because this is a dream come true day."

15

CHARLOTTE SAT AT HER OFFICE DESK SCROLLING THROUGH THE latest batch of fan mail. Cupcake rested his head on her lap and looked up at her with his big goo-goo eyes. She hunkered down, rested her cheek on the back of his neck, and gave him an enormous hug. "You're my darling. You love me unconditionally. George loved me that way too, but I pushed him away. I was scared I suppose. Do you think this dating lark will work?"

Cupcake's body tensed. His head swiveled toward the doorway and he emitted a low growl. A millisecond later there was a knock at her front door.

"Looks like we're about to find out," she said, glancing at the time on her computer. "He's early. Hopefully he'll whisk me off my feet."

She stood up and ran her hands down over her hips, brushing at the stray dog hair making her new dress look more, shaggy than chic. Uncharacteristically, she had laid out a mind-numbing amount of dollars, and bought something to caress and accentuate her curves instead of drowning them in layers. A little black dress. And boy was it little. But the store assistant had insisted she looked amazing and Charlotte, astonishingly, had found herself agreeing.

Wobbling dangerously in her very new strappy red heels, which made her legs appear slimmer and longer than she'd ever imagined them to be, she wended her way down the hall, terrified her legs would shoot out from under her and she would split a seam or something.

She was going to have to bake the store assistant a Little Black Dress Shortcake as a thank you.

Cupcake, the sweetheart, didn't even try to bolt for freedom when she opened the door. He sat when instructed, and stayed. "Good boy," she said, thankful the puppy training sessions she'd been lugging him to were beginning to pay off. "No barking at strangers. No eating cushions. No drinking the toilet water. And do not lick the remote control. Especially after drinking the toilet water."

"Well, gee," George responded, a twinkle in his deliciously dark eyes. "Spoil all my fun, why don't you."

Charlotte tried very, very hard not to laugh and failed. She continued to speak to Cupcake. "If you're a good boy, I'll give you an extra-special treat when I get home."

George bent and patted Cupcake. "Thanks."

Charlotte glanced up. "Not you, silly."

"Well, it's a treat for me just looking at you right now." He stood back and stared, as if seeing her for the first time. "You are absolutely ravishing."

"You're looking particularly handsome yourself in that fancy suit of yours. Shall we skip dinner and ravish each other instead?"

George laughed outright and when he settled he said, "I'm tempted, but no ravishing permitted on a first date."

Which meant there would be another date. Charlotte took a mental note to fit more clothes shopping into her busy schedule.

Charlotte was showing off her curves and they were in all the right places. How was he going to keep her at arm's length when every inch of her screamed *eat me*?

He tamped down the surge of attraction rampaging indiscriminately throughout his body and waited while she tossed a treat ball into the hall for Cupcake who obligingly scampered after it. When she pulled the front door closed he took her elbow and guided her down the path to his car parked behind hers in her small driveway at the side of her house. He opened the passenger door and inhaled as she wafted past him to take her seat. He loved her earthiness, but this new sophisticated woman had shifted the goal posts and he hadn't seen it coming.

"Where are we going?" she asked once they were in traffic.

"I've made a reservation at La Lumière."

He deduced Charlotte was suitably impressed when she asked, "What did you have to promise to get a table there? Did you offer to lick the maître 'd's boots?"

"Almost." George didn't mention that all he had done was mention Charlotte's name and they were more than happy to 'find' a table for them despite it being 'such short notice'.

"Licking, I recall, is one of your favorite things."

His foot slipped off the accelerator and the car bunny-hopped. George felt his cheeks grow warm. Just as well it was night and the light in the car minimal. "It's the prospect of being with you," he managed.

"I'm loving all this sucking up."

"You've got a fair bit of sucking up to do as well."

The light was muted but he could see enough to acknowledge she was the best thing since shortcake had been created.

As if she could read his mind she said, "I've baked up a lot of dates – the boyfriend variety - these past few years. Most have turned out to be crumbly and dry with no zest to speak of. You not only have zest, you are chock full of interesting delicious flavors and worthy of extensive research into how you are put together.

He glanced at her. "You look like you want to eat me." He swallowed and told himself to concentrate on driving and not on what those bites might entail.

"You're not wrong there," she licked her lips. "I don't imagine anything is going to be as succulent as you."

"There's no tasting the date tonight. The only thing your lips will be touching is the food at La Lumière."

She reached out and squeezed his thigh with her hand. Adrenaline shot with alarming accuracy to places that made him squirm in his seat.

She said, "If this is a game then you have to accept I'm going to do everything I can to get those tasty lips of yours on mine before the night is out."

He let out an amused bark of laughter. "Not a chance." He glanced at her as he pulled up outside the restaurant, more than thankful they'd arrived at their destination. "My game. My rules."

She pouted, a challenge in her eyes. He knew there was no way she was going to give up, plus he was going to have a hell of a time keeping his hands off her tonight.

But he was determined. He needed to be absolutely certain Charlotte believed she was good enough in her own mind. Absolute trust in a relationship was essential. Because this time, if they got back together, he wanted it to be for the long-haul.

The maître d' greeted them like royalty and took them to the best table in the house next to floor to ceiling windows where they could enjoy the glittering night lights of the city and harbor.

"I'm impressed," Charlotte told him honestly. "I never realized you were *so* important that you could get the best table here at such short notice."

He swaggered on the inside. "Thank you." But he had to

admit the truth. "It really wasn't hard once I mentioned your name. It seems the maître d' is a huge fan of yours."

"Really?" Charlotte was momentarily flummoxed. "I never realized I was that recognizable."

"You have never appreciated how highly regarded you are."

"The only people who matter are those closest to me."

There was a pause as they both gazed out at the view. George wished like hell he hadn't worn a tie, and loosened the knot. At the same time, he was grateful for his Calvin Klein suit. The pants were roomy enough to accommodate the action taking place down below without being overtly obvious.

"So," Charlotte said without turning to him, and he realized she was just as nervous as he was. "What do we do now?"

"We relax and enjoy dinner."

A discreet cough had them turning to their waiter, who handed them a menu each. "Can I get you anything to drink?"

George looked to Charlotte. He would have ordered a bottle of Veuve Cliquot, Charlotte's favorite, when he made the booking but felt it was too soon to toast the fact they were finally talking and possibly getting back together. "Do you want to start with a cocktail, or would you prefer wine?"

"These are your rules. You booked the restaurant. You choose the drink."

The waiter looked from George to Charlotte and back again.

"A Golden Dream for the lady," George told him, knowing it was her absolute favorite. "And a whiskey for me. On the rocks." Leaning back in his chair he opened the menu and saw the prices and began to cough uncontrollably. Miraculously, as if this happened often, a waiter appeared with water.

"Do you want me to pat your back?" Charlotte asked, all politeness, when he continued to splutter and his eyes filled with liquid.

He shook his head. "No," he rasped. "I'll be better in a minute." The meal had better be Michelin star worthy.

"My menu doesn't have any prices," Charlotte declared from behind her menu.

"Order whatever you want," he replied from behind his own.

"I'm famished." She shut the menu and placed it on the table. "I know what I want."

He figured she wasn't talking about food from the way she was eyeing him up, a teasing twinkle in her eyes. "Give me a moment," he told her. "I can't decide."

"Spoilt for choice," she added. "Leave room for dessert. I've got your favorite back home for afterwards."

"After what exactly?"

Charlotte winked. "After dinner of course."

"Sorry, but I have a new favorite now."

She didn't believe him for an instant. "What might your that be?"

"If you can guess, you can have me tonight."

"Strawberries dipped in chocolate."

He laughed. "Good try. But wrong. You'll never guess."

"If I guess your new favorite you're likely to lie and say it isn't."

"I might prevaricate, hedge or change the subject, but I never lie."

She picked up her Golden Dream which had discreetly arrived seconds before. "I believe you." For three months she had condemned this man, thinking the worst, tossing accusations of an affair with Sally when it was she, Charlotte, who was the one who had lied. She had lied to herself because she was afraid. George was right. She had trust issues.

"Start guessing," he encouraged. "I desperately want to taste whatever you have to offer, but this is a date with a beginning, a middle and an end. There's a ninety-nine percent probability I'm going home without tasting your bountiful delights tonight."

He thought her delights were bountiful. That made her happy. "Well, what about a kiss on the lips then?"

"On a first date?"

"I'll start guessing, and if I'm right I get a kiss. No. Make that a lip-locking smooch. Chocolate Dipped Strawberry Cream Shortcake."

"Tempting." He shook his head. "But wrong. If there is any lip locking it will be on my terms."

"But Chocolate Dipped Strawberry Cream Shortcake has always been your favorite. Remember? I was the shortcake and you did the dipping."

He shot a look toward the tables nearby. "Not so loud, minx. You're incorrigible."

"No, that honor belongs to Goldilocks. Ginger and Pear Shortcake Crumble."

"Nope. Give up. You'll never guess."

"By the end of the night you're going to be begging for a little slice of..." She paused and winked saucily. "Banana Caramel Pecan Pie?"

"Not even close."

She narrowed her eyes. "What has Sally done to you? Have her tarts spoiled your taste buds?"

"There is nothing better than one of your shortcakes, Charlotte."

She appeared appeased. "I love it when you grovel."

"That wasn't groveling. I'm stating a fact. They are the best."

Charlotte had polished off her Golden Dream. Her cheeks were rosy, her eyes sparkly and oh, so temptingly wicked.

"So what you're saying is there's no chance of me coercing your favorite out of you by nefarious means tonight?" Without waiting for his reply she said, "Black Forest cake with Drunken Cherries."

George's heart warmed and he admitted, "I'm drunk on you."

Charlotte's voice was serious when she said, "How could I ever have doubted you?"

"Only you can answer that."

She paused and stared at him intently, before stating, "I like this dating lark. It's like baking. First you add the right ingredients, combine them, and then place everything in an oven and hopefully it will, ah, rise to the occasion."

He reached over and grasped her hand, his thumb rubbing the sensitive pad near her wrist. "I might not be able to keep my promise."

"What promise? I don't recall you making one".

"One I made to myself. To keep my hands off the goods tonight."

"Broken already." She stared pointedly at their entwined fingers. "Kiss Me Quick Apple Charlotte."

He blinked and tamped down the urge to throw caution to the wind and whisk her home to see if her baking theory worked. "Nope! But it sure sounds delicious. Are you ready to order?"

Charlotte nodded.

George signaled the waiter and ordered their meal and wine.

"I sense sugar cinnamon success," Charlotte teased and continued throughout the meal to concoct all sorts of delicious desserts to tempt him, but she still hadn't guessed his favorite by the time they left close to midnight.

George didn't know whether he was happy or sad. He placed a hand at her back when she stood and he guided her out of the restaurant into the night to wait for the car to be delivered by the parking attendant. The warmth of her body intensified the scent she wore as it mingled with the crisp night air and he literally had to fight back the urge to pull her into his arms right then and there.

She grinned up at him, as if she knew exactly how he was feeling, but when she spoke her voice was serious. "I can't remember when I've enjoyed a night out more."

He felt the same. "You still haven't guessed my favorite shortcake."

"That's okay." Her voice washed over him with a promise of things to come. "You're worth the wait. I'll work on my guesses for the next date." She suddenly looked uncertain. "There will be another date, won't there?"

He ran an index finger down the length of her nose and wondered how long he could keep this game up before his will crumbled. "You bet."

16

———

Viggo couldn't fathom how Sally had sweet-talked him into taking her with him star-gazing, but, damn it, she had. He pulled his car into the curb, left the engine idling and flicked open his mobile to text her. *Am downstairs outside security gate.*

He'd told her he would not come up to her apartment despite her giving him her access code to get into the complex, having the feeling that if he went into her home, he might never come out intact.

He texted again. *Will wait in car.*

It wasn't long before he had his reply.

Come up. Apartment 4B.

He hauled air into his lungs, shut his eyes and let the oxygen back out in a rush. *Sorry. Can't wait. Come now or not at all.*

Fingers on one hand tapped the steering wheel while he scrolled through his mobile with the other and wondered what the delay could be. He had set down conditions for this field trip when Sally twisted his arm with the promise of another tart. He was going soft. He'd never taken a woman – well, one who knew nothing about astronomy – out star-gazing before. Ever. It was his special thing he shared with no one other than professional and amateur astronomers. Not even George or Myrtle. He was a nerd. An impatient one at that. He knew it. His family knew it. Sally was yet to figure it out.

Osiris meowed his thoughts from the back seat. Viggo glanced over his shoulder at his feline friend who went everywhere with him, especially on star-gazing nights, although he spent most of the time curled up on the back seat asleep. What would Sally think, he wondered? He silently thanked the universe that he'd managed to extract a promise from her to not bring Snuggles. Her little yappy thing would disturb not only his concentration but Osiris as well. Keeping the two of them from killing each other was not part of his plan for the evening.

Just as he was about to send Sally an I'm-not-waiting-any-longer message, he heard the click of heels on the pavement and then she peered in the passenger window. God, he should have mentioned she should wear flat shoes and casual clothes. They were best for this kind of adventure. Dressed in some kind of designer track suit, she wouldn't look out of place at a pool party or BBQ.

He jumped out of the car and rushed around to open her door, and it was just as well he did, for balanced in one hand was an enormous container – his tart, he presumed – and in the other, a large handbag. Also, weighing down both shoulders were two enormous bags.

"What the hell have you got in those," he grumbled. He relieved her of the container and her handbag and placed them on the back seat next to Osiris, who sniffed them both with interest.

Sally gasped. "Oh my giddy aunt. Your cat is in the car. Did you know?"

"Of course I know. He goes just about everywhere with me." Viggo moved to take one of the bags off her shoulder, but she had a grip on the strap so tight there was no way she was going to relinquish it without a tug-of-war.

"It's fragile." She flushed slightly, a flicker of guilt in her eyes.

He shot her a sharp, assessing glance. "What have you got in it?"

"My camera. A book on the do's and don'ts of star-gazing. I've been boning up on the subject."

The fact she'd taken time to undertake some research on the night sky impressed him. "I can understand the camera being fragile, but what on earth do you want a book for? You won't be able to read in the dark."

"The book is on my iPad. I have a backup torch just in case. Plus, there's all the other necessary accoutrements."

He arched an eyebrow. "I hope there's also a pair of sturdy shoes in there."

"Uh huh." She nodded. She indicated her left shoulder. "Take this one. It has napkins, a thermos with tea and a thermos with coffee. Plus milk and sugar. I like to be prepared. Although I didn't bring a knife as the tart is pre-cut. Plus, no plates. I thought we could use the napkins instead."

"Are you sure that's all you have in those bags?" He didn't hide the sarcasm in his voice. She was so darned cute standing lopsided in front of him

She looked him straight in the eye, bit her lip, hesitated, and then said, "Yes."

She lied so badly he almost laughed. He'd bet all the stars in the sky there was a Chihuahua in one of those bags and wondered whether to bother taking the time to draw the truth out of her but, she looked so guilty he found himself letting her get away with it. "Surely you've a jacket. There's a chill in the air tonight."

Sally indicated the bag on her right shoulder. "It's in this bag. It rolls up small," she elaborated, when he stared disbelievingly at it. "I'll carry this one on my knees."

Yep. Snuggles was definitely in the one she planned to rest on her knees. He opened the back door, and slid the other bag off her left shoulder. Osiris looked down his imperial nose as Viggo deposited the bulky bag on the floor.

"No marking your territory on the bag," he instructed the cat. He opened the passenger door for Sally and eyed the remaining bag. The straps were now tightly gripped in her hands. "You sure you don't want to put that one in the boot?"

Alarm flared for a brief second in her eyes. "No. it's fine."

He chuckled to himself as he made his way round the driver's side.

"Where do the stars hang out?" Sally asked him conversationally as she slipped the seat belt into its slot and rested the weightier bag on her knees as if it were precious cargo.

He frowned at the question as he strapped his seat belt on. "Where do you think?"

"You're the one who does the watching."

"Watching?" He shot her a momentary glance. She looked alert and interested. God help him for agreeing to let her come with him tonight.

"You said we might lose our spot if we don't hurry."

But his attention was diverted by movement coming from the bag on her lap. "Hadn't you better let your snapdragon out so he can breathe?"

Sally's hand smoothed tellingly over her bag. "Snapdragon." She didn't bother pretending not knowing he was on to her. "How did you guess?"

"My acute powers of deduction and observation. Your bag appears to be moving and you're a terrible liar."

She pouted. "Are you going to make me take him back inside?"

"You have everything else, so I expect you also have a leash in one of those bags?"

Her eyes twinkled and her pout morphed into a giggle that literally gave him goosebumps all the way up his spine to his scalp. "Of course. Like I said, I'm prepared." She twirled the bag around on her knees, and he discovered it was actually a dog carrier and Snuggles had been in no danger of suffocating at any stage. His little snout rested on what he guessed was Sally's jacket, rolled into a small ball just like she'd said.

"Good. Osiris's claws are dangerous and so are his incisors. It's not a good idea to leave them both alone together."

She unzipped the carrier and Snuggles' head popped out and immediately began to lick her hands in gratitude.

Viggo shook his head at his insanity in agreeing to let Snuggles come along with them, flicked his indicator on, and pulled out into the traffic. They drove out of the city in silence. Sally seemed happy to stare out the window and cuddle Snuggles, cooing every now and then while ignoring the I'm-going-to-claw-your-dog's-eyes-out meows from Osiris in the back seat.

Eventually Viggo flicked the indicator to the left and pulled off toward the coast, before driving the vehicle up a steep metal road.

"Is this a shortcut?" Sally asked as Snuggles pressed his little nose against the passenger window and lapped at the glass, his tongue leaving smears of slime behind.

Viggo kept his mouth shut about the mess Snuggles was making of the windows he'd only just cleaned a scant four hours ago. How could he complain when Osiris often did the exact same thing? "No. There is only one way up and one way down."

She blinked. "Okay." She found a clean spot on the window to press her nose against to look out as well. "I'm intrigued."

"We're nearly there. Not far to go now."

They continued in silence for another five minutes before Viggo pulled into a makeshift lot where six other vehicles were parked. "Not many here yet," he said, and grinned. "Our spot might still be available."

Sally frowned. "I fail to see how we could spot any stars from here."

"We're not there yet. This is where you need to change your shoes. You better get your jacket out too. It gets windy up here and there's a definite nip in the air. Put the leash on Snuggles as well before you get out of the car. You wouldn't want to lose him up here. There are no street lights from now on, the pathways are uneven and badly lit. If he gets lost we'll have real trouble finding him."

Grasping Snuggles' collar, Sally shoved off her strappy shoes and dug in her bag for her sneakers. "Just how far are we walking?"

Viggo opened her door. "Five, ten minutes at the most. I'll lead the way. Just stay close to me." He glanced upwards. "We have a myriad of stars to guide us. But bring the blanket from the back seat. You can wrap yourself up in it if you get cold."

Sally shot him a grateful look. "Are you always this prepared?"

"I do this every chance I get," he told her conversationally. "I'm prepared for most eventualities." Except, he told himself as he moved round to the trunk to retrieve his equipment, for Sally and her tiny perfect self as she shrugged into her jacket and put the lead on the snapdragon.

She emerged from the car and zipped up her jacket. "Don't you have other interests besides this?"

"Nope." he said with a grin. "This is my first love."

Her nose twitched and her mouth pursed into an expression he could only construe as disappointment. She waved her hand over the dark terrain. "What? Wandering about in the dark, spying on stars?"

He hefted out his telescope and slung it across his shoulder. This was exactly why he never took a date stargazing. Not that this was a date. At least he didn't think so. Perhaps she did! "I wouldn't call it spying."

She gave him a doubtful glance, and he wondered what the hell was going on in her mind. She was staring at him as if he was a pervert or something. "Not every night," he admitted. "Sometimes visibility is poor."

"Is that the only reason you wouldn't come out here?"

He kept a handle on his temper. "This isn't the only spot I go to. There are others, depending on the time of the year and the location of the stars."

"Your life is devoid of variety."

He blinked back his astonishment. "What? I love what I do."

"You're in danger of becoming one-dimensional."

He didn't appreciate being criticized. Especially when George had pretty much accused him of the same thing on far too many occasions to count. But he was family. They had a past together. George was allowed to criticize. "Talk about double standards. All you do is make tarts." Damn it. He regretted his words as soon as they left his mouth.

She blinked. She shut up for all of two seconds, and when she replied, her tone had softened. "I deserved that." She perked up almost immediately. "I guess we'll just have to learn more about each other then."

He gave her a brief, still irritated nod, tugged his backpack out of the back of the Jeep and lugged it over his other shoulder, the heavy weight hitting him in the back. He grunted again, then pulled out a torch and switched it on as it was now twilight and would be dark soon. The torch illuminated Sally for a second, and he glimpsed her expression before aiming the light toward the pathway which would lead them to his regular spot to set up his telescope. She was looking at him as if he was an alien. Maybe he should just shove her back into the car and give up tonight as a lost cause.

"I'm sorry," she said. "I didn't mean to offend you."

"You have every right to your opinions. But, at least wait until the night is over before expressing them."

She zipped her mouth with her fingers. "Sealed. Not another word of criticism shall pass these lips." She reached into the back seat and lugged her oversized and overweight bag out. Osiris looked up and meowed loudly.

"I thought Osiris was coming too."

Viggo shrugged. "He'll be happy in the back seat curled up on his rug."

"Are you sure he'll be okay all by himself? I thought he owned the mountain or something?"

Viggo arched an eyebrow. "He owns the car as well."

Sally shot him an amused glance. "I can see that."

"Cats can look after themselves." He looked pointedly at Snuggles, who was tugging at the lead in her hand. He would have been swallowed up into the night with one single bound of his tiny legs if he'd been free.

"Does Osiris always stay in the car?"

"I have a lead for him too. But since you have Snuggles, it's best if Osiris stays where he is."

"It seems mean to leave him here all by himself." She reached in to tickle Osiris's neck and a rumble of a purr vibrated through him.

"So now I'm mean as well as boring," Viggo harrumphed.

"It was a question, not a criticism."

He took the heavy bag from her hands, and she reached in and retrieved the Tupperware container.

"That tart of yours better be good. You're going to need to do a lot of sucking up to me afterward." He closed the door before Osiris could get out.

"I don't suck up to anyone," Sally told him haughtily, and followed him as he turned and guided her up the path with the torch illuminating the way. "All my tarts are exceptional."

"I'll give you my opinion *after* I've tasted it." He turned in the dim light and shined the torch toward her, catching her pissed off glare as she tottered in so-called casual shoes behind him. They were open-toed sling-back things with a tiny heel. He had the presence of mind not to laugh.

"This stargazing lark better be good otherwise I'll not be coming out here again," she threatened.

He huffed. "I'm devastated."

Her gaze turned as frosty as the night was promising to become. He spun around and began walking before she could volley a reply right back at him.

By the time they reached his spot twenty minutes later, she was completely out of breath. "I thought," she huffed vigorously, "you said it wasn't far."

"It's not with long legs. I had to walk slowly so you could keep up."

"Hmmmm," was all she said between puffs.

Surprisingly, Viggo was enjoying himself. Sally had gumption and stickability. He found himself hoping she would want to come out and bicker with him again. He'd even let Snuggles come if he had to. But looking at her current displeased expression, he guessed that maybe she wouldn't volunteer her company quite so readily if there was a next time.

She turned slowly in a circle. "So where are the other star gazers?"

"Oh, they'll have their spots somewhere." He dropped his bag to the ground. "This is my spot."

She looked uncertain. The ground was bumpy and uncomfortable looking. "It is?"

"Yep." He looked up to the heavens. "Such a clear night. Perfect in fact." He shrugged his telescope gently off his shoulder and took off the cover. He set it in the ground and then attached the rest of it to a tripod.

"I'm impressed," she told him as she dug around in one of her bags. "Mine is so much smaller."

"What is?" he asked absently, as he spread out a groundsheet and then a blanket over the top so they didn't have to sit on the damp grass. He placed the torch base down on the blanket so the light shone upward into the sky. He would switch it off soon, but would wait until Sally had herself sorted.

"This." She waved a camera under his nose. "I'm not going to get a good picture of the stars with this. I thought they would be much closer."

"Very funny. Love the humor."

She paused and fixed her gaze on the telescope. She blinked. And then looked at him as if something had just clicked into place in her brain. She started to laugh. Not one of those silly, simpering woman laughs, but a deep from the belly roar emerged past her lips. She clutched her midriff and doubled over before collapsing to the ground. The woman was a complete mystery to him. All women were, but Sally was more so.

"I suppose," she managed eventually, when he leaned down and offered a hand to haul her back to her feet, "we're not going to get close enough for anyone to sign this either."

Viggo shone the torch on the little book in her hand as she rifled the pages under his nose. The cogs clicked into place when he realized they had been talking at cross-purposes all evening. His lips curled upward into a grin, and within seconds, laughter – good, hearty, unrestrained laughter – echoed in the night air.

Sally laughed even harder, her voice mingling with his. "Now that's funny," she said. "Even if the joke is on me."

Snuggles grew so excited by the hilarity of his mistress that lifted his leg and peed on Viggo's shoes. Viggo let out an almighty curse.

Sally covered Snuggles ears. "Don't listen to the bad words, my baby."

Viggo grabbed a cloth from out of his bag and dabbed at the wet patch. Snuggles' reaction to his humor only added to the hilarity of Sally's misunderstanding and her earlier comments about his hobby. Stargazing would, definitely, never be the same again.

He dropped the cloth into a plastic bag and tied it tight and pointed to his telescope. "It's an optical telescope for looking at the stars in our universe." He fought to regain his composure. "The stars I watch are in the sky."

Sally fossicked about in her bag and pulled out a small packet of tissues. "Sugar. I haven't laughed so hard in years." She reached into her bag once more. "Vinegar," she explained as she placed a small bottle in his hand. "It will help neutralize the doggy smell on your jeans."

"Why am I not surprised you've got vinegar in your bag." He

waved the bottle away. "I'll worry about the smell later. If there is one." He was more focused on getting her to grasp his real purpose in coming out to this location. "I suppose the only way for you to understand what my passion is, is to take a look."

"I was really looking forward to getting a movie star's autograph."

"I know they're regarded as celestial bodies in some circles, but the only ones I care about are the ones in the sky." He looked into the telescope and focused on one of those stars then indicated for her to come stand in front of him. "Come take a look."

She didn't hesitate, and squeezed herself between him and the telescope. Her scent a heady mix of moonlight and citrus, caused an unexpected and totally alarming yearning for more to unfurl in his stomach and wend its way into his chest.

Spanning his hands about her narrow waist, he said, "Allow me to introduce you to a different type of star."

She leaned over the eyepiece, looked and stared into the telescope for what seemed an eternity. Her body grew still even with the distraction of Snuggles circling around them, ensnaring them together with his lead. Eventually she spoke, the air rushing out of her as she gasped, "It's so beautiful."

She twisted round in the small space between him and the telescope. His hands left her waist and he thumbed moisture from her cheeks. "You're crying." God, he so didn't understand women.

"It's not you. It's that bright thing in the sky." Then she broke the moment by whacking him hard on one arm with her tiny hand. "You got me good." Her head rocked back and she exploded into gales of laughter once more, and it was as if the stars in the heavens twinkled merrily in her eyes.

He knew in that instant, he was in very big trouble.

17

CHARLOTTE WAS IN HER KITCHEN WITH GEORGE, FREAKING out big time.

They'd managed to squeeze an appearance on Sally's show into her busy schedule for the following Tuesday due to a guest cancellation. "What was I thinking?" she wailed to Cupcake and George as she bustled about the kitchen with a large bowl tucked under one arm and a wooden spoon in the other.

Cupcake woofed his adoration at his mistress. George would have woofed too if he thought he could get away with it. Watching Charlotte at work in her kitchen was his favorite pastime. Perched on a stool near the end of the countertop closest to the dining room, he sipped on a Mai Tai complete with umbrella and fruit perched on the edge of the glass, as he watched her.

"You'll be wonderful," he told her. "I have every confidence in you."

Clearly she wasn't as freaked as she wanted him to think she was because, quick-smart, she came back with, "Sweet talking might get me naked."

"Kissing comes before naked."

"Kissing and naked go together like strawberries and cream."

"I could go for some of that," he admitted. "But first comes trust."

She banged her butter and sugar mix down on the counter. "I need stress release. Sex is a great way to calm the emotions." She broke an egg into the mixture and resumed beating.

"So is baking."

"If you're not going to agree with me, then get out of my kitchen."

He chuckled. "I'm not going anywhere. I'm enjoying the spectacle of you whipping up butter and sugar with your wooden spoon."

She waved her glop-laden spoon at him. "I'll whip your butt if you're not careful."

"Promises, promises. I love it when your boobs jiggle," he said as she beat another egg into the mixture.

"See." She thunked the bowl down and the spoon clattered onto the countertop. "That's why I shouldn't do television. Everything about me is wobbly. I'm a big girl." She signaled to her boobs and then smoothed her hands down over her rounded hips. "The camera will make me even more enormous than I already am. I'll be a wobbling spectacle."

"A gorgeous sexy spectacle." He slid off the stool, ambled over and snaked an arm about her waist. She glared at him for a second, then all the air deflated out of her like a light-as-air sponge. She dropped her forehead onto his shoulder and he inhaled her inherent sweetness. It fizzled about him in a heady wave and his body responded by rising into a painfully hard erection. "You're wonderful."

"You're just saying that to make me feel better." She looked up, a glimmer of teasing humor tilting the corners of her lips upward. "Although, I'd say something down below likes me a whole lot."

"It's staying behind the zipper until your trust issues are resolved."

She leaned in closer, testing his willpower, which was, heaven help him, wavering. He stepped back, and she pouted, picked up the bowl and the spoon and resumed beating and jiggling.

"I'm scared shitless," she admitted. She measured flour into a bowl.

Resuming his spot on the stool, he said, "Everyone is nervous the first time they appear on television. It's natural to feel some fear."

"And that helps me how?"

"By knowing you're not alone."

She picked up a measuring spoon and dipped it into a small container. "I'm hoping I'll just blend in, just like this baking powder," she told him as she sifted it into the flour she'd measured out earlier. "But somehow, next to the pint-sized Queen of Tarts, I'm going to look like an unshapely blob of marshmallow."

Several hours later, after Charlotte had finished baking the same shortcake four times and also practiced how she was going to present it for Sally's show, George took her down to the waterside.

Earlier in the day, before leaving his house, he'd pulled out a cooler and loaded it with bread rolls filled with chicken and salad, two apples, a bar of Belgian chocolate to share, and a bottle of bubbles to wash it down with. They sat on a park bench, the cooler between them, facing out to sea. The tide was on its way in, the water choppy, and the breeze brisk and cool even though it was mid-summer and supposedly in the middle of a heat wave.

Charlotte huddled into her jacket. "When you said let's go somewhere refreshing, I thought you meant a bar. Indoors. With lots of warming alcohol."

He raised his glass and clinked it with hers. "We have

bubbles. Champagne never fails to warm me up. I guess it will warm you to. You've been indoors all day. You need to clear your head. Tuesday will be here soon enough. You know the recipe backward, and you've memorized the patter and practiced it a zillion times."

"I thought I was the one prone to exaggeration."

He bit into his roll and made her wait for his reply. Eventually he said, "I'm not exaggerating. Plus, Sally has the patience of a saint."

"I'm not sleeping, worrying about all the things that could possibly go wrong."

Just yesterday, Charlotte had visited the studio with Viggo as an observer, to get a feel for what it would be like when she finally stood in front of the camera. "You weren't exaggerating when you said Sally is the easiest person in the world to work with."

She unwrapped her roll and bit into it. "Nothing fazes her. She doesn't even have a rehearsed script. She doesn't trip over her words, and says all the right things and finishes each segment right on time. I don't know how she does it."

"Experience and lots of practice," he told her. "Maybe not as many times as you over the past couple of days in your own kitchen, but then she's never had trouble with confidence."

She nearly choked on her roll. "Rub it in, why don't you."

He patted her back. "I'm stating facts. Nothing more."

"Couldn't you coat the facts in honey or something?"

"Relax. Let your personality shine through and everyone will love you."

"I almost believe you."

"I almost believe you believe me."

"I believe you believe you're attempting to build my confidence."

"I believe you believe I am and I believe you're right."

Charlotte slapped the half-eaten roll down on the wrapper on her knee. "I believe you believe you think you are soooo unbelievably clever."

"I believe I am. That's why I chose you over every other woman on the planet to be my girl."

She went all gooey inside, just like one of her Sticky Caramel Shortcakes. She wanted to shove the cooler out of the way and offer him a slice of her sweetness. Her mouth parted and her tongue moistened her lips. She stared at him and her heart beat fast and hard in her chest. She could tell he *do* wanted to break his rule.

"You want to kiss me, don't you," she teased. "You want to eat me in one big gulp." She could tell he was practically salivating for her.

"You know the rules. Trust first. Kisses second."

Compelled by his gravelly, sexy as hell voice she just had to ask, "What comes third?"

His eyes darkened to liquid molasses, his gaze raked her body like a hungry man, and she was left in no doubt as to what the third rule was. "We will have to wait and see."

18

CHARLOTTE MET SALLY OUTSIDE ALL BUTTERED UP BRIGHT and early on Sunday morning. Apparently it was the latest, hippest café in town. Charlotte's eyes were barely open. She wasn't a morning person and it was showing. Sally on the other hand looked bright-eyed and excited.

Charlotte scowled. "How can you be so cheerful this early in the morning? It's indecent."

Sally laughed, the sound musical, joyful even, and it hurt the brain cells in Charlotte's sensitive head. "I'm permanently happy."

"Like Pollyanna."

"Exactly. I'm also excited to be having breakfast with you."

Charlotte found herself explaining her grumpiness. "I'm always grouchy until I get some caffeine and sugar into my system."

"Well then. We definitely need to fuel up before shopping for clothes or we'll make all the wrong decisions."

Pondering on whether she should reveal she had already refueled on last night's leftovers in the hope it might wake her up or at least generate some enthusiasm, she said, "I should eat light. Something healthy so I don't stretch the stitching on all the clothes I'm about to try on."

Sally grinned. "If only I had your shape. You're a bohemian goddess."

Charlotte couldn't help the burst of pleasure at Sally's comment about being a goddess, although she wasn't so sure about the bohemian part. "I have trouble finding things to fit." She waved a hand across the front of her bust. "These creatures here don't conform to the average sizing rules in stores."

"All you need is a good cut and quality material," Sally said as they entered the café and made their way to a table. "I've a nose for design."

"That sounds expensive."

"True. But worth it in the end. Just you wait and see."

Charlotte didn't argue. The little black number she'd bought for her first date with George fitted her like a glove and had cost the earth. "I guess this means you're expecting me to part with vast sums of money this morning?"

"Huge. But it will be worth it. Trust me. I know what I'm doing. But first we need to refuel our brains and our bodies so we don't make poor judgments. Which is why I chose this place as our starting point. We need a good, honest, healthy breakfast to fire up those brain cells."

Charlotte's cells were waking up one at a time it seemed, but there were enough of them to realize she was in her own version of hell. This cafe was a no-added-sugar-zone. Her nose wrinkled in displeasure. The couple opposite them were tucking into enormous bowls of organic fruit salad, yoghurt and runny honey. "Just how healthy are we talking?"

"All Buttered Up uses natural sweeteners in its food. No white or brown sugar here. Fresh is best. No grains. No bad anything," Sally depressed her even further by adding, "Even the bread is made from ground seeds. There's bacon cured with

Maple syrup. No preservatives or water pumped into it. Wait 'til you try it. It's amazing. Oh, and you must try the organic free-range eggs. They really are soooo delicious."

Charlotte made a gagging sound.

Sally's laugh tinkled and Charlotte cottoned on to the fact that most of the patrons had recognized their local television star and were staring in their direction. Sally seemed to be refreshingly unaware of her celebrity status, or of the customers and staff who were plainly and in some cases rudely, staring.

"Making something without sugar or grains doesn't mean it's tasteless. I make genuine, honest-to-goodness fresh food all the time. I'm currently working on a cookbook where all my recipes are sugar free. Just like this place. I often stop in to get a fruit, nut and coconut yoghurt for breakfast. Now, this is my kind of fast food."

"I call leftovers from the night before good, honest fast food."

"You crack me up." Sally laughed again.

Charlotte failed to see how this was amusing. "But you're the Queen of Tarts. Everyone will be expecting you to eat loads of sugar on a daily basis."

Sally laughed even harder. "I adore what I do. I love tarts. But it doesn't mean I eat them all day long. I balance the load by eating healthy the rest of the time."

Charlotte could feel eyes focused on them and she fought against squirming in her chair. She didn't like being stared at. Oh why, oh why had she agreed to appear on Sally's show? Maybe she could break a leg by Tuesday. If she dashed out now she could throw herself in front of a car. She would blame it on brain fog due to lack of sleep, no grains and no sugar. "People are staring at us."

Sally blinked in surprise. "They are?" She looked around and nodded to those staring and even waved to a young girl who was pointing in their direction. "Isn't that lovely."

Charlotte failed to see the lovely right this second but didn't want to admit her failings to Sally. Such as the fact she ate way more sugar than Sally clearly did. "Let's get a move on then." She pointedly tapped her watch. "Time's marching."

"Oh, I already know what I want," Sally told her, and signaled for service. "What about you?"

"I'll have something buttery and rich," Charlotte said, feeling as if she had to support the decadent side of her nature. "Perhaps the creamy scrambled eggs on paleo seeded bread topped with camembert and organic champagne ham. That sounds pretty good to me."

"I thought you were going light so as not to stretch your seams."

"Looks like I don't have to." Charlotte licked her lips and decided she needed to order some of those sugar-free Sweet Potato and Chocolate Brownies in the display cabinet. "I'm a bohemian goddess after all."

With Charlotte's brain sufficiently refueled and her waistline two inches thicker, Sally revealed the delights of shopping for clothing in all the expensive places. Where Charlotte would never have looked at items on the racks, Sally plucked them off and tossed them with reckless abandon onto the growing pile in Charlotte's arms then shoved her into changing rooms with alarming regularity.

"I already have a black dress" she called out after one such journey to a cubicle. "I don't need another one."

"What if it's at the cleaners or in the wash?" Sally responded. "You need a backup."

Charlotte emerged from the cubicle and ran her hands down over her hips. "I look fat in this."

"You look.... Rubenesque."

"Rubenesque *and* bohemian." Charlotte wailed at the mirror.

"It makes me look like a woman in mourning. It's too... too..."
She struggled to find the right word. "Black."

"What about this one?" Sally shoved a bright emerald
number under Charlotte's nose. "This will contrast amazingly
with your red hair."

"I'll have you know my hair is not red, it's golden." Charlotte
grabbed the item from her and disappeared back into the cubicle.
Secretly she'd been looking forward to trying the emerald dress
on. Her eyes had zeroed in on it within seconds of entering the
store. The texture of the material was smooth and slid over her
skin in a sensual flourish.

She gasped at the reflection staring back at her. Where was
her mother earth figure? "Oh. My. God."

"What's wrong?" Sally called from the other side of the
changing room door.

Charlotte couldn't reply. Her eyes filled with liquid and her
heart did a little twirl in her chest. She looked as if she'd stepped
direct from the silver screen via some magical stargate.

"It can't be that bad, surely," Sally called out. "Champagne
and emerald should look amazing together."

Charlotte swiped a wayward tear from a cheek. She twirled
in the strappy heels the attendant had provided, inspecting
herself from every angle.

Sally called out, her voice laced with concern. "It's okay.
We'll find something else."

But Charlotte opened the door, and Sally was rendered
speechless. Her mouth dropped open and Charlotte's lips trembled into a glimmer of a smile. She figured Sally wasn't easily
silenced.

"There's no need to look elsewhere." Charlotte moved to
stand in front of a row of floor to ceiling mirrors. "This is
the one."

But Sally was still silent and doubt filtered into Charlotte's
head. "Unless you don't consider it's right for television?"

Sally found her voice. Thank God! "Oh, Charlotte. You look

amazing. Incredible. It's perfect for television. You're going to knock everyone's socks off. Especially George's."

"I'm hoping to knock more than his socks off," Charlotte responded as her confidence returned. "I have plans involving other parts of his anatomy as well, and this dress is likely to slay his resolve and get us both horizontal sooner rather than later."

19

CHARLOTTE HAD REHEARSED AND REHEARSED AND THEN rehearsed again, even going so far as to wake up and find herself reciting her patter to an attentive Cupcake, his large head resting on her thigh, while his ever-increasing girth anchored her to her bed. The pup was turning into a giant fluff ball, and he'd taken to skulking onto her bed in the wee small hours, after abandoning his perfectly good one on the floor in the corner of her bedroom.

She appreciated his loyalty and constant company. It was lonely in bed all by herself. Some nights she even hugged her pillow, pretending it was George wrapped in her arms. One morning she'd woken to find she'd been snuggling Cupcake's rear end. Phew. It didn't help that he'd eaten something definitely not from her kitchen the night before.

On the day she was to appear on Sally's show she arose at 1.42 in the morning to be exact and made her chosen recipe for the show one last time. It had been a total disaster. The marshmallow had melted and oozed over the sides of the dish onto the kitchen bench. She'd cried with frustration and had to resort to spending the rest of the night worrying about the dark circles under her eyes. In the end, she'd run a bath, made a homemade face pack of avocado, olive oil and honey, and plastered it on her face.

"I'm exhaustipated," she told Cupcake as she blobbed like a frustrated whale in the bath while he peered over the rim at the bubbles floating around in the water. He made a little woof before his tongue snaked out and slurped a few bubbles up.

"It's going to be a disaster. I just know it. I'm scared and definitely no slimmer than last week." She sighed and ignored Cupcake when he hiccupped a bubble out of his mouth. She placed a cucumber slice over each eye, leaned back and wallowed a while longer in her own self-pity. "God help me."

Apparently God had been listening to her plea. Charlotte stared into the mirror, hardly believing her eyes. It was amazing what a spot of war paint could do. She twisted this way and that under the dressing room lights. The makeup artist, Erin, was a miracle maker. Charlotte's skin was smoother than she'd ever thought possible and was the color of fine porcelain china. The dark circles the cucumber had failed to soothe away had miraculously disappeared under this amazing thing called concealer. She really ought to get some. Combined with the dress she'd bought the other day, she had been transformed into someone she hardly recognized, but liked a whole lot.

"Can I take you home with me?" she asked Erin. "You can live in my wardrobe. It's large and comfy in there."

Clearly, Erin had other ideas about living in a wardrobe, no matter how spacious. "Thanks, but I like the box I work in now."

"Pity." Charlotte sighed and tried to look dejected. "With you in my arsenal, I need never have another bad hair or makeup day ever again. What about if I sweeten the deal by baking a couple of dozen cupcakes for you and your family each week."

"Tempting, but sorry. No. Don't worry though," Erin told her. "I can teach you a few tricks of the trade. This way you'll save a fortune because I don't come cheap and my waistline will remain where it is."

Charlotte twisted and turned in the chair before the mirror, looking at her reflection from every angle. The coiled frizzy tendrils of her hair were, for once, sleek and shiny. Where was the real Charlotte hiding? She smoothed her hands down over the emerald dress. It was vibrant and bold. Sally had totally understood her free spirited nature. She left the chair and twirled, and the folds of the dress twirled with her. "I look incredible."

"You bet your sweet shortcake you do," Sally concurred as she walked into the room. "It's all you, you know. Erin has accentuated your wonderful features. But you've a natural beauty that shines through even without makeup."

Charlotte couldn't help herself. She grinned at her reflection and then laughed, suddenly wondering what she had been so worried about all her life. She turned and impulsively hugged Sally. "Thank you. You look incredible too. But then, you always do."

Sally passed a scrutinizing eye at her reflection in the mirror. She grinned. "Thanks. I do. But not half as good as you. Most women would kill for a figure like yours. I'm straight up and down, nothing much out front or back to speak of. I have to work hard to find the right garments to make me look as if I've got something going on under here."

Flabbergasted, Charlotte realized Sally meant every word. "Don't forget I saw you almost naked on my kitchen floor. There's nothing straight up and down about you. You're incredibly sexy."

The smile on Sally's lips was positively naughty. "But would you turn gay for me?"

Charlotte pretended to consider the question but her lips refused to co-operate and they tilted upward. "I'll keep you in mind if it doesn't work out between me and George."

The filming wasn't half as bad as she'd thought it would be. There was a small studio audience who clapped and oohed and aahed in all the right places. She'd had barely enough time to put the finishing touches to her shortcake before it was time for her to cut into it.

That was when disaster struck. Cupcake, who had been sequestered in a corner with Viggo during the recording of the show, managed to let out a series of large barks, drowning out everything Charlotte was saying to the camera. Seconds later Snuggles raced past in a blur, fortunately out of range of the cameras. Startled, Charlotte's hand jerked and the stuff of her nightmares came to fruition. Somehow, the slice she'd cut catapulted through the air and landed with a splat on Sally's face. A moment of stunned silence ensued and then everyone broke out into raucous laughter. Charlotte's eyes darted from side to side in her eye-sockets, her mouth agape and at a complete loss for words. The camera zoomed in on her horrified expression and then onto Sally's delighted face as she, without hesitation, swiped her finger through the strawberry marshmallow and sucked the sticky sweetness off.

"Oh my," Sally said, and her eyes rolled shut in bliss. "That is the best ever." And then she laughed so hard tears streaked down her cheeks as she recorded the ending of the show and filming came to an end.

The entire disaster hadn't gone live, yet, but Charlotte just knew the crew would talk and she would be in the news and possibly not in a positive light.

As Sally wiped away the sticky mess with some kitchen towels, she called for Snuggles. Cupcake, who was sitting on the couch Sally used to interview guests, looked up with a big dopey grin on his chops. "Woof!"

"Snuggles," Sally called again.

Cupcake woofed again.

Snuggles, it seemed, had vanished.

Charlotte shrugged out of her apron. Sally, oblivious to the stain from her shortcake seeping into her designer dress, began searching all the dark recesses of the studio for her fluff ball.

Viggo began searching for Snuggles, along with a cacophony of calls from studio staff.

"Snuggles."

"Where are you Snuggles?"

"Come out, come out, wherever you are."

"I've got a treat for you."

Although Cupcake looked up when he heard the word *treat*, there was nothing but the sound of his woofs and of his tail thumping madly against the back of the couch.

"Find Snuggles," Charlotte told him as she scanned the room holding a dog biscuit she'd dug out of her bag. "Find Snuggles for mama."

Cupcake's tail banged more wildly and he sat up and stretched his neck to rest on the ridge of the back of the couch. Charlotte looked behind the large piece of furniture. Nothing. But she paused, listening. She was sure she'd heard something.

"Quiet everybody," she yelled, and the room fell silent.

Sally ran over to the couch. "Have you found him?"

"Shhhh," Charlotte said. "Snuggles. Is that you?"

There was a muffled bark and Viggo joined them to listen as well. "I'm sure I heard something," he said.

"Snuggles," Sally cooed. "Where are you?"

"He's here somewhere," Charlotte insisted. And then they all paused again. Yes. Another muffled bark.

Sally hunkered down and peered under the couch. "He's not here." She got up and made a wide circle around everyone. "Snuggles," she called. "Where's my darling snuggly-wuggly?"

"He's likely to be hiding out of sheer embarrassment," Viggo muttered. "You can't call a dog snuggly-wuggly."

She shot him a frustrated glare. "He's my baby and I'll call him whatever I want."

"You don't understand," Charlotte told him. "You're not a dog lover."

"I don't hate dogs, but there are limits to names when speaking of animals."

"He's not an *animal*," Tears welled in Sally's eyes. "He's my baby and I love him."

Charlotte was swift to place an arm around her shoulders. "Don't worry. We'll find him." She sent a *stop-teasing-this-is-serious* glare at Viggo, who in turn changed his look to one of suitable concern.

"Oh, God help me," he uttered as they looked to him as if he was the one to solve all their problems. "I'll find him for you." He cleared his throat. "Snuggles," he called, his tone short, sharp, almost like a bark. "Come."

"Not like that," Sally insisted. "You'll frighten him."

"He needs to hear authority. I'm pretending to be the leader of the pack."

Charlotte stifled back a strangled sound of laughter.

Cupcake made a low growl in his throat, and Charlotte moved to grasp his tail so it wouldn't thump, thump, thump against the arm of the chair. "Call him again," she instructed Viggo. "Quick. I can't hold this tail much longer. It's like handling a wriggling snake."

This time Viggo's voice was gruffer. "Snuggles. Come."

Cupcake jumped up, placed his huge paws on Viggo's shoulders, and licked his face as if he were a delicious pudding.

And suddenly Snuggles' bark was no longer muffled. Charlotte sucked in air and felt her eyes grow large and round.

Viggo glanced over Cupcake's shoulder and exploded into gales of laughter.

Sally screamed her relief. "Snuggles."

And there he was, wedged in the crevice between the cushion and the back of the couch. He wiggled, but remained stuck. Cupcake gave up licking Viggo's face and turned to licking Snuggles.

"My baby," Sally cried, and shoved at Cupcake. "Get out of the way you great hulking beast. He's eating Snuggles. Oh my God, he's eating Snuggles."

Charlotte didn't know whether to laugh or be horrified. Surely Sally wasn't serious? "He's not eating Snuggles. He's licking him."

"To the death by the looks of things," Viggo offered unhelpfully.

Charlotte shot him a tight-lipped glare, ever conscious of the audience and crew still in the room watching the entire debacle unfold with not a small amount of hilarity. Sally was crying real tears. Charlotte felt a smidgen of guilt for laughing, and Viggo sobered considerably. Sally was genuinely upset, even if it was obvious to everyone that Snuggles was not suffering from his confinement. In fact, he seemed perfectly happy.

Viggo pried the offending cushions apart and Sally reached in and tugged Snuggles free. He wiggled with joy and licked her tears away.

But then, to Charlotte's sheer astonishment, Sally turned on her. "Your dog nearly killed Snuggles. Get him out of here now."

"He didn't do it on purpose," Charlotte protested.

Sally buried her pert little nose into Snuggles' neck, then spun on her designer heels and ran from the room, shouting, "Cupcake is banished from this studio. Never let him in here again."

So the perfect Miss Sally had a weak spot. It was gratifying to know she wasn't quite so perfect after all. Charlotte waved a hand at Viggo. "Go, make sure she's okay. I'm fine." And she buried her face in Cupcake's neck. "We're both fine."

20

VIGGO DASHED FROM THE ROOM, HOPING LIKE HELL HE COULD remember his way to Sally's dressing room, but couldn't help wondering if he had fallen down a rabbit hole like Alice in Wonderland.

He barged uninvited into Sally's dressing room. Even with makeup streaked with tears, she was the most beautiful creature he'd ever seen.

"What are you doing here?"

"I was worried about you."

She sniffed. "You were?"

He fought an insane urge to bundle her up in his arms and whisper soothing noises in her ear. His fingers twitched and he reminded himself such an action wasn't acceptable agent behavior.

"I'm fine," she hiccupped.

Clearly, she wasn't. "No, you aren't."

"Snuggles might have been suffocated. I don't understand how he wasn't."

Frankly, Viggo wondered the same thing. "I doubt Cupcake was trying to kill Snuggles on purpose."

She wiped her cheeks dry with the back of one hand and squared her shoulders. "I'm not so sure."

So she had a screw loose. Good. It would be easier to keep his hands at his sides and not tangled in her luscious locks. "I'm sure he wasn't."

She narrowed her eyes at him. "You think I'm crazy."

"Fruit-loopy." And sexy as hell.

"I'm serious."

"That's what I'm worried about."

"You forget I've seen you and Osiris together."

"Osiris isn't anything like Snuggles. I don't speak goo-goo noises to him."

"You take your cat stargazing."

"I accept Osiris is different but, we're talking about Cupcake and Snuggles here." Or they had been.

"Sorry. You might have guessed Snuggles is like my own child. I'm overly emotional about him." She lightly kissed the top of Snuggles' little head. "I just love this little snuggly-wuggly dog."

Viggo didn't roll his eyes even though he wanted to. "You need to apologize to Charlotte. It was my fault Cupcake got away from me in the first place."

She was calming down. The tears were diminishing. Sanity returning. "No. It was my fault. I allowed him into the studio. They seemed to be getting along just fine. I guess I hoped they were forming a friendship similar to me and Charlotte."

It didn't seem to matter which way Viggo looked at Sally, happy, sad, determined or apologetic, she made him horny as hell. Even now. He wanted to rip her clothes off and get it on with her on the day-bed over in the corner of the dressing room. He figured it could soothe her worries. It would certainly soothe his rampaging desire to lick her all over.

He had to get out of here before he did or said something stupid. "I have to go." He spun on his heels and marched to the door. "It was a good show. We can do another take of the ending. All is good."

"I know." Sally surprised him by agreeing. "But we won't redo the ending. It was television gold. In fact, I want to do another show with Charlotte."

He looked over his shoulder in astonishment. "You do? The way you spoke to her earlier made me assume you never want to see her ever again."

Sally gave Snuggles a huge smooch on his fury cheek before placing him on the ground. The tiny rug-rat trotted over to his bowl and scoffed down biscuits faster than Viggo could eat a slice of Sally's tart.

"I was upset about Snuggles." Without waiting for a response she said, "We should do a bake-off. We're good together on camera."

"Are you mad? There's every probability she'll not want to do another show. Gossip will be rife right across social media. Plus, she believes you never want to see her again."

Sally looked worried for all of ten seconds. "Everything will be fine." She crossed her middle finger over her index finger. "We're buddies. Or we will be again once she realizes I was scared something had happened to my little snookums'."

"Maybe you and snookums should wait for the results from the public before issuing another invitation."

"The viewers will love the show."

"I admire your confidence, but Charlotte isn't you. Being on television is a big deal for her."

"You saw her. She was fantastic."

He had to admit Charlotte had been a natural, and from his vantage point behind the cameras, she had looked incredible. George would be proud of her. He was too. "Yes, but will you be able to convince her of that fact?"

"She won't need convincing. Once she sees the show she'll be over the moon."

As Viggo walked into GVM some time later, he acknowledged to himself he was in deep, deep, do-do. He'd never met anyone as sweet as Sally. She wasn't the kind of woman to fool around with, to satisfy an urge and then move on. The kind of woman he preferred dating involved no emotional entanglement. That equaled no heartache. No one to abandon you when you needed them the most.

He strode through GVM, past the empty reception desk, and began opening doors, searching for Myrtle. Osiris trailed along behind him, meowing madly as if Viggo had been gone a week, when it had been a matter of three hours at most.

He found her in the tiny lunchroom at the back of the building. "Myrtle. I need you."

Quick as a whip, she replied, "Sure thing. Where do where do you want to do it? I guess your office is best as we don't want to be interrupted."

Good thing he knew she was joking. "Nothing is going to happen between us."

"Ah-ha! We're not blood relatives so it doesn't count." Merriment danced in her eyes. "I've given you years of adoration and you cast me aside so easily."

"The only thing you adore is yourself," he snorted.

"You have to love yourself before you can love anyone else," she shot back without hesitation. "You never date anyone long enough to find out what it's like to feel any emotion at all."

"Not you too. George has been at me as well." How could he argue with her when she was right? "Get out of my business."

"It's what family does. They get in each other's business."

There was no way he was admitting he'd been drooling all over the thought of Sally in his arms a short half hour ago. "No one messes with my business."

"Did you bring me a slice of Charlotte's shortcake? I'm sure to forget all about you if you did."

"Nope."

"I'm hungry. I haven't had lunch as I thought you were bringing me something."

"I bring you nothing but bad news."

Her eyes lit with a wary interest. She leaned forward and rested her elbow on the lunchroom table and propped her chin in the palm of her hand. "Gossip is almost as good as food. Go on, tell me more."

"It's as well the show wasn't being filmed live is all I can say. Charlotte splattered shortcake all over Sally. Cupcake disrupted the ending of the show by chasing Snuggles across the set. He sat on Snuggles, almost smothered him, and Sally yelled at Charlotte."

Myrtle's mouth gaped. Her eyes danced with merriment. "A tall caramel latte from the café on the corner will go towards keeping my mouth shut."

But, later that afternoon, shortly after the show went to air the Viggo crumbled into a chair at the tiny table in the GVM lunchroom and raked his hands through his hair. Greenspan had gone with the original take and also a short segment on Snuggles being rescued from underneath Cupcake. Which also meant, he was inadvertently, on television too. It was a blessing no hint of Sally's distress was revealed on camera. Only her relief on Snuggles being found.

"It didn't take me long to screw things up," he muttered.

"Screw things up." Myrtle was rubbing her hands in what appeared to be glee. "It wasn't you who flicked shortcake all over Sally. The calls and emails are already flooding in and reviews are nothing but positive. From what I can tell, the public want to see more of the same. There's already a request in my in-box for Charlotte to appear on Cooking with Daisy."

His eyebrows shot up. Daisy was the number one show across the country. So Sally was right in her assumption the public would love Charlotte. "What does George think?"

"I haven't heard a peep from him. But he's not stupid. He'll know this will be good for business."

Viggo shot her a disbelieving stare. "I'd like to believe you."

"Look around. He's not here to kick your sorry ass outta here. I'd take his absence as a sign he's okay with everything."

"I'm surprised he wasn't at the studio, seeing as he's in the process of attempting to win Charlotte's heart back."

"There is no heart to win back. It was never lost in the first place. Besides, he listened to me for once and stayed home. He's chased Charlotte since their split. It's Charlotte that needs to do the chasing now."

Viggo wasn't convinced. "Last time he took your advice he ended up in hot water, if I recall."

"What is it with you men? You only remember the bad stuff. What about all the good advice I've dished out over the years? Surely that outweighs the bad."

He struggled to remember any good results when Myrtle meddled, but he wisely kept his thoughts to himself. "I certainly hope you're right."

21

CHARLOTTE STOOD TRANSFIXED IN FRONT OF THE TELEVISION, her hands clamped over her mouth. Her mobile lit up. She ignored it as she tried to take in what she'd just witnessed. They'd used the piece where the shortcake had splattered over Sally. And Cupcake sitting on Snuggles.

The phone buzzed again. She glanced at it. It was Myrtle. She picked up the phone but didn't even get to say hello before Myrtle said, "Your backbone seems to have over-asserted itself."

"I didn't do it on purpose. And why didn't they get me back in to shoot a better ending?"

Myrtle let out a raucous laugh. "Because it makes good television. The phones are ringing hot. My in-box is full."

"Sally must really hate me."

"You have never been more wrong. Sally does not hate you. In fact, she loves you."

Charlotte instinctively stood taller. "How much does she love me?"

"Enough to invite you back for another show. Viggo told me so."

"Oh, fudgciles. No. I'm never doing television again."

Myrtle cackled like a disbelieving old witch. "Right."

After her conversation with Myrtle, Charlotte went online to read the local newspaper. And there she was. Front page news, along with a giant photo of Sally with shortcake all over her face. She stared at it for several long minutes, waiting for... something. But instead of plunging into the depths of despair, she found herself chuckling. The journalist had taken an amusing approach with a clever turn of phrase. If she was in the paper, there was every likelihood she'd made the televised news as well. A quick check revealed her instincts were correct. Yep. She was there too.

According to Myrtle, she was trending on Facebook, Twitter and Instagram as well. But it was when a national news channel picked it up that her phone began to vibrate incessantly. How the hell they'd got her number she didn't know, but in the end she flicked the sound to mute and stuffed it under a cushion on her couch.

She valued her privacy. She valued the quiet so she could create new recipes. She didn't want continuous interruptions each and every day. Her life was planned out for the next year with cooking demonstrations, classes and a book release, and now it seemed the rest of the world wanted a piece of her as well.

How in the world did Sally do it every day?

Instead of hiding in her house and devouring more sugar, Charlotte pointed her car toward George's run-down, ramshackle house on a hill looking out over the bay. The view and the land meant it was worth mega-bucks.

The house itself was an eyesore that should have been demolished years ago. But George had seen its potential, and loved that it had a history, and so had she. She held a closely-guarded fantasy in her heart that they would both live in it, eventually. But then she'd spat the dummy, been jealous about nothing, and they'd split up.

So when Charlotte pulled up outside the property, she was astonished by just how much work had been done on the house.

George hadn't been skulking around doing nothing in his spare time. For a second she forgot all about herself and stood at the end of the garden path under an arbor abundant with the heady scent of the climbing roses she'd planted several months ago. She inhaled and felt the breeze wash away her worries.

George was, apparently, a building genius. The ramshackle villa was ramshackle no longer. Every board had been sanded and painted a warm ivory. Every window fastidiously planed and repainted an antique white. The wide, covered verandah surrounding the entire circumference of the house was exactly as she'd always imagined it would be. In fact, it resembled a photograph she had once pulled from a magazine, right down to the outdoor wicker furniture and padded cushions now situated in a cozy corner on the front verandah.

Shock rooted her to the spot. George had built the home Charlotte had always dreamed of living in. All these months, when she'd been cussing his name, calling him a two-timing bastard, he'd been diligently turning his ramshackle house into a home.

She went weak and her knees buckled. She reached out to steady herself and found her palm pierced by a bunch of thorns. Tears filled her eyes as she nursed her hand and blindly tried to pull the small sharp thorns out.

Cupcake leaned into her thigh and looked up at her with concern. And then George was there, rushing down the path to rescue her. He likely thought her tears were pain induced, and they were, but it was the sheer magnitude of her past erroneous thoughts and actions that caused her to feel so much sadness and regret.

"You're hurt," George murmured, holding her hand as if it was one of his fragile roses and began to gently pull out the rest of the thorns.

It didn't help that he'd removed his shirt. His biceps were contracting almost as much as her womb in response to his near nakedness. The tears in her eyes dried in an instant. Moisture was needed elsewhere. Careful not to drool and make a complete and utter fool of herself, she'd already done so on television, she looked down at the back of his neck as he inspected her hand, and inhaled his masculine scent. He reminded her of a combination of leather and cinnamon apple cake. He was yummy. So very, very yummy, and she wanted to eat him all up.

He'd built her a house made from her dreams and an arbor of roses to ensnare her heart. Well, okay, she'd planted the roses, but he'd kept them alive and nurtured them to an abundance of blooms cascading over the entrance arbor.

Compulsion seized her. She needed to show her gratitude the only way she knew how outside of a kitchen. Her head dipped, and pressed her lips to the sun-warmed skin at the back of his neck.

22

"WHAT ARE YOU DOING?" GEORGE DUCKED AWAY BEFORE HE did something that involved naked bodies, entwined legs, and thorns in both their butts.

"Thanking you," she told him simply, and her hand reached out to flick a strand of wayward hair off his brow.

George had watched Tempting Tarts before heading outside to sand the windowsills, prior to giving them a final lick of paint. But mostly, he'd headed outside to stop himself from calling Charlotte to see how she was coping, hoping she would come to him instead of retrenching to her kitchen and eating as she normally did when life got tough.

It was a strategic move on his part, and it looked as if it had been a success. He waggled a finger at her. "No kissing or touching allowed."

But he wasn't quick enough. Her hand clamped around his finger, and she looked at him, moisture brimming in her eyes. "Those are your rules. I've my own and they include kissing you as often as I can."

He looked to the heavens and wondered how long he could

keep this dating thing without the naughty bits going. "I saw the show."

A cloud of doubt invaded her eyes. "Oh. Right. So you know then."

"It was a good show."

"It would have been. Everything went perfectly until the end."

"It was funny. Sally handled it like the professional she is."

"Are you saying I'm not?"

Ah. The prickly pear was back. Much easier to deal with than sultry kisses. His level gaze conveyed exactly what he thought of her comment. "I said no such thing."

She increased her grip, refusing to relinquish her hold when he attempted to pull away. "Well, then. What did you mean?"

"It was a good show," he told her again. "In fact, my gut instinct tells me the public will love it too."

The doubt was still there in her eyes, but she relaxed a little. "They do. It's all over the media."

He was downright pleased. "Plus, you looked amazing."

"I did?"

"You know it. Was it as bad as you thought it was going to be?"

Charlotte paused, and he knew her mind was doing a run-through of the entire show. "No. It wasn't."

Her admission was a big deal. He grinned and finally managed to withdraw his finger, flung an arm around her shoulders and began to guide her up to the house. "I'm proud of you."

She turned her head, her mouth a few paltry inches from his. "You are?"

He withdrew his arm and put space between them before he gave in to the compulsion to kiss her. "Very."

A light twinkled in her eye, and she beamed. "I'm proud of me too. You don't know the rest of my story though," she said. And as he led her up onto the verandah, she enlightened him on how Cupcake had nearly killed Snuggles, and how Sally had banned him from the studio. "Probably forever," she told him.

She hooked Cupcake's lead under one of the wicker chairs and sat down in it so he couldn't run away with the chair.

"Viggo never mentioned that." And neither had Myrtle. He perched on the balustrade, his arms crossed against his chest. "It's a good thing you don't like appearing on television then."

Charlotte hesitated. George knew that look. She wanted to do it again. He nearly laughed out loud.

"Viggo said Sally wants me back again."

George grinned. "And what do you want?"

"I'm still thinking on it. But let's not talk about me. I want to know about this house. I can't believe what you've done to it."

"You like it?"

"Like it? Are you kidding me? I love it."

"I did a lot of the work myself." Pleasure at her appreciation coursed through him. "With me no longer in demand at GVM I'm considering adding building services to my CV."

"I've told you, I'll take you back as my manager."

"I prefer you as my girlfriend."

"But I'm not, am I?"

"Yes, you are."

Her cheeks warmed to a delightful pink. "We're not sleeping together."

"We need to get your confidence sorted before any sex happens. Be assured that when we get together in the bedroom, there will be no sleeping involved."

She looked inordinately pleased. "I thought sex and relationships went hand in hand."

"I don't want to ruin what we have. This time we're doing it slow."

She groaned her frustration, shut her eyes and locked her knees together.

He knew how she felt.

But then her eyes popped open and she changed tack. "Are you going to show me around?"

"If you want."

"I want to see the kitchen."

"Don't you want to see the bedroom first?"

She tossed back her long golden locks and leaned back into the chair. "Kitchen first."

"Hmmm." Their very first physical encounter had involved a kitchen, a bowl of cream, and strawberries. Maybe it wasn't the best room to start a tour of the house.

He held out his hand and she slipped her fingers into his, and he tugged her to her feet. Given the opportunity to escape, Cupcake took off into the garden with the chair flying behind him, one wicker leg trapped in the lead.

"Cupcake," Charlotte called out. "Come back right now." But Cupcake was chasing an imaginary rabbit and wasn't hearing anything right now.

"Leave him," George said, as the chair was liberated on the lawn. "The property is surrounded by a fence and it's too high to jump." He fished a small device out of his pocket and pushed a button. "I've closed the main gates. There's nowhere he can go."

"Except straight off the cliff. There's no fence there."

"I'm pretty sure he's a happy dog. I don't imagine he's going to throw himself into the bay intentionally. Come on."

With one last look at Cupcake, who continued to race about the wide green expanse as if he'd won the lottery, Charlotte followed George into the house.

Charlotte stood in the doorway of the kitchen and her heart flip-flopped in her chest, a wild surge of hope causing her throat to close up. She gasped. It was everything she had ever imagined the perfect kitchen to be. Old-fashioned and yet modern with a large table at the epicenter, the benches were wide, made from gleaming natural timber – she didn't know what kind, but they looked like New Zealand's native reclaimed kauri. She'd always wanted kauri benches ever since she'd viewed pictures in an Architectural Digest magazine at the dentist years ago. How he'd managed to get a hold of kauri was unfathomable. The cupboards, although new, had an old country kitchen feel and were painted a soft dusky blue. The windows were new and bi-folding and stretched along the entire far wall, providing an uninterrupted view of the bay.

Outside, Cupcake sat on the lawn, his canine nose raised in the air, the light breeze ruffling his increasingly unruly fur into a dance of its own. He looked supremely happy to have so much lawn to play on.

Charlotte understood how he felt. Joy swirled around her heart and cooked up a little batch of imaginary, light-as-air angel cakes as she fell even more deeply in love with George.

She ran her hand over the countertop. "Its..." Oh God, she was going to cry. "Stunning."

"Really?" The slightly anxious flicker in George's dark choco-late brown eyes disappeared. "I tried to imagine what... what a cook would want," he admitted. "So that's what I went with."

Please, please say it was me.

"I was listening when you told me what you needed in a kitchen. Plus, kitchens sell properties."

Disappointment deflated the angel cakes fluttering around her heart. "You intend to sell?"

"Possibly. This is a family home. It deserves to be filled with children."

Charlotte agreed. But she wanted those children to be theirs. "Surely you want to live in it after all your hard work."

But George just nodded and said, "Perhaps. Come on. I'll show you the rest of the house." And her disappointment turned what was left of the angel cakes into hard rocks of discomfort that made her feel nauseous and so dreadfully unhappy.

23

WHEN CHARLOTTE HAD ACCUSED GEORGE OF INFIDELITY ALL those months ago, George had retrenched to his villa. After two weeks of moping around the house like a lovesick moron, he'd begun to work in earnest. He had taken solace in physical exhaustion. At first, the work kept his mind busy and his body too dog-tired to worry about what he was missing.

As the weeks passed, he'd emerged from the cloud of unhappiness to discover he enjoyed working with his hands, and so he'd continued throughout the long hot summer mornings and evenings as well as most weekends. Now, he understood Charlotte's awe. Even he was awed by what he had accomplished.

Most important to him though, was Charlotte loved what he'd done with the villa. He'd built it for her and he knew she was angling for hints but he wanted to be sure before he committed his home and heart into her hands again.

An hour after her unexpected and totally welcome arrival, they were back in the kitchen eating store-bought chocolate chip cookies and drinking freshly made cappuccinos from a state-of-the-art coffee machine he'd bought in a moment of extravagance.

"You still haven't guessed my new favorite dessert," he teased.

She inhaled the aroma of fresh cinnamon sprinkled over the top of the frothy milk. "Don't worry, I'm building a list. I've been writing my guesses down so I don't repeat anything."

He laughed. "Anytime you're ready, start guessing."

"What's the point when there's no hanky-panky in our fore-seeable future."

"But if you guess, it's fast-track all the way. That was the deal. I never renege on a deal."

"But then I won't evolve into the woman you want."

"I need you to be the woman you want to be, Charlotte." His tone grew serious. "Other than trusting me, I don't want you to be anything other than yourself."

She blushed. "I value your opinion more than any other. I don't want to disappoint you."

His eyes warmed to a dark chocolate, and he reached out and cupped her cheek. "I want you to value your own opinion more."

"So what's your opinion on Pear and Ginger Torte?"

"I'd value it highly, but it's not my favorite."

She flung her hand out and waggled her fingers toward her handbag on the kitchen counter. "Pass it over, will you."

He reached out and snagged it for her. She delved in and pulled out a notebook and pen. "Pear and Ginger Torte," she repeated as she jotted it down at the bottom of a longish list, and then scratched a single line through it.

She nibbled the end of the pen. "Whatever way you look at it, I win. I mature into the woman I want to be, and once I guess your new favorite sweet treat I get to nibble it off that chiseled body of yours."

He actually snorted. "I don't recall that part of the bargain."

"Well, you did say I could taste your bountiful delights."

"We were talking about *your* delights."

"You're just being picky."

"Believe me, I'm very picky when it comes to sampling some-one's bounty."

"Oh, my God," she giggled. "You're so bad it's wonderful. Your new favorite dessert is Chocolate Cream Pie."

"Sadly, it's not. But I sure won't object to tasting one."

She wrote down her guess in the book and scratched it out. "I've no objection either. Shall I make one now?"

She so wanted to test drive this amazing kitchen. Her fingers itched to open the cupboards and fridge to see what they harbored. She shot from her chair and started searching. She pulled out a pantry on glide rails and inspected its contents. "Flour. Baking powder. Sugar. Chocolate." She opened the fridge. "Cream. Check. Butter. Check." She looked about for eggs. "Yes," she cried when she spied them in a bowl on the bench. At room temperature too. She shot George a flirtatious glance. "Anyone would wonder if you'd set this kitchen up with me in mind."

All she got were raised eyebrows and a growl as he rose and dug in a cupboard, and pulled out a set of mixing bowls. "Get started, woman. I've a hankering to watch you bake. There's nothing I'd like better."

Charlotte arched her eyebrows in return, disappointed he hadn't immediately spilled his heart onto the table and admitted that yes, the kitchen was made especially for her. "Nothing?"

"Darling," he growled as he also retrieved a set of electronic scales and measuring cups, "You are incomparable when it comes to cooking in the kitchen."

"Oooh. I feel all warm and fuzzy. I don't need those. I measure by eye."

George put them away again. He ran the tip of his index finger down her nose and handed her a wooden spoon instead. "There's nothing sweeter than you."

"So you're saying my baking is sweeter than my loving." She felt so smug right now. She finally knew what his favorite treat was. He'd practically told her outright, but instead of falling into his arms and revealing what she'd figured out, she grabbed a stick of butter and the sugar, dumped them into a mixing bowl, and whipped up a light-as-air creamy mix. She had a hankering to prolong the anticipation as long as she could.

"Well then. One outrageously delectable Chocolate Cream Pie coming up."

She glanced out the window and saw Cupcake bounding past, chasing a butterfly as it flit from here to there on invisible currents of air. "Do you have anything Cupcake could eat? Baking this pie will take forty minutes or so and it's past his dinner time."

24

MYRTLE WAS IN HER ELEMENT. THE INCOMING PHONE LINES were ringing one after the other and she reveled in the excitement. Viggo, on the other hand, retreated to the office, wishing like hell he'd never agreed to representing Charlotte and Sally.

He didn't know if the churning in his stomach had anything to do with the attraction he had for Sally, or the fact GVM was being bombarded by the media, which meant he was *it* when it came to decisions about their futures. Myrtle was doing an awesome job schmoozing. Thank the stars, because he didn't have a single schmoozing bone in his body.

He'd been trying to call George on his mobile for advice on what to do for the past hour, but he wasn't picking up. "George," he bellowed at the work phone as if it could answer back. "Where the hell are you?"

His landline rang, and he stared at it, wondering at the synchronicity, but it wasn't George's number on the screen. Ignoring the call, he let it ring. He stood, with the intention to track down and torture his soon-to-be-dead business partner in person for putting him in this position when Myrtle burst into the room, a wide-eyed look of crazy excitement in her eyes.

"What the...?"

"Answer the stupid phone," she rubbed her palms together. "You'll want to hear this."

Alarmed at her tone, he stepped backward, feeling wary. "Why?"

"It's the best news ever."

"You tell me first."

"You're going to want to hear this." She picked up the receiver and shoved it towards him.

Call George, he mouthed. *Let him handle whatever it is.*

But she instead turned on the audio button and said, "Viggo's right here. I'll put him on."

He shot her an I'll-get-even-with-you glare and reluctantly, spoke up. "Viggo here."

A voice boomed back. "I understand you are assisting with the management of Charlotte and Sally?"

Oh so reluctantly. "Yes," he replied.

"We're interested in putting together a live televised one-off show featuring the two of them in a bake-off. If we're lucky it will be picked up by the major food networks across the country. Those two are dynamite together."

"Who is this?" he asked, stalling for time. He mouthed to Myrtle, *Get George on the phone. Now!*

The voice came back. "Kevin Spade. Senior producer for Greenspan Television."

For once, Myrtle obeyed him, but it took her several excruciating minutes to get an outside line due to all the incoming calls from the media. Viggo wasn't entirely convinced she wasn't fudging it, so he had to continue speaking to Kevin.

Then she pressed a button and George was suddenly patched in. And thanks to all the stars in the universe, he took over, negotiating terms, discussing dates and contracts, yada, yada, yada.

Viggo collapsed back into his chair as the details were discussed. Eventually Kevin hung up, leaving George on the speaker phone. "I'm not equipped for all this shit." Viggo had

had enough. "Stop playing builder and get your sorry ass back in here now."

"I'll review the paperwork when it arrives," George said. "Meanwhile, you're still in charge. So drop the attitude and I'll meet you first thing tomorrow morning. We'll nut out the plan on what you need to discuss with Sally. Charlotte's already here. I'll run the idea past her now."

"Will she agree?"

"She will take some convincing. Myrtle. Are you still there?"

She was grinning like the cat had got the cream. "Yep."

"Don't you say a word to anyone. Nothing is signed on the dotted line. I don't want the papers or social media hearing about this until all parties are agreed. Got it?"

"Got it." She pretended to zip her lips with her thumb and index finger. "All zipped. Not a word to anyone."

George was thankful Charlotte was outside filling a water bowl for Cupcake from the garden hose when the call came through. He wasn't sure she would say yes to the offer. And yet, she hadn't been as put off as he'd expected her to be by her first outing on television. But this was a far bigger deal than any of the had expected.

Charlotte meandered across the grass and onto the patio. She slipped off her shoes and walked through the bi-fold doors into the kitchen, a picture of happiness. He could envisage her living here with him. He could envisage his life being spent at her side. He could envisage their having children together. Hell! He'd been envisioning this scenario all these long lonely months.

What he couldn't envisage was her agreeing to do a show that may or may not be picked up by major food networks across America.

"That pie smells cooked," she said as she wafted past him, grabbed a couple of mitts and opened the oven door.

And he was cooked too, if he didn't approach this right. "You know how you said you might accept another invite from Sally."

She paused and he caught the flash of suspicion in her eyes at his tone. "Yes. There were parts I really enjoyed. And then there was the part where Sally yelled at me."

"She must be over it or she wouldn't want you back on her show."

"I guess it's true, but I need to speak to her to make sure everything is square with us." The blush on her cheeks had nothing to do with the heat from the oven when she admitted, "I really like her."

He broke into a grin. "I never thought I'd hear you say that."

"I never thought I'd say it either." She put the pie crust down on the bench to cool and began to prepare the chocolate cream filling. "I was wrong. About her. But most of all, about you. I should have trusted you."

Unable to resist, he came up behind her and wrapped his arms around her middle, and nuzzled the back of her neck as she stirred melted chocolate into the mix on the bench. "So would you trust me if I said it would be good for you to accept her offer?"

She leaned back into his body and chocolate ended up on the bench instead of the bowl. He reached out and swiped some of the chocolate onto his index finger and smeared it down the side of her neck, then devoured it off her skin.

"I'm considering it," she said, and attempted to pull away from him, but she was caught between him and the bench.

"You better hurry up and guess my favorite shortcake, or I might have to take matters into my own hands."

She dipped a finger into the bowl, turned round, smeared the mix down the length of his nose and surprised him by stating, "I already know what it is."

Oh he sure wished she'd tell him. He was going insane with desire and it was taking all his will not to succumb. "No, you don't, or you would have said already."

"Don't you know, I've been toying with you." She grinned but said, "There's something else on your mind and it has nothing to do with us getting down and delicious right now."

The minx. She had been leading him a merry dance when he could savor more than a chocolate cream pie in this kitchen. "Oh, but it does."

She gave him her best *I don't believe you* glare.

He relented and backed away. It was safer that way. "Okay. There is something, and I'm not sure how you're going to take this, but the call I just took while you were feeding Cupcake was from Greenspan. They want to do another show with you." He held out a hand to stop her from speaking. "This is not about Tempting Tarts. They want a televised bake-off between you and Sally. A special one-off show called Tart vs. Shortcake."

"A bake-off!"

Her voice had turned all squeaky, and she'd grown pale. He guided her to a chair at the dining table. "Sit down before you fall down."

She shook off his arm. "I need to finish the filling for the pie." But her legs crumpled and she sat as instructed.

He picked up the cream filling and brought it to her, and then collected the pie base and brought it over too. Pulling out a chair, he sat next to her. "Finish your pie while you think it over. It's a good offer."

She rubbed her forehead, leaving traces of chocolate cream behind. She ran both hands through her curly hair, leaving it as wild as the fear in her gorgeous emerald eyes.

He sat, giving her time to digest this news.

Her eyes were open, big and wide. Her long lashes batted as she blinked. "What are Sally's thoughts?"

"I don't know. Viggo is going to speak to her tomorrow."

Charlotte nodded. "She'll be super-duper excited."

He nodded. "I expect so. The question is, are you super-duper excited too?"

She pushed the cream mix out of the way and rested her forehead on the table. "I'm in shortcake hell. I'm super-duper scared."

He bit down on his bottom lip to stop himself from chuckling. "It's a wonderful opportunity."

She moaned. "I knooooooow."

Better get it over with. "That's not all."

"Tell me now," she moaned again. "And then I'll kill myself and Sally can find someone else to have her bake-off with."

He laughed outright. "It's Greenspan's idea. Not hers. There's a real possibility the show will be broadcast live nationwide on at least two of the top cooking channels."

Her head popped up and she looked at him as if he'd developed two heads. "That's not funny."

"No. But you are." He brushed a hand over her hair, and it bounced right back. He smoothed his palm down the side of her cheek and then gripped her chin lightly between his thumb and forefinger. "It's one of the wonderful things I love about you."

Her lips quivered. "If I say no, then Sally's dream flies out the window. How can I possibly do that to her?"

His heart warmed and he thought he couldn't love her any more right this second. "If you do say no, there will be other opportunities for her."

"So you'd accept a no from me if I don't want to do it."

He nodded. "And Sally would too. I want you to be happy. I'm not going to force you to do anything you don't want to do."

"Oh, George. You are the best manager ever. Let me think it over. Plus I need to talk with Sally first."

"I am not your manager and okey."

"That's right. I forgot for a second. Viggo is the best manager ever. You are the best boyfriend in the history of the universe. Even if we aren't doing *it* yet."

25

Viggo drove over to Sally's apartment after his meeting with George. He told himself he was going to Sally's because he wanted to see her reaction to the good news. He was fooling himself of course. He just plain wanted to see her in person.

Plus, she might have something sweet to taste. Of course, as that thought arrived in his mind, so did an image of her mouth pursed in a teasing pout.

Oh boy. He so wanted to taste those lips. He hadn't counted on her surprise attack at the studio the other day when she'd planted one on him. She had been as delicious as one of her tarts.

Don't go there, he told himself as he stepped out of the car. Be professional. She's your client. Do not get involved. He almost rolled his eyes as his libido kicked in and stirred up a wicked brew of need.

Willing his wayward mind to behave itself, he walked through the apartment complex and found his way to her front door. He wondered if she would be dressed yet. He hoped so. He was pretty sure he'd lose it altogether if she wasn't fully dressed.

He lifted his hand and knocked. He heard Snuggles bark and the scrabble of paws on the door.

He knocked again.

A voice called out. "Who is it?"

"Viggo." It went quiet for a second, and he frowned. "Can I come in?"

"I wasn't expecting you." Sally's voice was somewhat muffled. "Give me a minute."

She was half dressed. He just knew it. His imagination took flight and so did the traitor between his legs. He chose to ignore it. "I have news you'll want to hear in person."

"I'll unlock the door. I'm in the middle of showering. If Snuggles tries to make a run for it stop him, will you? I have no desire to spend half the morning searching for him."

He swore under his breath. She was naked – or wrapped in a towel. His imagination was far more creative than he'd ever imagined it could be. "Believe me. Neither do I."

She laughed. "Good."

Maybe he should turn and run before all was lost. He didn't do relationships. He didn't do commitment. He carried a deep distrust of all women because of his past. So just having these thoughts about Sally told him, despite his head telling him not to go there, the rest of him was willing and perfectly able.

But, she'd already unlocked the door and opened it a fraction. He stood there for more than a minute considering his options. Snuggles continued to yap. Viggo lifted an index finger and pushed at the door gently, so it wouldn't swing open wide enough to let the little escape artist out. Snuggles pushed his nose into the gap and wiggled his way through. But Viggo was ready. He swooped down, caught Snuggles, and extended his arms out and away from his body so the dog wouldn't attempt to lick his face off. Nudging the door the rest of the way open with his shoulder, he stepped inside the apartment and shoved it closed with his butt before putting Snuggles down.

Snuggles sat at his feet and stared up at him, his little behind wiggling excitedly, his barely-there tail whipping backward and forward.

"I'm in," he called out to Sally.

No answer.

He walked from the small entranceway into the living room and toward the alluring smell of coffee brewing in the kitchen. He could do with some caffeine, and he'd bet his wages that Sally's coffee would be as good as her tarts.

The size of the kitchen shocked him. It was pokey and, well, unexpectedly boring. He searched one of the very few cupboards for a cup and poured himself a drink, then leaned back against the counter. He'd expected a working kitchen like Charlotte's. Big and gleaming. He'd be surprised if Sally cooked anything in this apartment. Just to check, he opened the fridge. On one shelf was a plate made up of a roast dinner. Left-overs he presumed. There were a few other items, but it was the enormous fruit tart with a glossy glaze over it that caught his eye. He salivated and closed the fridge door before he caved and put a huge dent in it.

"Wow."

"Wow?" Sally appeared in the doorway looking fresh, dewy and damp. Her hair, usually blown dry into perfectly straight blonde locks, dripped at the ends onto her shoulders. Her cheeks were pink and she wore no makeup at all. She was wearing skimpy casual clothes that clung to her skin as if she hadn't quite dried herself off properly from her shower.

Oh yes, he was hungry. But not for the tart in the fridge. "Wow," he said again, as he searched for the words his brain refused to provide. Instead, he grabbed another cup from the cupboard, poured her a black coffee, and handed it to her.

"What's wow?" She held the cup between the palms of both hands. She looked up at him, her gaze open, and interested.

"This kitchen." Was it his imagination or did she look slightly disappointed at his response? "How do you make your tarts in such a tiny space?"

She shrugged. "I keep my work and home life separate. I

generally don't use this kitchen for anything other than breakfast and dinner. If I really want a big meal, I head over to my mom's. I might be the Queen of Tarts, but she's the Queen of Roasts."

"So I shouldn't have brought business to your door?"

Once again she seemed disappointed with him. "Is that why you're here? Business?"

"Yes. I wanted to tell you in person."

"It better be good, otherwise you're going to ruin my day off."

Her tone had lightened. But he wasn't so sure about the calculating look in her eyes. It meant trouble was on its way. "Greenspan wants to produce a televised bake-off between you and Charlotte. They want to call it Tart vs. Shortcake. And there's talk of it going nationwide."

Her eyes lit up. She literally bounced on the balls of her feet and clapped her hands like an excited child. "Really?"

Some of her excitement rubbed off on him and he grinned. "Really."

"That's not just good news. It's the best news ever."

She eyed him up as if he was a delicious ice cream before launching herself into his arms. Uh oh. There went all his resolve to remain detached. Unconnected to his brain and mostly connected to his groin, his willpower evaporated. His arms wrapped themselves around her. Catching a whiff of her fresh citrusy scent, his body went into overdrive and a deep primal groan rose in his throat.

Sally, the minx, knew exactly what she was doing. She leaned back, looked at him briefly, kissed him soundly on his lips, and he was lost to a sudden rush of need to kiss her back.

The kiss went on far longer than it should have. Surprisingly, Sally pulled back first and he experienced a sense of loss.

"I don't kiss random guys," she told him.

"I'm not random."

"I know. I want you to know I fancy you like crazy."

A knot formed in his stomach. "We can't do this." He dragged up an excuse to keep their relationship on a business level. "Look what happened between Charlotte and George. You're a client."

"But you fancy me?"

How could he deny it when he had a boner like never before? "It doesn't mean we have to act on our attraction for each other."

"I have a hankering to make love to you under the stars."

He narrowed his eyes and tried hard not to reveal just how turned on he was right now. "You're a wicked, wicked woman."

She laughed and he swore her eyes twinkled. "I know."

He loosened his grip on her, intending to put space between them, but she clung tight and hitched herself up high enough to wrap her legs around his hips. "I know what I want. When I do, I go after it."

"You're looking at me as if I'm one of your tarts and you want to eat me all up."

"You're not wrong," she said, and leaned in and licked at his bottom lip.

"That's not fair." His voice was a traitor. It was all-out husky, and he was fast losing the will to look for excuses. He wanted to return the favor and kiss her. Head to toe and then back again.

"Tell me you don't want this," she said as she nuzzled his neck.

His head rocked back as a thrum of lust rocketed through him. "I want it, but we can't do anything about it."

She lifted her head. "Give me a good reason why not."

"Like I said, we work together. Can I remind you that you fired George and hired me? Relationships with clients are tricky."

"I'll fire you and rehire George. Will that help?"

He found himself somewhat amused. He could see straight clear to her soul, and it was all sparkly and shiny and oh so determined. "No. You will still be a client."

"But until I met you, I had no idea you existed. You can

return to your books and stargazing at night. We can have an illicit liaison. Doesn't that sound juicy?"

It sounded so juicy he was having trouble staying coherent. His hands were gripping her butt as she clung even more tightly to him and well, she was a perfect fit.

"I don't do relationships. I'd hurt you in the end by walking away once the lust for you was satiated."

The light dimmed somewhat in her eyes. "How is a liaison a relationship?"

"My guess is you're not a one-night-stand woman. Or a two-night-stand either. I don't do commitment. You say you want a liaison, but at heart you're looking for something more permanent."

The twinkle left her gorgeous eyes, and she loosened her legs around his hips and deliberately slid down his torso until the balls of her feet touched the floor. But she didn't back away. "What are you afraid of?"

A question he didn't care to answer. Very few knew his past or the reasons why he avoided long-term relationships. "I'm not afraid of anything."

She stepped backward, putting space between them. "You're fighting your attraction to me and I don't know why. But you know what?"

He arched an eyebrow even as he missed having her wrapped around him. "What?"

"I'm not giving up. You may think you know me, but you don't. Persistence is my middle name."

She grabbed the coffee she'd placed on the bench earlier, and took a gulp of the cooling liquid. There was a quiet determination in the jut of her jaw and the direct gaze she gave him. "You look tired."

The change of topic put him off balance. "I was up most of the night stargazing, then I had a business meeting with George first thing this morning."

"You need something to eat. I'll make you something before you go home."

He really should go but his stomach, the traitor, gurgled. He looked around the spartan kitchen. It was almost as empty as her fridge. "That I'd like to see."

"Well, then," she said as she began to bustle around him as if he was a kitchen island. "Be prepared to be amazed. I'm going to cook my way into your heart."

Yep. He was in deep, deep, do-do.

The sight of her humming as she moved about her tiny kitchen turned what he would have classed as a chore into a work of art, and all with the minimum of fuss.

It was like alchemy, he thought as she led him onto the small balcony that looked out onto the apartment courtyard. Sally's breakfast was as yummy as one of her tarts. "You're a magician." He dug into his decadent eggs Benedict. "This must be the best I've ever eaten."

She waved her fork at him. "I don't make this for just anyone."

She beamed her naughty smile and he felt a foot not belonging to him search for the hem of his trouser leg. He shifted his leg out of the way. "Playing footsie isn't on the menu today."

"Does that mean it might be tomorrow?"

Damn it. She made him laugh. "Maybe. Maybe not." He could see she wasn't going to give up easily. "You're going to have to go to church and pay penance for all those illicit thoughts of yours?"

She waved a fork at him. "I have a sparkly clean soul. I don't have anything to confess. Plus, it's possible your sins may be greater than mine. I'll go if you go."

He grinned and waved his fork at the sky. "My church is the universe."

She made a gagging sound.

He handed her a glass of water. "Sounds like you need some of this to purify your mind as well as your soul."

"Don't you know the rules of dating at all? Never talk about religion or politics."

"We're not on a date so it doesn't count."

"I'm calling this a date. We're here together. Sitting in the morning sun, eating good food and enjoying each other's company. I'm certainly enjoying yours, even if you don't want to take this further. So. Are you heading out tonight to look at more stars?"

He paused, wondering if that was a trick question. "I'm considering it. It will depend on whether the skies remain clear."

"And if they don't?"

"Sleep."

"With me?"

Oh boy. He cleared his throat and his mouth engaged before his brain. "Dinner. I'll pick you up at seven." For some reason his voice had gone all croaky. He stood, picked up his empty plate and walked back into the kitchen.

Sally followed. "Are we going on a real date?"

He turned, knowing he shouldn't answer. "We'll see."

"Stargazing and dinner sounds like a real date to me." She grinned and he found himself transfixed by honesty.

He leaned down and pressed a light kiss on her cheek. "So are you coming?"

"Stargazing as well as dinner?"

"Yes."

"Can I bring Snuggles?"

"If you do, dinner will have to be a burger somewhere and nothing fancy."

"I can do burgers."

He'd imagined she was a fine-dining girl. "If the skies stay clear, we could have a makeshift picnic."

"It's a date."

Damn!

26

THAT AFTERNOON CHARLOTTE CALLED SALLY AND THEY MET
for a walk along the waterfront before making their way into
Pike Market, one of her favorite places in the world. Sally was
recognized instantly, but then a number of people were pointing
at Charlotte too. With Sally at her side, Charlotte discovered she
didn't mind the attention as much as she thought she would.
Especially as most of it was complimentary. The number one
question they were both asked was, would they be doing another
show together?

Sally just tapped her nose and said, "You never know."

Charlotte pasted on a grin and hoped it wasn't too cheesy and
tried her darnedest not to apologize for her disaster every time it
was mentioned. It seemed, as Sally, Viggo, George and Myrtle
had all said, the audience loved the incident of the flying
shortcake.

They found themselves at a counter purchasing coffee and a
dozen delicious mini cinnamon donuts to undo all the goodness
their brisk walk would have done. Finding a bench to sit on, they
discussed the offer from Greenspan.

"What do you think?" Sally asked Charlotte. "It'll be a little competition between us, but we'll make it a fun thing. We'll have to pre-film some scenes, just like the other day, and then we'll film the final segment with the judges live on air."

"I'm terrified. If I say yes, you have to promise me if I stuff up this time, you won't include it in the final version that goes to air."

Sally was apologetic. "I can't promise you that. I won't have control over what they edit out or in."

A combination of fear and excitement curled in Charlotte's stomach. "Who would be the judge?"

"There would have to be more than one judge." Sally rattled off a couple of big-name celebrity bakers, her eyes alight with happiness. "Viggo could act as our deciding judge if there's a tie."

Charlotte snorted rudely. "Good luck with that."

Sally grinned. "Don't worry your golden locks about him." She held out her pinkie. "I've got him wrapped around my little finger. All he'll have to do is taste both tarts and announce his preferred choice if there's a tie. If there isn't, he needn't say anything at all."

"Granted, it would be good to have someone I know nearby, although I'd prefer it was George. Appearing on your show as a guest is one thing, but a bake-off just for the two of us?" Charlotte shuddered, remembering what had happened last week.

"I know you're afraid disaster will strike twice. But it won't. That was an anomaly. And I really, truly am sorry for yelling at you. No dogs will be allowed in the studio if that's what you're worried about. We'll get a minder. Or George or Myrtle will do it.

"I suppose they could be locked in one of the dressing rooms at the studio."

"Separate rooms are probably best." Sally nodded.

"Still worried Cupcake will eat Snuggles?"

Sally colored prettily. "I can't help it. He's my baby."

Sweet shortcakes. Sally even blushed prettily, whereas she,

Charlotte, looked like she'd just stepped out of an oven. "What if we do a test in a controlled environment with the two of them?"

"What kind of controlled environment? You mean put them in a room together with the doors locked and see what they do to each other?"

Charlotte chuckled. "We'll be there to keep an eye on them. They can have leashes on. I'll get George to hold Cupcake's leash if you like. He's much stronger than me."

George popped into her thoughts, in all his bare-chested deliciousness with enhanced builder biceps, and her eyes closed as sticky honeyed desire trickled through her veins and she felt a pulse of need in her whooseywhatsit.

She really was going to have to do something about all this pent-up lust.

"You're drooling," Sally leaned back as if Charlotte was about to pounce on her. "What on earth are you thinking?"

Charlotte snapped back to attention. "You don't want to know."

Sally's lips tilted upward. "I bet I can guess. It's sex. Right? Although I fail to see how talking about Cupcake and Snuggles led you in that direction."

"I was picturing strong muscles and well developed biceps," Charlotte admitted. "George's." She still felt horribly guilty. She'd been so wrong about Sally. It made her wonder just how often she'd been wrong about everything else in her life.

Sally flushed. "I'm so sorry, Charlotte. I really had no idea you thought George and I were an item."

"You're a much better woman than me, Sally. You've no idea how badly I treated him. I'm working on my trust issues."

"Don't give up," Sally insisted. "He loves you. I'm sure of it."

"What about you?" Charlotte turned the conversation away from herself. All this introspection was making her feel regretful and was doing nothing to ease her need for George. "Do you have a man in your life?"

"I've found the man I want," Sally informed her. "I'm just

biding my time, waiting for it to dawn on him he can't live without me or my tarts."

She and Sally had far more in common than she'd thought possible. "Do I know who it is?"

"You must have had your head buried in the oven to notice. It's Viggo."

Charlotte reared back shock. "Viggo!"

Sally sighed and collapsed back against the bench seat and looked to the sky as if she was offering up a silent prayer to God. "I'm head over heels."

Charlotte texted George early that evening.

Charlotte: OK. I'll do it.

George: Really?

Charlotte: Yes.

George: F**k! What! No arm twisting!!!!! I'm proud of you.

Charlotte: Me too.

Charlotte pulled out an enormous tome of recipes from under the kitchen counter. It was her precious bible of sorts, bursting with recipes her mother had passed down to her, and even a handful from her grandparents on both sides. She was already thinking about what she wanted to make.

Charlotte: I had a long talk with Sally. I'm going to face my fear head-on. My shortcake incident doesn't seem to have hurt my career any.

George: So what are you going to make?

Charlotte: Don't know. I've got my bible out.

George: LOL

Charlotte: I mean my recipe bible?

George: I figured.

Charlotte: I'm sorry.

George. What for?"

Charlotte: For giving you such a hard time. I'm hoping this will be good for me. That it will be good for our relationship too.

There was a very long pause and Charlotte nearly fainted from holding her breath while she waited for his reply. Then he began typing and she breathed again.

George: The fact you recognize your weaknesses and are working on them fills me with hope.

Charlotte: I'm crazy about you.

George: I'm coming over.

Charlotte: No. I need a little more growing up to do. On the inside.

George: Well damn!

Charlotte smiled. She felt warm and gooey all over.

Charlotte: I really do know what your favorite tart is.

George: I'll be waiting for when you're ready. I'm not going anywhere.

27

THEY COULDN'T HAVE PICKED A BETTER NIGHT TO DRIVE OUT to Snoqualmie Valley. It was gratifying to see Sally blink back tears as she stood on the observation deck, transfixed by the sheer magnificence of the falls.

"They're magical," she gushed. "I can't believe I've lived my entire life so close to something so beautiful and never been here before."

Viggo looked down as she looked up at him and found himself revealing a desire he'd never actually verbalised before. "I have a dream of owning a house out this way one day instead of living in the city. Out here, you can inhale clean air, the sky is dark and the stars more visible."

"It's a good dream," she said simply.

She was a born and bred city girl. He didn't expect she'd ever want to live the kind of life he desired.

"I feel so small and insignificant," Sally said. "Sometimes, I forget there's more to life than the studio, cooking and family." She looked back up at him for a second. "Thank you for bringing me here."

They stood there for as long as they could, absorbing the beauty of their surroundings, but as the light began to wane, they had to move or be ushered out of the park officially.

"Come on," he said. "Let's head out to Fall City. I know of an excellent place where we can get gourmet burgers and then I'll show you another of my secret spots where we can safely put out a couple of blankets. If we're lucky we'll see a shooting star or two."

Two hours later, replete with food, Viggo was more than happy to be horizontal. He kept telling himself he should set up his new telescopic camera, but right now, he didn't want to move.

Sally lay beside him. He turned his head and found her looking at him.

She smiled. "This is nice. I've never done this before. What happened to set you on this path? Why do you love astronomy so much?"

He lay quiet for some time, his eyes focused on the heavens, but his mind and body attuned to Sally. Her hand was so close to his that he could have curled his fingers around it if he wanted.

He turned his head and found her waiting for an answer. Something deep welled within him. Memories connected to his past. Gazing at stars had kept him sane when his life had fallen to pieces.

"I'm fascinated by what's out there," he told her, not wanting to break the moment. He wasn't ready to tell her the truth. He didn't know if he ever would be. "There must be life out there somewhere. It's something I used to do with my grandfather. We'd lie outside on the grass in the summer and he'd point out the Milky Way. Sometimes, he would wake me in the middle of the night just to show me an eclipse. He was a keen sailor and taught me a lot about how sailors navigated the oceans by the stars."

"How wonderful to have someone like that in your life," Sally whispered, as she turned her attention back to staring at the sky.

"I've never seen so many stars. They seem brighter, closer here than in the city."

"Light diminishes their visibility." He began pointing out the different stars, and they lay side by side contentedly, just observing, listening to the night sounds. "What's your star sign?"

She looked at him curiously. "I didn't take you for one who believes in astrology."

He chuckled and pointed upward. "At certain times of the year some of the constellations represented in astrology are visible. I was born late January and my star sign is Aquarius." He got up and rummaged in his rucksack for his phone and googled the relevant image of the stars representing that sign. "See. Here's what it looks like." He pointed back up to the sky, and following his line of sight, Sally eventually located what he'd shown her on the screen of his phone.

"I see it." She practically vibrated with excitement. "I'm a Leo," she said. "Is my star sign visible?"

"Unfortunately, no. But we can come back another time so you can see it when it becomes visible." He lay back down on the blanket and tucked his hands behind his head.

She hitched herself up onto one elbow and looked down at him. "I'd like that. Thank you." She looked indecisive for all of two seconds and then blurted, "This is the best date I've ever been on."

His heart warmed just a little more. "You think so?"

She grinned. "I know so. And Snuggles agrees with me."

They looked at the small dog curled between them. Viggo had given her a stake to secure his lead so he wouldn't run off into the night, never to be seen again. The little dog, curled up in a ball, lifted his head long enough to let out a contented woof and then went back to sleep.

"See," Sally laughed. "He loves it. And so do I." She leaned over further and planted a kiss on Viggo's cheek. "Thank you for bringing me here."

Instinctively, his arms came up and curled around her. Taking care not to disturb Snuggles, she rested her head on his chest, and sighed. "I could stay like this forever."

He didn't say it, but Viggo was thinking the exact same thought and it scared the hell out of him.

28

"You're looking way too smug," George noted as he ordered a whiskey for Viggo at O'Flanagan's.

"I have no idea what you mean," said Viggo. "I always look like this."

"No you don't. Something's going on with you."

Viggo frowned. "You're imagining things."

George's eyes narrowed - it was clear he didn't believe him. There was no way Viggo wanted to get into a discussion on how much he'd enjoyed Sally's company the other night. In fact, he wasn't even going to tell him he'd been out with her. No doubt Sally would talk to Charlotte and Charlotte would mention something to George. But right now his brother knew nothing, and that's how it would stay. For now.

Thankfully, George gave up and said, "Charlotte and I discussed the bake-off. She mentioned that Sally suggested you as the deciding judge if there's a tie."

Viggo bolted upright in his chair as if he'd been shot out of a cannon. "Like hell I will."

"Tell me how you really feel, why don't you?" George leaned forward, ready to do battle. "Listen. The station has lined up a couple of really famous bakers, but they need someone in case there's a tie."

"I'm no expert. I am not going on camera. Are you mad?"

George raised both palms up and leaned back in his chair. "No need for insults. It was just an idea."

"A very stupid idea," Viggo said. "You need someone well-known. Someone the public trusts, not some two-bit manager who prefers to remain behind the scenes."

"Have you read the contract?"

Viggo scowled. "No. Why? What's in it?"

"I suggest you read it. Greenspan has signed off on it. We'll only use you if there is a tie."

"I haven't signed anything."

"You didn't have to." George paused, knowing Viggo was going to be furious. "I signed on your behalf." It wasn't unusual for him to do so but as he wasn't supposed to be acting as Sally's manager, he knew he was treading deep water.

Viggo looked like he would combust. And he didn't disappoint. He verbally exploded with a series of expletives, then shook his head like a wounded bull. "I'm not doing it. Myrtle can. Or you. But not me. No way. Never going to happen." Viggo surged from his chair, ignoring the waiter who had just brought their drinks to the table, and leaving most of the patrons watching as he stormed out of the bar.

George picked up his drink and knocked it back in one gulp. "That went better than I thought it would."

He texted Sally.

Watch out. He's about to read the contract. You may have to bake him a dozen conciliatory tarts.

Sally, pulled out her kitchen scales. She needed something quick and enticing as all-heck to sweeten the irritation right on up and out of Viggo. If she had a conciliatory tart recipe she'd definitely be making it right now.

It was close to 8.00pm and she had just had a shower and wasn't dressed for company. She looked down at the slinky, pale pink satin slip that made her think of frosted icing. The cream lace across the top hid most of her important bits, but little glimpses of skin could be viewed if she stood, just so, under the kitchen lights. Her nipples were already perky with anticipation. She made the decision not to change. If baking didn't work to appease him, then how she was dressed just might.

Hoping she had time, she whipped up a quick batch of double chocolate fudge brownies. They were still in the oven when Viggo knocked at her front door. She peeked through the peephole. Oh boy. She could practically feel the heat of his anger zapping her eyeballs. She rocked back on her heels and contemplated not opening the door. Maybe she should pretend she wasn't home. Give him the night to cool off. But then Snuggles began circling her legs and yapping up a storm.

"Open the damn door, Sally. I know you're in there. You wouldn't leave that little snapdragon alone and I can smell something burning?"

Flicking open the locks she made a mad dash for the kitchen. She slipped her hands into oven mitts and rescued her brownies. "Crap!"

Viggo loomed behind her with Snuggles in his arms as she rested the tray of darker-than-she-wanted-around-the-edges brownie on the stove-top.

Well darn it. There went the tempting sweet treat. But there was still her, in her sexy-come-hither slip. She spun on the balls of her feet to face him, squared her shoulder back so that there was no chance he'd miss her very happy nipples poking at the sheer material.

She tilted her head and blinked slowly. "I wasn't expecting you."

His Adams apple bobbed in his throat and he looked as if he

was having trouble containing his irritation. She guessed it was that, but heck, she hadn't expected this degree of anger.

"I don't know why not," he ground out through a jaw so tight she thought he might have lock-jaw. "Did you expect to charm me into agreement after the fact?"

There was no use pretending. "Something like that."

"You're far too used to getting your own way."

Sally scrunched her nose. "I am not."

"Not from where I'm standing." He placed Snuggles in her arms. "You're going to have to find someone else to be the deciding judge. I'm not doing it."

"It's only if there's a tie," Sally put Snuggles down on the floor and the little rascal ran circles around their legs. "It's a matter of sixty seconds or so on screen."

"As far as I'm concerned, that's sixty seconds too many."

Well darn it. He was digging his heels in well and good. "I'm sorry," she said. And she was. "I'll find someone else."

But there was the issue of time and finding someone to agree. They'd scheduled the bake-off hot on the tail of their show together, so that interest didn't wain.

"I'll get George onto it," Viggo muttered, his anger deflating as quickly as a collapsed sponge.

"I really am sorry," Sally said and then uttered, softly, "Perhaps it's true."

"What's true?"

"I'm too used to getting my own way." She frowned. "I don't want to be one of those demanding stars."

His eyebrows arched. "Stars?"

"You know what I mean. When Charlotte mentioned she'd be happier if there was someone on-set who knew her well in case she experienced, and this is in her own words, "a case of the collywobbles", I thought of you and may have mentioned your name?"

"May have?" Viggo frowned down at her.

"Alright. I did, and Charlotte was happier thinking you would be there as emotional support."

"Well now you know it was one of your worst ideas ever."

Boy, did she. "Want some brownie. It will be all gooey and warm in the middle. I'll cut off the burnt edges. I have whipped cream to go with it. Or yoghurt if you prefer."

"Don't change the subject."

But she saw his eyes dart to the brownie, and the hungry flick of his tongue over his bottom lip.

She wanted to dance a victory jig. Instead, she pulled out a couple of plates and cut two large slices of brownie from the center of the pan. She inspected each piece underneath and scrunched her nose. Grabbing a knife, she scraped it down. "It will still be good," she said as she dived into the fridge and brought out a bowl of whipped cream and a pottle of yoghurt.

She sure as heck hoped this would sweeten him up. "Don't worry, she said. "We'll find someone else to be a deciding judge." She indicated the plate and handed him a fork and then made sure she was standing under the light so that he got a good view of her as she delved into her portion. "Dig in while it's still warm and gooey."

She shoveled another large forkful into her mouth, before she said something she oughtn't, like *I want you to make me gooey all over.*

29

A FEW DAYS LATER, NERVES ROILED UP A STORM OF ACID IN Viggo's stomach, making him feel as ill as Osiris when barfing up a fur ball. Sally and he were still talking, business only, as he had not fully forgiven her, or Charlotte and George for putting him in this position.

Granted, both Myrtle and George had spent hours searching for a alternate judge, but he wasn't so sure either of them had been totally honest when they declared they hadn't been able to book anyone else to take his place.

Once he'd read that diabolical-behind-his-back contract he'd pretty much realized he was screwed and had no choice but to say yes, otherwise Sally's dream of taking her show nationwide would be on the rocks. She'd used him to get what she wanted and he wasn't happy.

He looked in the mirror as Erin, the makeup artist, patted his skin dry for the third time. "You're wasting your energy," he said. "I'm going to break out in a case of perspiration and possibly hives the moment the cameras start rolling."

"Don't fret," she told him. "We'll pat you dry and touch up

your makeup if you have to go in front of the camera. I've dealt with worse."

"I don't know how I let them do this to me," he mumbled, more to himself than to Erin, who applied yet another layer of powder to his face. "It should be George doing the judging."

Myrtle spoke up from the doorway. "I'd give anything to be a judge. I don't understand why Sally didn't ask me."

"I wish she had." Viggo could see her reflection in the mirror. "In fact, why don't we swap places right now?"

Delight and then fear passed in quick succession across Myrtle's features. "It's you she wants."

He wasn't surprised Myrtle had shown up unannounced. She'd been so excited about the bake-off from the second she'd heard about it. "Who's minding reception at GVM?"

"George. Charlotte doesn't want him here. She believes he'll make her too nervous and she'll screw everything up so he promised to stay away. As soon as the show has been filmed, I'll head back to take over."

"Then why did she suggest me as the deciding judge."

"She's not in love with you, dimwit. You're not going to make her nervous"

Damn it! "I'm not going to be a biased judge."

Myrtle snorted. "Anyone with eyes can see you're besotted with Sally. Of course you're biased."

"I am not besotted.

"You *are* so."

"I am not."

Myrtle nudged his shoulder and handed him a bottle of water. "I'd prefer it if you were besotted with me."

He laughed at her attempt to take his mind off the nerves threatening to have him throwing up any second now. He took a good slug of water from bottle. His mouth was dry and he thought he might be having an out-of-the-body-experience. "The only thing closely resembling besotted, is my love of astronomy."

"Astronomy won't keep you warm at night."

"I have an electric blanket."

"If you're not serious about Sally, don't play with her feelings. She's too nice. You'll break her heart."

"I've no intention of breaking anyone's heart. We are not in a relationship and after her manipulating me like this, I'm not sure I want any kind of relationship with her."

Exasperation edged the corners of Myrtle's lips downward and when she opened her eyes, all sign of humor was gone. "She's already halfway in love with you. I wouldn't be surprised if she wasn't working on your wedding tart as we speak."

The comment rattled Viggo, but he wasn't about to let Myrtle know she had got to him. "Right now she's preparing for this show. She's not thinking of anything except making her tart better than Charlotte's shortcake."

When Myrtle would have screwed with his mind further, he held up his hand. "Don't meddle, Myrtle."

She slapped a hand over her chest. "Meddle? I never meddle. I offer advice."

"Well, thank you for the advice," was his terse response. "This time I choose to ignore it."

A gleam he didn't like lit Myrtle's eyes to a feisty chocolate brown. "You'll be sorry if you let Sally slip through your fingers. You're missing out on the best thing that's happened to you since Alice and Bill adopted you into the family."

—————

The director called for the sound and lighting technicians to make their final check, and asked Charlotte to stand behind her counter, walk to the oven and back, and then walk over to Sally's bench. He asked Sally to do the same. There were some other final checks, and then it was time to begin.

"All quiet on set," the director called. The chatter of the audience decreased as the director silently counted down with his fingers from ten to zero, and then pointed to Sally. *You're on,* he mouthed.

And like a pro Sally was off, taking charge of the bake-off between herself and Charlotte.

"Modern versus old fashioned. Fast food versus slow food. Tart versus shortcake. Which is best? Of course, I believe my tarts to be the best ever. But then, Charlotte reckons her short-cakes are better than mine. Industry experts have graciously agreed to taste the finished products and give us their verdict. Let me introduce them to you now." And she rattled off the names of two of the most influential pastry chefs in the country as they made their way on set. The audience roared their approval. It was television heaven.

Adrenalin pulsed through Charlotte's body, making every-thing tingle with an awareness that all eyes were on them. Time was going so fast that it became a blur. She'd watch the play-backs later. If she dared.

As the clapping diminished, Sally continued. "In case of a tie, we've roped in our agent from GVM Media – yes folks, Char-lotte and I share the very same agent – to cast the deciding vote if we need it. And here he is, the very delectable Viggo Freedlander."

The camera focused on Viggo as he walked up on cue and joined the judges. There were wolf-whistles from the audience and a lot of laughter as he towered over everyone, although, surprisingly, he seemed calm and wasn't melting his makeup off. But Charlotte knew, as did Sally, he wasn't happy with either of them right now.

Sally continued talking and Charlotte's attention was drawn back to the present when she heard her name. "Charlotte loves to cook the old-fashioned way. It will take a little longer for her to prepare some aspects of her shortcake, so we will begin the show with her as she puts together the base for a Strawberry Crumble Shortcake. This recipe is from her number one bestseller *Short-cakes To Live For.*"

Sally was definitely a marketing whiz and not shy on promotion. Charlotte could learn a thing or two from this woman.

"I will be making a Lemon Surprise Tart," Sally continued. "The baking time between our recipes is essentially the same." She turned toward Charlotte and the camera switched to a shot of them both, Charlotte at her workstation and Sally at hers. She nodded encouragingly, but, there was a competitive twinkle in her eye. "Over to you Charlotte."

Oh sweet heaven. What had she got herself into? Charlotte's knees shook so much they knocked together. She was on a show that would beam its way around the country in a few hours' time. She opened her mouth, and somehow, her prayers were answered and words fell out. Although, who knew what she said, because it was as if she was talking down a long dark tunnel, and she could barely hear herself. Whatever it was she was saying appeared to be right, as Sally nodded her head encouragingly.

"I always butter and flour the pan," Charlotte said to the camera. "Nothing sticks. There's no need to buy all those newfangled bendy silicone dishes. A good old Pyrex dish does just as good a job as those fancy ones Sally uses."

She measured out ingredients, the patter she had practiced over and over spilling from her lips with an ease which astonished and pleased her. The familiarity of dealing with butter, flour and sugar calmed her frazzled nerves and a calmness took over as she blended and created what she knew would be her best shortcake ever. She continued until the base was made and placed in the oven for its initial bake.

And then it was Sally's turn. Backward and forward they went, and as she relaxed, she found herself being able to make the odd feisty comment about Sally's techniques. The crew were smiling. The judges were smiling. Even Viggo's lips were tilted upwards. The director was nodding his head. All was going according to plan.

Feeling more relaxed, Charlotte opened the oven to check her base was cooked. "Another minute," she said and closed the door and started her prep for the strawberry topping. "I like to eat my shortcake slightly warm," she spoke to the camera as she finally took the dish out of the oven and placed it on the bench. "It won't matter if it's not cold before you eat this. It's fabulous either way."

She added sugar to the strawberries and swished a small amount of Cointreau into the bowl as well for good measure. "For a little decadence," she said. "If you don't want to add alcohol, then cut an orange in half and squeeze the juice into the strawberries instead."

The time whizzed by in a blur. It felt like a million years. It felt like five minutes. Next thing she knew, they were both placing their creations' side by side on cooling trays, and Sally moved over to the couch area to interview the judges before going to a commercial break.

Everything was going so well. Just like her first and only appearance on Tempting Tarts. She wasn't about to congratulate herself on making it through the entire process until the tart and shortcake were judged.

Commercials over, Nancy Driscoll, the doyenne of all things sweet now stood with Anita Baker – was it really her name – who was from one of the city's most famous patisserie stores, *A Touch of Sweetness*, between Charlotte and Sally.

Sally appeared to still be her calm unflappable self. On the other hand, she, Charlotte, had been okay until she'd had to stand right next to her heroine. Now she was struck dumb in adoration and filled with extreme trepidation, because Nancy had picked up a fork and was plunging it into her Strawberry Crumble Shortcake.

Anita had got in first though, proclaiming her shortcake gooey, decadent and delicious. But Charlotte could tell, she preferred Sally's tart because of the beatific expression that crossed her features when she'd sampled it. Despite this, it was Nancy's good opinion which mattered the most to Charlotte. She didn't care about losing. She did care about Nancy loving her shortcake.

Nancy swallowed and took another bite, something she hadn't done with Sally's tart.

Sally spoke up, breaking the palpable tension in the room. "So what do you think?"

"Incredible," Nancy said. "It should be called Strawberry Sensation. It melts in the mouth. I've never tasted a better short-cake in all my years of baking. And that hint of Cointreau is just perfect. Outstanding."

Charlotte released a breath she had not realized she'd been holding. "Really?" Nancy Driscoll thought her shortcake outstanding. She wanted to throw her arms around her, hug her, then dance a jig about the room. She wanted to whoop for joy and clap her hands in glee, instead she managed to miraculously say, ever so calmly, "I'm absolutely delighted."

"So, Anita," Sally said. The camera zoomed in on the other judge. "You first. Who are you voting for."

Anita paused, and then said, "They are both delicious, but in the end, I'm choosing yours, Sally."

The studio audience erupted into cheers and clapping.

Without missing a beat, Sally graciously acknowledged the win and then spoke to Nancy. "And how about you Nancy. Tart or Shortcake?"

Nancy's expression gave nothing away. "Sally, your tart was absolutely exquisite."

Charlotte's heart dipped. It would be fantastic to win, but she wouldn't be devastated. Nancy's comment that her shortcake was incredible and outstanding was enough for her. As far as she was concerned, she'd won already.

"But Charlotte's shortcake..." Nancy shook her head as if unable to comprehend how wonderful it was, "...is sensational. I have to go with the Strawberry Crumble Shortcake."

Charlotte witnessed the small flicker of disappointment in Sally's eyes, but like the professional she was, she focused her gaze on the camera. "So it looks like we have a tie. It looks like we're going to have to ask Viggo Freedlander to cast the deciding vote. We're taking a short break and will be back with you shortly."

Everyone erupted into a spontaneous burst of applause.

30

VIGGO SLUGGED BACK A LARGE GLASS OF WATER AND BROKE out into a visible sweat. The makeup artist rushed on during the break and dabbed the moisture away.

Sally spoke to Charlotte after ensuring their microphones were off. "I'm still pinching myself."

Myrtle rushed over from her corner. "It's going fantastically well."

In awe, especially now that her nerves had evaporated, Charlotte declared, "Nancy Driscoll loves my shortcake. I've won no matter which way I look at it."

Sally patted her on the back. "Will you still be happy if Viggo declares mine as the best?"

Charlotte popped her lips as she gazed into her compact mirror to make sure she hadn't melted all her makeup off. "You bet. I'm exhilarated."

"It's called adrenalin," Myrtle handed her a bottle of water.

Charlotte winked and took a sip. "It's as good as sex."

"There's something seriously wrong if starring on television is better than bonking George." Sally hooted with laughter.

"Alas, there's no bonking as yet and I wouldn't tell you even if we were." The women erupted into gales of laughter.

"I thought you and George were an item already," Sally frowned.

"We're taking it slow."

"What's wrong with you? Jump him quick before he gets away," Myrtle said.

"There's one thing I know now that I didn't before we broke up."

"What's that?"

"George really does love me."

Myrtle and Sally rolled their eyes in unison, but it was Myrtle who said, "It's obvious to everyone he's head over heels."

"To you maybe. Me. I was an idiot. But I can tell you this, when it finally does happen you'll see the fireworks from the balcony of your apartment, Sally."

She figured it was time she and George got horizontal. Hopefully they would stay like that, living together in the house he'd built, until they were wrinkled and shriveled like old prune shortcakes.

Charlotte giggled at the image, and then they were ready to pick up where they'd left off. Myrtle scuttled back to her corner taking Viggo and Charlotte's bottled water with her.

During the break, someone had sliced the shortcake and tart and put them on plates ready for Viggo to taste.

Sally caught Charlotte's glance as the microphones were switched on. She winked and then then she spoke into the camera once again without missing a beat. "So which one will Viggo love best? Will his choice be biased? But of course my tart is definitely more to his liking."

"Ladies, I love you equally," he said, his tone serious as he stood between them. It was clear his nerves were clamped as tight as his locked knees to stop them from shaking.

Charlotte nearly lost it with laughter. Did he really just say that? She bet they wouldn't edit it out either.

"Oh, I'm sure you do." Sally winked. "But right now all we want to know, is..." She paused and grinned. "... which is best? Tart or shortcake?"

Sally knew him well enough by now to recognize genuine fear when she saw it. He possessed a deer in the headlights look in his eyes.

Viggo picked up a fork.

"Mine is way more than incredible than Sally's," Charlotte elbowed his arm. "Nancy Driscoll says it's sensational."

Viggo forked a decent amount of Sally's tart into his mouth. There was a palpable silence in the room as they all waited for his verdict.

"Not bad," he eventually said.

"Not bad?" Sally teased. "Come on. You can do better."

"I need another taste."

She grinned. "He loves it so much he's going back for more."

"He's just greedy," Charlotte volleyed in return. "It's time to try mine now. He can practically eat an entire shortcake all by himself."

He picked up the plate with the shortcake on it and dug in.

Individuals from the audience began calling out their preferred winner all at the same time.

"Charlotte."

"Sally."

Viggo ignored them all and shoveled in another decent sized piece of Charlotte's shortcake.

It was clear he was feeling a whole lot more relaxed when he said, "The shortcake is incredible. The strawberries are tart, a perfect foil for the sweet shortcake base. The hint of Cointreau gives it an extra dimension.

Sally's eyebrows arched in surprise as he waxed lyrical.

Charlotte shot her an equally astonished look. Suddenly their manager was very chatty.

Viggo turned to Sally. "Your tart was diabolically delicious, but Charlotte's concoction is equally so."

He waved his fork in a dramatic arc over the remains of the shortcake, and Charlotte wondered if he'd suddenly developed a fever. "I need some more of that tart."

"Absolutely." Sally cut him another slice, her expression smug. "It's the best I've ever made."

It was as if there were only three people in the room, Charlotte, Sally and Viggo, despite their two guest judges standing to one side waiting for the final verdict.

Viggo stabbed at the tart with his fork. "Down the hatch," he said and shoveled half the slice into his mouth.

Sally and Charlotte collectively gasped. The audience broke out into laughter. Viggo rolled his eyes, taking his time to savor the tart.

Charlotte stifled her amusement behind one hand. Sally stood transfixed. Neither of them were sure what to make of this new Viggo. He looked kind of funny too. His cheeks were getting redder and a fine sheen of sweat glistened his brow.

"Sally," he proclaimed as he once again shoveled tart into his mouth. "You are the only thing more amazing than this tart."

Charlotte developed a serious case of the giggles. Sally caught the bug within seconds. Everyone else, including the audience, taking the cue from them, began to laugh uproariously.

Sally managed to say, "Well thank you, Viggo. But right now what we would like to know is which is best? Tart or shortcake?"

The sheen of perspiration on Viggo's brow turned into droplets. He loosened the collar of his shirt. "God, it's hot in here. Someone turn on the air-conditioning."

"It is on. Your decision, Viggo," Sally prompted as the director began to make frantic movements from behind the camera. Time was ticking away and they needed a result. Fast.

"Decision?" Viggo frowned. "What decision?"

Charlotte playfully slapped him on the arm. "Come on. It can't be that difficult. It's me, isn't it, but you don't want to hurt Sally's feelings."

But when her palm touched the skin on his forearm, she

noticed he felt very, very hot. Stay calm, she instructed herself, as she realized Viggo's behavior might not be because he was teasing.

"Tart or shortcake?" Sally prompted again.

"Tart or shhhhhortcake." Viggo was slurring his words. "I declare the winner to be Strawberry Crrrrrumble Shhhhortcake."

Charlotte instantly forgave Viggo for being such an idiot, punched a victorious fist in the air, and performed a mini-jig on the spot. "Yes."

Sally, ever the professional, hugged Charlotte and announced, "We have a winner. Charlotte's shortcake is the best." And then she started wrapping up the show, a tad faster than usual, because in the background Viggo continued to jabber, his deep strident tone overriding Sally's despite the fact his microphone had been turned off.

"Isn't Sally wonderful? She's the most amazing thing since sliced bread. But so are you, Charlotte. Hey Sally, did you know Charlotte writes for Drive Men Wild. Funny, huh? She doesn't drive me wild. You do though. Oh, my God. I feel so hot." His eyes glazed over and he loosened his collar further as if he was having trouble breathing.

Why hadn't they stopped filming? The studio was in an uproar and Charlotte could see the audience, despite the blanket rule no-one was to video anything on their phones or cameras, were doing just that.

She glared at Viggo as her brain tried to work out what demon had taken hold of their agent. She'd known him for years. This behavior was completely out of character.

"George so wants you back. Take him back, Madam Delicious." Viggo rocked unsteadily on his feet, and without further warning, fell backward in a dead faint.

Sally, who was never lost for what to say or do, screamed and threw herself down onto the floor next to him. The audience rose in unison from their seats, trying to see, but he was out of their line of sight behind the counter.

But they heard everything Sally said because her voice was bordering on hysterical. "Viggo." Sally slapped his cheeks. "Wake up." She turned and glared accusingly at Charlotte. "You've killed him."

If the statement hadn't been so ludicrous, Charlotte wouldn't have laughed. It was nervous laughter she knew, but it was likely no one knew that. "I did no such thing." She leaned over Viggo as well, and rested her cheek just above his lips. "He's breathing. He just fainted. It was the stress of being on television."

Sally grabbed his shoulders and shook him, her voice now frantic. "Viggo. Wake up. Someone call an ambulance."

Myrtle, who was paler than Charlotte had ever seen her, started fanning a book over Viggo's face. "He must have been discombobulated from appearing on the show? I've never seen him behave like that, ever."

"It started happening within seconds of eating your short-cake." Sally shot what Charlotte could only describe as dagger-eyes at her.

Charlotte kept what she really wanted to say about that remark to herself. She looked up to Nancy and Anita. "Do either of you feel unwell?"

They both shook their heads. Everyone turned in unison to glance at the remains of the shortcake and tart, and then back to her.

"Nobody else touch them," Sally instructed. "Just in case."

Charlotte shot Sally a pissed-off glare, but the pint-sized woman was leaning over Viggo, her hands cupping his face. There was no mistaking the very real fear in her voice as she tried to wake him. "Please wake up Viggo. Oh my God, he's so hot. He's burning up. Where the hell is that ambulance?"

31

GEORGE'S FOSTER BROTHER AND BEST BUDDY HAD COLLAPSED. May even be dead for all he knew. Such a pity, because right this second, he really wanted to kill Viggo himself.

What the fuck! Viggo had revealed Charlotte's secret identity to the world and word was spreading. Social Media had taken over. There were tweets and photos everywhere, including those of Viggo's feet poking out from behind the counter as he lay unconscious on the studio floor.

Abandoned and without any living relatives, Viggo had come to live with George's family as a young teenager and never left. Just like Myrtle had. Eventually, George's parents had become Myrtle and Viggo's legal guardians. Viggo might not have been born into his family, but George considered him a blood brother.

He wiped away the sweat from his brow and ran his hands through his hair. He was sick to his stomach with worry. He slumped into a waiting chair and leaned forward, his elbows resting on his knees, his head cupped in his hands, his heart heavy and his mind a muddle of emotions he never expected to feel.

George looked over to Charlotte standing at the window

staring out onto the emergency entrance. Sally had gone off to find them all coffee. Myrtle had gone back to GVM to field calls, speak to their parents and then lock up before coming in to the hospital.

"What the hell happened?" he muttered to himself.

Charlotte turned, concern evident in her eyes. "I really don't know.

She crossed the floor and sat next to him. She took one of his hands in both of hers. "I began to realize something was wrong when he started blabbering. He never blabbers. And he was hot. So hot. But we couldn't shut him up. He was perfectly well one moment, and the next... he started acting so oddly. I don't get it."

Neither did he. George shook his head, his response calm, but he could feel the tension building in him. "I just can't make any sense of it."

"Sally half-thinks I poisoned him."

He'd thought she would be more upset about Viggo revealing her identity as Madam Delicious. "Poison?"

"Maybe he's developed a sudden acute allergic reaction to one of the ingredients. He's eaten my Strawberry Crumble Shortcake on numerous occasions. If anything, it's more likely to be Sally's tart that felled him."

"I heard that." Sally had returned, hands loaded with coffee and passed them out. "I can't believe what I'm hearing."

"And I can't believe you accused me of poisoning him."

Sally had the grace to blush. "He's the love of my life. I was so scared."

George coughed, mid-swig of his coffee. "What the...?"

"I'm going to marry him," Sally elaborated and patted George on the back.

"He hasn't said a word to me." George spluttered.

"That's because he doesn't know it yet," Sally said. "But we're meant to be together." Tears welled in her eyes and she rubbed her sternum as if in pain. "He's not allowed to die. We have a whole lot of living to do. Together."

"No one's going to die." Charlotte was suddenly the sensible one. "You heard the medic in the ambulance. His life signs are stable."

"But what would make him behave so weirdly? Then pass out?"

"Like I said. I'm guessing he's developed an allergy to something in the food," Charlotte surmised. "Apart from a serious case of nerves he was fine before filming started."

"Well he's not now." Sally wrung her hands into a tight ball of white knuckles. "He clocked his head pretty hard when he hit the floor. He's likely to have concussion as well."

"None of this is helping," George interrupted. "If you're going to natter inanely, I'd rather both of you went over there." He pointed to the far end of the room. "Where I can't hear either of you."

Sally slumped into the chair on the other side of George and grasped one of his hands. "Tell me about Viggo."

George stared down at the floor, wishing she'd leave him alone. If Viggo wanted to tell Sally his story, then it was up to him. "That's for him to tell you."

"That's just it. He holds everything so close to his chest," Sally said softly, almost to herself. "It's like he doesn't have a history. Except for his grandfather. Did you know he used to lie out on the grass in the park across from his grandfather's house when he was a little boy. They'd lay side by side for hours, gazing up at the stars. That's where his interest in astronomy started."

George turned to fix her with a probing look and wondered just how serious she was about loving his brother. "You're lucky he's told you as much as he has. It's more than he tells most people. If you really want your relationship with Viggo to work, it's going to take patience and staying power."

What could he say without breaking his brother's trust? "If you do care about him, you're going to have to be patient. And believe me when I tell you, his trust isn't easily given."

Tears glistened in Sally's eyes. "I guess coercing him into being a judge on the show hasn't helped. He's still angry with me." She shrugged, looking lost and so unlike the confident Sally he'd come to know. "I took one look at him and fell head over heels you know. I can't explain it."

George squeezed her hand. "I know how you feel." He turned to Charlotte who had remained quiet throughout his exchange with Sally and his heart jumped a beat in his chest. Somewhere, over the past few weeks, something had happened to Charlotte. She was learning it was okay to fall over. All she had to do was get back up and try again. She seemed to be taking being outed as Madam Delicious far better than he'd thought she would. She also didn't seem to mind that he currently had his hand clasped in Sally's smaller one.

And then the doctor came through the door asking if they were family, and the moment was broken. George rose from his chair. "I'm his brother. How is he?"

The doctor smiled. A smile was good. Right?

"All his vital signs are normal, including his heart rhythm. We're not sure what caused him to become incoherent and pass out," the doctor admitted. "We've taken additional bloods and sent them off to toxicology, but, it will be a few hours until the results come back. Not knowing what to look for makes it harder to diagnose.

The tension in George's neck and shoulders eased. Viggo was in no immediate danger. "Is he awake?"

"Yes. But he sustained a mild concussion, so we've sent him off for a scan as a precaution. He'll be fine to go home in a couple of days provided there's someone there to keep an eye on him. In the meantime, family visitors today only."

_____

32

CHARLOTTE STABBED AT THE HEADLINE ON THE FRONT PAGE OF
the next morning's newspaper and read it out loud. "Maybe
Charlotte Meyer should rename her bestselling cookbook *Shortcakes To Die For.*" She shook the paper under George's nose.
"Everyone believes I've poisoned Viggo."

She had turned up at his house the next morning before the
birds in the trees had left their nests, steaming more than the still
warm blueberry muffins she'd brought with her.

The sun was only just beginning to rise. She looked like she
had been up all night. Her hair was a wild halo about her head,
as if it hadn't seen a brush for several days. She had Panda eyes
due to smudged mascara and, her clothes looked as if she'd
picked them up off the floor and put them on in the dark,
because her t-shirt was on inside out. He wasn't going to tell her
though, because, to him, she still looked wonderful.

"It's just sensationalism. It sells papers. The good news is
your book sales will soar as a result."

"Is that really a good reason to sell more books?" She read
the article out loud. "Charlotte Meyer has been outed as Madam
Delicious, the anonymous writer for national car magazine Drive

Men Wild. The identity of Madam Delicious has been a long-held secret, but Viggo Freedlander, partner at GVM Media, revealed the writer to be Ms. Meyer before collapsing during the live broadcast of a one-off show with Greenspan, called Tart vs. Shortcake. Mr. Freedlander was rushed by ambulance to hospital where he is currently undergoing a series of tests to determine what caused his collapse."

Charlotte stabbed the paper again. "Where's Sally in all this? Why haven't they mentioned he ate Sally's tart too?"

"Sally's there somewhere." Having not slept either, George had read the headlines online before Charlotte's arrival. He ripped the paper from her clenched fists, scoured the article and found what he was looking for. "Look. Here she is." He pointed to the beginning of a new paragraph about halfway through. "Sally, Queen of Tarts, the new darling of daytime television, is also being investigated to rule out any possibility of collusion with Ms. Meyer. Both shortcake and tart have been impounded and are undergoing a series of forensic tests."

Charlotte tucked her hands under her thighs, a sure sign she had something else on her mind and was doing her darnedest not to blurt it out.

"Come on," he said. "Out with it."

She blinked. "Out with what?"

"You want to say something and you're not sure whether I'll like it or not."

One of her hands eased out from under a thigh, and she rubbed her tired eyes. He resisted the urge to hug her. One hug would lead to another and then there would be lips touching and then who knew what would happen. Plus, his parents were upstairs.

"We need to focus on Viggo."

"He's going to be all right." He reached out and grabbed her hand before it could retreat back to her thigh, and squeezed gently. "Come on. What is it?"

"Madam Delicious. What are we going to do about her?"

"What do you want to do?"

"Well, I know this is going to sound odd coming from me, but I don't really mind that I've been outed. Somewhere along the way, I seem to have redeveloped the backbone Myrtle said I'd lost. But what will the editor of Drive Men Wild say? Will they want me to continue writing for them now there's no mystery to it all?"

George nearly fell off his chair. He'd thought she'd be devastated, but here she was, sounding sane and in control. He fell, right then and there, a little more in love with this crazy, wild-haired woman who looked like she hadn't slept a wink in the past twenty-four hours.

He squeezed her hand again. "I believe the question is, do *you* want to continue as Madam Delicious?"

She turned in her chair to face him, her knees brushing his as he also did the same. "I hadn't thought it would be an option."

"The media machine will drive sales for Drive Men Wild. Pun intended. The problem as I see it is that having your alternate identity revealed might not seem as titillating to their readers. The other problem is – and to me, this is far more important – whether you want to continue, knowing everything you write for them will impact your life as Charlotte Meyer, teacher, cookbook writer and now television personality. Do you want to be all those things? Are you prepared to handle the scrutiny on a daily basis?"

"Do I have a choice? Could I let Madam Delicious go?"

"Your contract has another seven months to run. I'll make an appointment with the lawyer to discuss our options with the legal team later today. You tell me what you want. I'm on your side. Always."

Uh-oh. Her eyes were filling with tears. "You truly are the most amazing man. I do love you, you know. More than I ever thought possible. I trust you to make the right decision." She shrugged. "If they insist I go early, I will. I'm not going to be devastated. If they want me to continue, I will do it. I've enjoyed my time writing recipes for them, but I have to admit that without having you to practice on, it hasn't been as much fun."

His Charlotte had come a long way in such a short time. "Where did the old Charlotte go?"

"She's here. She's just been afraid to truly trust for fear of rejection. I'm now Charlotte the Brave."

He brushed a hand down the side of her face and then cupped her cheek. "I'm loving this new real Charlotte very much."

"Me too." She grinned.

He leaned in, intending to steal a kiss, but she leaned back. She wagged an index finger in front of his face. "Nah-uh-ah. I haven't guessed your favorite shortcake yet."

He grinned. "You told me you know what it is."

"That's right. I did." She matched his grin. "Once this debacle with Viggo is over, I'm going to make you the best short-cake you're ever going have in your life."

Which couldn't come soon enough as far as George was concerned.

33

DAYLIGHT HIT VIGGO'S EYES, AND ALTHOUGH HE BLINKED several times the picture remained the same. Had he been abducted by aliens?

"He's waking up." Oddly, it sounded like Alice, his foster mother.

"Thank God," said another that sounded like George.

What the hell? Where was he? His sore eyes tracked George as he paced backward and forward alongside the bed. He was in bed! Why was he in bed? But then a pain lanced through the back of his skull, and he groaned. Alice leaned over and grasped one of his hands. They were so tiny. Almost as tiny as Sally's, he thought. They made his look so big. He looked up at Alice and saw shiny tears in her eyes. Why was she crying and holding his hand?

He looked at the walls. At the ceiling. And it dawned on him where he was. He was in hospital?

"What... happened?" he croaked.

George paused mid-stride. "You don't remember?"

"My darling boy," Alice clenched her hands around Viggo's. "You collapsed. Yesterday."

George flopped down into the chair on the other side of the bed. "Man, you were acting weird. Wait 'til you see the playback."

Viggo grit his jaw. That damned show he had no business being on! All he could remember was how hard and fast his heart had been beating as he attempted to be light-hearted and at ease in front of the camera.

"How weird?" It looked as if he was going to have to admit he couldn't recall much of what had happened on the show. It didn't help that his head felt as if it had been used as a football.

George arched an eyebrow. "Definitely weirder than usual."

Viggo looked to his foster-mother, knowing she would tell him the truth. "Did I embarrass myself?"

Alice hesitated. "I never realized how photogenic you were until yesterday," she said. "When the camera first zoomed in on you I imagine all the women in Seattle swooned just a little."

George rolled his eyes. "Mom. Don't. His head's big enough as it is."

"It's the truth. Admit it. The camera loved him."

George shrugged. "One has to be sane as well as photogenic when appearing on television."

"I was insane to agree to judge the stupid contest in the first place," Viggo muttered. "Oh that's right. I didn't agree. I was coerced into it."

Alice pushed back the hair on his forehead, then leaned down to plant a kiss where her hand had just been. "It's true it didn't end well. Announcing Charlotte as Madam Delicious to the world wasn't your best moment."

Viggo groaned. "No. Really?" Snippets of memory that he thought had been a dream were turning into an unwelcome reality. "I was hoping I'd dreamed the whole thing."

George enlightened him. "Unfortunately, the audience captured some of the drama on their cellphones and began posting to media immediately. Reporters wasted no time in whipping up a froth of headlines to go along with those images. It's media heaven. Or hell, depending on how you look at it. I've yet to discover what the Editor in Chief of Drive Men Wild will want to do now you've announced who Madam Delicious is."

Viggo saw the narrow-eyed-glance Alice gave George. "You can worry about this later. We just want you to get well, Viggo," she said. "George will take care of everything in the meantime."

But Viggo wasn't deterred. "What kind of headlines are we talking?"

"Exaggerated ones. I wouldn't be surprised if they've reached across the Atlantic as well. If the world didn't know Charlotte and Sally before, they do now. I have to give you credit where it's due. Your PR tactics might be extreme, but they worked." George grinned. "Just what we always wanted for them. Notoriety and lots of attention."

Viggo had the sinking feeling he was just as famous as Charlotte and Sally right now. But this diabolical train of thought was knocked askew and replaced by another when there was a knock at the door and a nurse entered.

"A detective would like a word with you Mr. Freedlander," she said. "Are you well enough to answer questions?"

Viggo frowned. "Detective! What the hell does he want?"

Alice shook her head as if to say *not now*, but George responded. "If he's well enough to argue with us, he's well enough to answer questions."

Viggo was baffled. "Is he going to arrest me for passing out or breaking some moral code?"

George tucked his hands in his pockets and grinned. "Maybe?"

"Don't listen to your brother." His mom patted Viggo's arm. "There's talk of you being poisoned. That's why they're here."

Viggo snorted, and winced when the action caused the pain in his skull to worsen. "Poisoned! Get real. How? When? More importantly, why and by whom?"

"They've whisked the remains of the shortcake and tart to forensics and are testing them both for unusual compounds."

Viggo was dumbfounded. "What? You can't be serious."

George actually laughed. "Charlotte has decided you've developed an allergy to something in the baking. A reasonable assumption. Sally, in the heat of the moment, suggested Charlotte poisoned you. Unfortunately, she said it loud enough for the audience to hear, so now the whole world thinks so too."

"Get serious." Viggo's intonation suggested it was George who should be the one lying in the hospital bed. "And I can't believe Sally would even contemplate poisoning me. It's ludicrous."

George shrugged. "She was upset when she said it."

Viggo thought this hilarious and laughed out loud, despite the throbbing in his temples.

At that point the detective – he assumed it was him – entered the room. Viggo looked at the nurse, the doctor, Alice and George. Maybe he *was* dreaming this entire scene? He closed his eyes, seriously hoping he was.

But the doctor spoke, and Viggo had to accept this debacle wasn't a dream and opened his eyes.

"It would be prudent for Mr. Freedlander to remain another night in the hospital for observation because of his concussion. Otherwise all his vital signs are good. The blood work is still to come back, and if it's clear of anything unusual, he'll be free to go home tomorrow as long as someone stays with him for a couple of nights."

"I'm more than capable of looking after myself."

"I'll look after him," Sally announced as she followed Charlotte into the room with an enormous chocolate tart in her hands. "He can stay with me."

Viggo found himself inordinately pleased to see Sally. He covered that pleasure up by frowning. It wasn't hard with the headache banging on the inside of his skull. "I'm not staying with anyone. I can look after myself."

Alice's lips were pursed with displeasure and she pointed at the tart. "No more of those for him until we sort out what felled him in the first place. In the meantime, my husband and I will look after him. We're staying with George as your apartment is too small, Viggo. We can look after you there." She patted Viggo's hand. "Your dad is dropping our bags off at George's house and he'll be in to see you soon."

Sally placed the tart on the table at the foot of the bed. "You don't really believe one of us poisoned him, do you? I was beside myself with worry."

"I don't believe it for an instant," Viggo nodded toward the detective, who'd remained silent throughout. "It's that guy over there you need to convince."

Sally looked to the detective. "Who is he?"

"A detective," George said.

Sally grew impossibly pale. "What?"

"There's no way I was poisoned," Viggo protested, wanting to reach out and comfort Sally. "The studio was in lockdown during filming. I can't see how anyone could have tampered with the tarts. The crew and Myrtle were there the entire time. I probably hyperventilated from being coerced into being on camera."

Sally had the grace to look guilty. And so she should, Viggo thought, although he wasn't really angry anymore. Just disappointed at being manipulated.

The detective interjected. "We have to follow procedure. Especially as everything was caught on camera. I want to speak with Mr. Freedlander first, then I'll speak with you Ms. Forbes, and then Ms. Meyer. As soon as possible, before time erodes your memories."

"No problem," Sally said. "But first, there's something we need to do." She reached into the bag slung over her shoulder and pulled out a large cake slice from her bag.

The detective's eyebrows shot upward, and without hesitation he lunged forward and grabbed her wrist.

"Ouch," Sally complained and tried to wrench her arm free. "What are you doing?"

"Carrying a concealed weapon is a criminal offence."

"This is not a concealed weapon," Sally protested. "It's a cake slice."

"No one is to eat anything made by you or Ms. Meyer until the bloodwork comes back and we've reviewed the results."

The doctor concurred by nodding his head.

Tears welled in Sally's eyes. "You really *do* think one of us poisoned Viggo." She turned to Charlotte. "I didn't mean what I said. You know that, don't you?"

"Of course I know it. You were upset. I've said far worse, believe me."

"But not on camera."

Charlotte conceded this was true. "True."

With the detective's attention diverted, and as everyone erupted into opinions of their own, all of them in defence of Sally, Viggo sat up, leaned forward and teased the cake slice from Sally's fingers. He tugged the table on wheels towards him and served himself a giant slice of tart despite not being hungry.

"Yum,." His stomach protested but he managed to hide that fact. He wanted this over with, and what better way to do so than to eat a slice and prove it wasn't anything to do with Sally's baking. As they argued, he ate.

Reaching out, he grasped Alice's wrist to get her attention and winked at her before clutching his stomach and groaning. "Oooh. I feel odd." He rolled his eyes backward in his head and flopped back onto the pillow, the cake slice sliding from his fingers to clatter onto the linoleum floor.

"He's dead," Sally screamed. "Oh, my God. I killed him."

"Death by Chocolate Tart." George was onto Viggo within a heartbeat. "I can see the headlines now."

"Viggo," his mother reprimanded. "This is not funny."

The doctor picked up Viggo's hand and checked for a pulse, before pulling his little torch out of his chest pocket and looked under Viggo's eyelids one at a time. "Hmmm. He's not dead yet."

Viggo's mouth twitched and he shot upright into a sitting position, despite the sudden lance of pain in his skull. Charlotte and Sally screamed. George erupted into laughter. Alice scolded Viggo, and the doctor just shook his head.

34

EARLY THAT SAME AFTERNOON, THE DOCTOR FLICKED through Viggo's chart. "Some unusual compounds have shown up in your bloods."

Viggo reached for the clipboard. "What kind of compounds? Show me."

But the doctor held firmly to his notes and Viggo had to let go before a tug of war ensued. "You said you're not on any form of medication?"

Viggo gave a short sharp nod. "Correct." He got the feeling the doctor didn't believe him. "I've never been sick apart from chicken pox and the odd cold or flu."

"Hmmm." The doctor wrote something on the chart. "If you could be honest with us, it would make our job much easier."

Viggo swung his legs off the bed and gripped the edge of the mattress, the sheet bunching beneath his fingers when pain lanced through his skull. "For God's sake!" His blood pressure rose. He could feel the color rising in his face. "You think I'm lying?" He stood up and began stuffing his belongings into the hold-all George had brought in that morning. He wasn't staying here a moment longer.

"You definitely took something," the doctor went on. "Whether it was willingly or not."

Viggo pinned a dizzy gaze on the doctor. "So what exactly do you think I've been ingesting?"

"One of the compounds in your system is often used for erectile dysfunction."

The doctor was pissing him off big time. "Believe me when I tell you I've never had any issues in that area. I have never taken, nor ever intend to take something to enhance my libido."

"Look, I've seen and heard it all," the doctor pressed. "It's not the end of the world if you have trouble in getting it up. Stress and depression are major causes. Have you been stressed lately? Are you depressed?"

Viggo glared at the doctor. The only stress he was experiencing was in fighting back the urge to flatten the doctor's nose with his fist. "I'm not taking anything."

It was clear the doctor held doubts. "Well then, let's hope the food allergy tests we took earlier show up something. The forensics on the food are yet to come in too. In the meantime, I suggest you proceed with caution."

"Neither Sally nor Charlotte are guilty of planting anything in their cooking. Why would they want to? It could be career suicide."

"I'd be happier releasing you if I knew all the facts."

"The fact is, I'm fine. I did not knowingly ingest drugs and I'm one hundred percent better than yesterday." Apart from some dizziness, that was, but he figured it would pass and he wasn't about to provide the doctor with ammunition to insist he remain in hospital one minute longer than he needed to. "I'll stay with my brother for a couple of nights to keep everyone happy and we'll just have to wait and see what the police have to say in a few days' time. I'm signing myself out early."

"Are you sure Viggo's OK?" Myrtle asked George for the umpteenth time. It was late that same day, and she stood in George's kitchen along with George, Sally, Charlotte, Alice and her foster-father Bill. Everyone had somehow converged on George's home and now Viggo had turned up in a taxi, having discharged himself from the hospital against the doctor's advice. He was now ensconced in one of the guest bedrooms and unpacking his overnight bag.

Osiris, who George had picked up the previous night on his way home from the hospital, was exploring the great outdoors. Somewhere. Possibly teasing Snuggles and Cupcake by the sound of all the barking coming from outside.

George slung an arm over Myrtle's shoulder and gave her a swift hug. "He's ninety percent better. Don't tell him I told you but, they did find something unusual in his blood work."

He felt Myrtle's tension increase at this news and the worry in her eyes was genuine. "They did?"

He hugged her tighter. "He won't tell me what that something was, but he reckons someone at the studio must have spiked his water, or the shortcake and tart."

"Spiked the water?" Myrtle squeaked. "Why would they assume that?"

Charlotte replied for him. "Maybe because Sally accused me of poisoning him?"

A flush rose on Sally's cheeks to match Myrtle's. "I can see I'm going to be saying sorry for the rest of my life."

"I wasn't there, so I know I didn't do it," George said.

"But why? Why would someone do something so stupid?" Charlotte demanded. "Although, I might try to poison Viggo once he's one hundred percent better. He's outed me to the big wide world as Madam Delicious, thank you very much."

"If I was going to poison Viggo," Sally said, as if Charlotte hadn't spoken, "I'd do it quietly and not when anyone was watching."

George coughed into his coffee. "I can't believe you said that."

"Neither can I," said Viggo as he sauntered into the kitchen.

Sally blushed. "I'm just speculating on how it could be done."

Alice pulled out a chair and waved to Viggo. "Darling boy. Sit down."

Viggo knew better than to argue with his foster mother so he sat and looked up at the sea of concerned faces surrounding him. He wasn't going to admit his head was banging and he felt weak and hungry all at the same time.

"I thought you were dead," Sally said. "My life flashed before my eyes."

"Isn't that supposed to be my line?" Viggo couldn't hide his sudden amusement.

Sally's cheeks bloomed a deeper pink "A slip of the tongue."

Alice interjected. "What did the doctor say?"

"I can't tell you." Viggo's reply was clipped, his tone blunt. It was clear to everyone he didn't want to discuss it.

"Can't or won't?" Bill, asked, undeterred.

"Won't." The detective phoned and asked me to keep what I know to myself while they investigate further. What I can tell you is somebody definitely spiked something, as there's no way this side of the galaxy I would have taken any form of illegal drug. And before you all ask, I'm not on any medication."

"Come on," George coaxed. "We're family. We're the people who should know. You must have more information than what you're telling us."

Viggo looked first to Charlotte and then Sally. "The two of you are under suspicion. I'm keeping the results to myself so as not to muddy the waters."

"What about the other judges?" Myrtle asked. "Nothing happened to them."

Sally shot Myrtle a grateful look. "Maybe Charlotte is right. Perhaps Viggo has developed a severe allergy to something."

"This is all so unsettling." Alice's voice wobbled. "We nearly lost you Viggo. I couldn't imagine what our lives would be like without you in it."

Bill, a man of few words, placed a comforting arm around his wife's shoulders and sent them all a warning glare that said *enough already.* "George, go set the table. Charlotte, Sally, Myrtle, if you're all staying for dinner, you'd better get washed up."

Nobody mentioned it was only five in the afternoon. Looked like they would all be eating early tonight.

35

Charlotte: *Come over. I have something you want.*
George: *When?*
Charlotte: *Now would be good.*
George: *I'm on my way.*

THE NEXT EVENING, CHARLOTTE LOOKED DOWN AT CUPCAKE, who was staring at her with his usual adoration. "If this doesn't work, nothing will. If we don't get back together tonight it won't be the end of the world. I am a bohemian goddess after all, and there are plenty of men out there."

Of course, she didn't want any other man. She *wanted* George. If he turned her down tonight she would be heartbroken. But her world would not end. Her life would continue and she would be wiser for the experience.

The doorbell chimed and Cupcake broke out into a series of barks, raced down the hallway and slid to a stop by banging into the door.

Charlotte had put on a pair of way too high red strappy heels Sally had convinced her to buy. Why? Because every woman should have a pair of red shoes. That's why! With one last glance in the mirror, she tottered down the hall to the door, wishing she'd taken time to practice walking in them before now.

"Let's hope it's George on the other side," she said. She'd taken the precaution of closing all the blinds earlier, even though it wouldn't be dark for another thirty minutes at least. "Or our visitor is in for a shock." She grabbed Cupcake's collar, tugged him out of the way and opened the door.

———

George nearly swallowed his tongue. The dimmed light from the hallway behind Charlotte accentuated her rounded curves, sending his mouth dry and his body into red-hot alert. He broke out into a raspy cough. He should be looking over his shoulder to see if the rest of the neighborhood was witnessing what he was seeing, but he couldn't take his eyes off her.

"Fuck!" It seemed the best word to describe how he was feeling right this second.

"Maybe," she said, a saucy look of promise in her eyes. She stepped back to let him in. "Everything depends on whether the tart I have for you is your new favorite."

Boy, was he hungry. "Oh, it is. I'm sure of it."

He reached out and wrapped an arm about her waist, feeling bare skin, and tugged her to him so he could plant a kiss on her lips, but she wriggled out of his grasp and held up a hand in a stop signal between them. "No touching the help."

His lips tugged into the beginnings of a smile. "The help?"

"That would be me." She batted her eyelashes at him, and turned on her extremely high red shoes, giving him an eyeful of an itty bitty tie folded into a bow at her waist and, well, pretty much nothing else except a scattering of freckles and smooth as silk, milky-white skin.

Fighting the nearly impossible task of keeping his mind out of the gutter and his hands to himself, he picked his wits up off the floor, locked the door behind him and trailed after her like a lovesick calf into the kitchen. "You're asking for trouble."

"I have a your new favorite waiting." Charlotte pointed to the items already on a tray on the countertop. He looked and adrenalin surged through his veins. There was cream and a bowl of deep, rich, cherries.

"Yum," said George, unable to keep the hunger in his eyes hidden any longer. "But where's the shortcake?"

"You're looking at her," Charlotte waved a hand down her front. Her almost see-through apron barely covered her nipples which jutted beneath thin, chiffon-like material. He swallowed and ran his tongue around his suddenly dry mouth.

He plucked a moist cherry out of the bowl and stuck it between his lips and bit down. "Her?" he questioned.

"Me," she said. "I'm your new favorite shortcake."

"Took you long enough." He reached for her, but she stepped backwards. "Oh no," she said.

"But I need a taste. To see if you're as delicious as you look," he managed, although his body was already telling him she was. He had a hard-on pressing painfully against his jeans and if she kept this up for much longer it was going to be all over for him before they even got started.

She turned and swayed those sexy hips over to the fridge. She opened the door and bent over to get something out, giving him a tempting view of her beautiful plump behind.

He groaned out loud, and she turned her head, a knowing look in her eyes. "Something wrong?"

"You're a wicked, wicked woman." A wave of heat flooded his veins. His heart rate picked up and began to race as he fought the urge to toss out what remained of his willpower, grab her backside and plunge deep into her while she stood at the fridge.

"Just how you like it," she said and turned back, her derriere wiggling invitingly. "Ah. There it is." She grabbed a squeezy bottle of something, straightened up and closed the door.

"What's that?" he asked, although he'd already guessed.

"Something you're going to love." Her voice had turned husky, dripping with innuendo. Her sultry emerald eyes, challenged him. Placing the bottle in the microwave she warmed it for a few seconds.

"I'm loving this recipe so far. But you'd better hurry up or I'll not last. It's been a long time coming, Charlotte."

"And the wait will be worth it," she whispered as she took the bottle out of the microwave and placed it with the rest of the items on the tray. "So have I guessed right?" she asked, her tongue moistening her lips. She looked as hungry for him as he was for her.

"You've nailed it," he groaned, the anticipation flooding his body, filling him with an aching need to bury himself deep, deep inside her and stay there forever.

A determined light in her eyes, she whipped the apron off so that she was standing in the middle of the kitchen floor naked, except for her dangerously high and oh-so-sexy heels. "You're overdressed. Take those pants off."

He didn't need to be asked twice. Off went his shoes and then his jeans. His boxers next. He hesitated, standing only in his shirt and nothing else. Then he bent down and pulled several condoms out of his jeans pocket and advanced toward her. "You're my favorite shortcake. Every delectable morsel."

She picked up the tray and once again presented him with a view of her rear. "Follow me," she said, and he did what he was told. Without question. All the way down the hall to the bedroom.

"This is going to ruin your sheets," he growled as he whipped off his shirt and came up behind her so that their bodies touched, skin to skin. His arms snaked round to cup her breasts and he nuzzled hungrily at her neck.

"I have more," she told him, and put the tray down on the side table, intentionally pressing her bottom against his penis that threatened to explode any second now.

She climbed onto the bed, grabbed the cream off the tray, lay down and proceeded to squirt dollops onto her breasts, and then a line down the centre of her rib cage, over her belly button and ending at the apex between her legs. He waited, knowing there was more to come.

Ah. Yes. She grabbed the bottle and drizzled warm chocolate sauce over the top, circling it round her nipples and then trailing it down over her stomach and hips. She paused, looked up at him and said, "Pass the cherries, please."

He licked his lips as he picked up the bowl and handed it to her. She tilted it and cherry juice drizzled out, along with a handful of whole cherries. She plucked a couple with stalks out of the bowl, lay back and placed them on top of the cream covering her nipples.

"What are you waiting for," she teased. "Your shortcake is ready. Come get a slice."

What could a man do when confronted by such a tasty morsel? He ate her up like the oh-so-hungry man he was.

To: theeditor@drivemenwild
From: Madam Delicious
Subject: Recipe for your next issue

Cherry On Top Shortcake

- *One basic shortcake mix*
- *A punnet of fresh cherries, pips removed (reserve a few cherries with stalks for decoration)*
- *Whipped Cream (if desired)*
- *One hungry honey pie (your significant other)*

Method:

- *Toss shortcake mix into back of pantry*

- *Place cherries into a large bowl and mash until the juices run*
- *Layer your honey pie as you will with cream, chocolate sauce and cherries (best to remove pips prior)*

Caution:

- *Cherry juice stains. Use old sheets unless you want them to take on a 1960s tie-dyed retro look*
- *Shower immediately after consuming. Reason: see caution No. 1!*

36

VIGGO SUSPECTED HIS BROTHER AND CHARLOTTE HAD FINALLY reconciled, and were busy rebuilding their relationship by getting down and dirty at her house. George had been out of the house more than in it, and had taken to kissing his mother on the cheek and telling her he loved her every five minutes when home.

All this blatant display of affection was disturbing Viggo's equilibrium.

Sally turned up this morning on the doorstep with a brown bag of ingredients and ignored the storm dark clouds he was sure were forming above his head. She was currently standing in the kitchen whipping cream to go with one of her delectable tarts. She had informed him it was his favorite, and he gathered from the distinct smell of chocolate that it very well could be.

The aroma of it baking in the oven was calming. Almost as calming as being outside studying the vast night skies.

Not waiting for the tart to cool once it was removed from the oven, she picked up a knife and cut into it. She placed a large slice of the warm gooey chocolate deliciousness on a plate and wafted it under his nose. "Eat up. You need your strength."

He sighed as he pulled the plate close and spooned a large dollop of cream Sally had whipped up earlier on to the plate. "I'm sorry, but I'm not hungry."

Sally snorted. "I can see that."

She sat so close to him that a different type of hunger edged past his willpower to keep her at arm's length.

"Go on. Eat."

He tasted the tart. Oh heavenly constellations. The concoction was the best yet. But he knew Sally would taste even better.

What he really wanted was to bury his lips in her hair, in the crook of her neck, in the dent between her clavicles. She was wearing a bitty dress with tiny straps barely tied in bows on her shoulders. It wouldn't take much to loosen them. Dropping the fork, he pushed the plate away. The light in her eyes diminished and disappointment took its place, until he reached over with a finger and thumb and tilted her chin, and leaned in to lightly taste her lips instead.

Fleetingly, he wondered whether drugs were still in his system because the second she had walked into the house, all bright, breezy and determined to impress him, he'd been knocked off his axis and was having trouble finding his balance.

Maybe he was more concussed than he thought. Especially when he found himself fingering one of those bitty ties on her shoulders and saying, "You are, by far, sweeter than any tart."

She didn't need further encouragement. She melted like chocolate into him. Her arms reached out and wrapped themselves around his neck, her fingers threading through his hair. "I'm a unique blend of ingredients you're never going to find elsewhere."

Of that, he was certain. But could he allow himself to trust her? What if Sally was an achingly beautiful but deranged Queen of Tarts? Would discovering she wasn't what she seemed to be sour his attraction and, he had to admit it, his increasing feelings for her refusing to be repressed?

He should pull away, but his mind wasn't cooperating and his hands splayed across her back, holding her firmly in his arms. She was so tiny. So fragile and yet so capable. He liked the fact she wasn't needy or clingy. Except for the clinch they were currently in. He was enjoying this kind of needy.

And then her lips touched base with his neck and his mind turned to mush and his body took over. His internal excuses evaporated along with the dark grumpy cloud over his head.

"Sally," he said, as she grasped his face in both hands and tilted his head down so she could reach his lips. "This will complicate things."

"It's a good complication," she whispered, and kissed him on the mouth with such open abandonment that an intense ache in his heart shot a bevy of zigzagged arrows through him, creating exquisite havoc on a pathway to his groin.

Who knew what would have happened if the front door hadn't slammed, jerking the two of them apart as if they were guilty teenagers.

Viggo felt like he'd been caught sampling something he shouldn't. Sally was addictive and he wanted more. But he was also a master of denial, so he utilized his willpower and shoved his chair back and stood up just as Osiris raced into the kitchen with Snuggles in hot pursuit. Not far behind were Alice and Bill.

Fortunately, Alice was diverted from making comment, because it was clear, Viggo thought, that Sally looked as if she'd been thoroughly kissed, when Osiris jumped on the table to get out of Snuggles' way, his fur bristled and puffed, as if someone had taken a blow-dryer to him. Despite this, somehow, the cat held an air of feline superiority as he positioned himself right next to the cream, lifted a paw and dipped it in then proceeded to lick the cream off as if he hadn't a care in the world.

Snuggles bounced up and down as if on a rebounder, trying to see more. Sally broke out into a fit of giggles and picked up the plate seconds before Osiris could lick at the remains of Viggo's tart as well. "Oh, no you don't. This is for humans. Cats can't eat chocolate." She also picked up the cream. After placing the dishes on the bench, way out of reach, she leaned down and picked Snuggles up, and cuddled the wiggly dynamo. "Hello my honey-bun. I'm so happy to see you've made friends with Osiris."

Viggo glanced at Alice and saw the worried expression in her eyes when she saw the tart on the table. She had a big soft heart, and he knew she cared for him as if she had given birth to him herself. She was the one woman he could trust implicitly. The one who had not only opened her heart to him, but had also given him a home when he'd had none.

But she still didn't fully trust Sally hadn't poisoned him. "Sally is not trying to kill me. Do you really believe she would be so blatant about it?"

Sally blinked. And her happy smile evaporated. But she didn't try to defend herself. She just stared at Alice, a challenge in her eyes. Viggo wasn't quite sure what that challenge was, but he had a feeling they were both staking claims on him as if he was real estate.

"Of course Sally wouldn't poison you," Bill said, and tickled Osiris's neck.

"Someone did," Alice responded, her tone more sour than any of Sally's lemon tarts. "And until we know who and why, I won't be trusting anyone." Her eyes gentled. "Except you, Viggo. And of course Bill, George and Myrtle."

"That leaves Charlotte and me," Sally said, her tone as frosty as Alice's. "Anyone else you want to add to your list?"

The two women glared at each other.

Oh brother. They were fighting. Over him.

Viggo walked to the bench. He cut an enormous slice of tart, slathered it in cream, and stuffed it in his mouth. It was sheer pleasurable torture. Every last morsel. "I've already had some," he told Alice. "Now I've had more and I'm still standing. I know you want the best for me, and you're being protective, but you have to believe me when I tell you it wasn't Sally, and I'm equally certain it wasn't Charlotte either."

He turned and cut two more slices, placed each piece on a

plate and handed one to Alice and one to Bill. "Eat up. You really have to try it. It's the best I've tasted yet. And Sally, if you'd made this on the show you would have won the bake-off, hands down."

———

After Sally left, taking a very reluctant Snuggles with her, Bill wandered out to the garden and began to weed a flower bed. Viggo and Alice stood at the kitchen window, watching.

"You're concerned about me," Viggo said. "You don't need to be."

"Tell me what the doctor said. What was it they found in your blood?"

He didn't want to lie, but it was too darned embarrassing and unbelievable. "You of all people know I would never take anything that wasn't prescribed for a legitimate illness."

Alice was shocked. "Does this mean they found an illegal drug in your system?"

Damn it. "Don't worry. What they found isn't illegal and I definitely didn't take it on purpose."

"Then why can't you tell us?"

He shrugged. "Wait until the tests on the tart and shortcake come back from the lab."

"You don't have to do everything on your own. You have us. We're your family. We love you."

"I know." He cleared his throat. He'd nearly said *I love you too*, something he'd never said out loud in all the years he'd lived with them. But they had to know he did. It was just that he had trouble saying those exact words to anyone.

Alice stopped staring out the window. She turned to him and waited until he focused on her. "Tell me about Sally."

"What about her?"

There was a fierce determination in Alice's eyes, and he realized she wasn't going to let him get out of this one without saying something. Anything.

"She likes you," Alice added. "I'd go so far as to say she's in love with you."

Oh boy! This was way too deep for a conversation like this with his mother. "I like her too. Very much."

"So what's going on between the two of you?"

"Nothing." There would have been something, if Alice and Bill hadn't come home when they did.

"I'd say she wants there to be something."

He shrugged. "She's a permanent kind of woman. I don't do permanent."

"I'd like to see you settled down."

He shot her a doubtful glance. "I got the impression you didn't like her."

Alice paused, and he could tell she was trying to conjure up a way of wording her next sentence so as not to seem pushy. "It's not that I don't like her, it's that I can't trust her right now."

"And when you find out she's innocent, will you still not trust her?"

"I don't want to see you get hurt. But I feel she'd be good for you. She reminds me of me. Persistent."

He chuckled. "She told me Persistence is her middle name. But how can she hurt me when we're not even an item?"

Alice grabbed his hand and squeezed it tight. "She doesn't hide her emotions. It's all there for everyone to see. Don't bother pretending you don't care for her as well. I know you well enough to see you care more than you are admitting. But remember, I know your past. This could end painfully for the both of you if you're not honest with her."

"We haven't started anything." Except for a kiss that had literally blown his socks off – or would have if he'd been wearing any.

"If you do, make sure you're fully committed. You could break that sweet girl's heart."

He shook his head and tried very hard to be civil. "So now you think she's sweet."

"She is sweet. But I'm not going to give my blessing until her innocence is proven."

He didn't need Alice's blessing. He nearly told her so. But he knew it would hurt her feelings, so he kept his mouth shut and turned his attention to watching Bill, who had wandered out into the garden, dig out a clump of weeds with a spade.

Osiris sat perched on the outdoor table, licking his paws, his tail flicking from side to side. The scene was all so domestic and heartwarming. Viggo found himself wondering what it would be like to be settled, in a loving relationship such as Alice and Bill's. A forever kind of relationship.

It was something he had believed would never happen to him. And he'd been okay with that.

Until now.

37

"Oh Lord. Give me the strength to do what I know I must even though I don't want to." Myrtle opened her eyes and assessed how she felt. She'd just taken a couple of drops. Just the recommended dose. Nothing more. She felt fine. The instructions on the side of the bottle said it was for both men and women. She put her reading glasses because the damn print was so small and there they were, which in all honesty, she didn't need glasses for, were the words in bold capitals. **USE ONLY AS RECOMMENDED**.

Who could believe something so innocuous could do so much damage? Myrtle gulped back on the guilt gnawing a hole in her gut as she stared down at the small indigo bottle in her hand. It was her. She was the one who had felled Viggo with a few drops of Love Potion Number 11 in his bottle of water. Well, maybe more than just a few drops. More like, half of the bottle. And he'd drunk the entire bottle!

Who could have known it would produce such a dramatic reaction?

She tossed the offensive item into her handbag, girded her so-called loins, attempted to pull her jacket over her breasts and do up the buttons, but the material sprang back to where it had been seconds before. She needed to look smart, and not at all like a deranged almost murderer. She had a confession to make. She'd tried several times to tell everyone it was her, but her mouth had refused to work and discovered it just got harder and harder to say anything at all. There was an elephant in her head and she thought she might lose all her marbles completely if she didn't fess up.

Unhooking the seatbelt, she climbed out of the car and looked up at the police precinct sign on the old concrete building. This was where criminals went. This was where she was going. After completing a full day's work she'd timed an email to go out at midnight to both George and Viggo about hiring someone new and what agencies were best to use.

It was just after eight and the light was waning. Fewer people to see her slink her sorry ass into the station. She felt sad for her future life. Or lack thereof now that she teetered on a precipice where there was the chance she would never see the light of day again. Sadly, she acknowledged that the detective who had questioned her as well as everyone else, was a hunky so-and-so and she was sure he fancied her. Damn it. He was hunkier than cake and romance novels. So sad. She would have liked a taste of him, but it was never to be.

As if she conjured him out of nothing, that very same detective walked out of the door and down the front steps. She almost peed herself from fright and considered turning tail and slinking behind the nearest lamppost. But she knew her boobs would poke out one side and her butt out the other.

He recognized her straight away and headed towards her. He tipped his head, like the gentleman he was. "Ma'am?"

"Detective Ranger." Her voice came out small and weak. She was losing her nerve, fast.

"Are you well?" he asked. "You don't look so good."

Don't be nice to me. I'm a horrible, horrible person. "Could be better," she mumbled, and then tears welled in her eyes without warning. Double drat.

And the floodgates opened. "It was me," she wailed, unable to keep her guilt inside any longer. "It was me who poisoned Viggo."

And then she burst into large heaving sobs, and before she knew it she found Detective Ranger's strong, well developed arms engulfing her against his gloriously wide chest. He smelt fresh, as if he'd just showered and somehow that made her cry even harder. He was about to lock her up and throw away the key. Forever.

"There, there." He patted her back and directed her toward the station. "Come inside and tell me all about it."

Surprisingly, he didn't arrest her. Instead he called a meeting at George's house and then led her to the slaughter... ah, his car. Too upset to drive after divulging all the horrid little details of her descent into crime, Myrtle let Detective Ranger help her into the vehicle. He leaned past her and clicked her seatbelt into place. Such a gentleman. While he was at it, she inhaled and locked his scent away in her mammeries... ah memory.

While he drove, she used up all the tissues he'd pressed into her hands as an after-thought.

"What's going to happen to me?" Myrtle asked as the car eventually pulled into George's driveway. "Will I be charged? Are you going to lock me away forever?"

He was silent for several agonizing moments, his mouth compressed into a thin line. Eventually he shook his head. "I doubt that will happen. What you did was stupid, but it wasn't done with malice. But because it became national news, there will be repercussions, and right now I can't say what they will be."

Her stomach fell clear through to the soles of her feet. She didn't know if she'd be able to walk to the front door, let alone fess up to everyone. She looked out and registered that both Charlotte and Sally's cars were already there, parked alongside Bill and Alice's.

The detective, like a true gentleman, got out of the car, walked round to her door and held out a hand. "Come on. Best to get it over with."

"George told me not to meddle."

A small lift in the corner of the detective's mouth was the only sign he might have been amused by her comment.

She squared her shoulders. Her breasts pushed at the jacket she'd just managed to do up, and the button few off into the garden. She sighed with a deep feeling of regret as they walked through the rose arbor. In her mind, she heard the ominous theme from Jaws.

Detective Ranger accepted a cup of coffee from Alice. He eyed the chocolate fudge brownies Charlotte was passing around and his eyes narrowed. "I have the results from the lab in relation to the tart and shortcake."

The detective glanced at each person before focusing on Viggo. "Perhaps you'd like to hear the results first before sharing them with everyone else?"

Viggo leaned back against the counter. His eyes narrowed as he looked from Myrtle to the detective and back again. He had a bad feeling about this. "Myrtle, how is it you came in the same vehicle as the detective.?"

"I was about to ask that too," George said and reached out for another brownie.

The detective's expression gave nothing away as he pulled out a chair before Myrtle collapsed into it. She blew her nose as a fresh bout of tears erupted in her eyes and cascaded down her cheeks. Her lips quivered and she opened her mouth to speak but nothing came out except a high pitched squeak.

Alice immediately placed a hand on Myrtle's shoulder. "Darling. What is it?"

Detective Ranger cleared his throat and spoke first. "There was nothing unusual in the tart or the shortcake. I was on my way here to tell you the results were negative for contaminants, and that we were closing the case when I bumped into Myrtle."

Viggo frowned, and his gaze shifted from Myrtle to the detective, and back to Myrtle again. He suspected he knew where this was heading. "And…?"

The detective hesitated and looked to Myrtle. "Do you want to tell them, or will I?"

If possible, Myrtle grew even more pale. Her lips trembled, her voice grew shaky and more squeaky. "I'll do it. I should be the one."

Viggo glanced at George, who in turn nodded slightly at him. Yep. They were both on the same page. Meddlesome Myrtle had been at it again!

"What's happened?" Alice collapsed into a chair. "Has someone died?"

Viggo snorted his derision, and pushed away from the bench. Sally grasped his hand and stood solid beside him, lending her support.

Charlotte, put the plate holding the rest of the brownies on the table, pulled out a chair and sat down opposite Myrtle. "Oh dear."

Myrtle's lips quivered. She blinked rapidly and gulped. Heaved in a deep breath and then the words rushed out of her mouth. "It… it was me that p… poisoned Viggo."

"With innuendo you mean?" George joked.

"I'm serious." She was wringing her hands. "It's my fault he collapsed."

Alice reared backward and pressed a hand over her mouth.

Bill's eyebrow's rose half way up his forehead. He slung an arm about his wife's shoulders and hugged her tight.

Now that she'd gotten the words out, Myrtle kept going. "I bought a love potion online."

Viggo glared at Myrtle. "Love potion? Online? Stop joking around, Myrtle. This is serious."

Sally winced, and Viggo realized he was squeezing her hand a little too tight. "Sorry." He let go and crossed his arms over his chest and held back on what he really wanted to say to Myrtle.

The detective held up a small bottle with a dropper lid. "This is the offending article. Apparently too much can cause symptoms resembling a heart attack."

Everyone turned their attention to the bottle and an eerie silence descended over the room, except for a small sob from Myrtle.

It was George who eventually said, "Viggo. Are you going to tell us what your blood results were now?"

That seemed to make Viggo even more furious. "If it wasn't in the tart or shortcake then how the hell did I ingest it?" He thought back, his mind racing as he tried to recall the day.

He remembered as Myrtle admitted, "It was in the bottle of water I gave you. You looked so stressed. I put more in it than I should have, thinking it would help."

Viggo recalled he'd downed a lot of water before heading over to stand in front of the cameras. He'd been so nervous, but now that he thought about it, the water had tasted a little... different.

Myrtle lifted her shoulders in a huge shrug. "I really didn't think a few drops would cause such a big reaction."

"You really didn't think at all." Viggo snapped his mouth shut, afraid he would say something he would regret.

"So what exactly is in this love potion?" Charlotte attempted to take the bottle off the detective and read the label.

"Sorry. I can't give it to you," he said. "This is now evidence."

"Evidence of what?" Viggo growled. "That my sister is stupid crazy."

"Now, now, Viggo," Alice said. "Your sister is very upset."

"I have news for you. I'm upset too," Viggo ground out, his outrage clear.

George though, looked as if he wanted to laugh. "What was it the doctor found in your blood?"

Viggo scowled. He was so furious he could barely string two words together. "I'm never going to forgive you for this." He cursed loudly and said, "It appears I had an overdose of something used for erectile dysfunction."

Silence. Then the sound of strangled laughter erupted from George. Charlotte's mouth dropped open in shocked silence. Alice gasped and Bill comforted her, but there was a merry twinkle in his eye. Myrtle was crying still… and Sally? Viggo glanced at her and discovered she was neither horrified nor amused.

"So Charlotte and I are no longer suspects?" She asked Detective Ranger, taking the attention away from Viggo, and he found himself liking her even more than he did before because of it.

"Yes. The question is, Viggo, are you going to press charges against Myrtle?" He rested a hand on Myrtle's shoulder. "Is this something you want the media to know? That you had an adverse reaction to a potion bought online?"

"You mean an erectile dysfunction potion," George laughed. "No. We don't. The question is, are you going to charge Myrtle or is this something we can settle out of the public eye?"

"As far as I'm concerned, the tests on the baking were clear. This innocent little bottle is not an illegal substance. I checked, before I brought Myrtle here. We are not going to press charges unless you want to do so yourself."

Viggo knew Alice would forgive Myrtle anything. That was what was so wonderful about his foster mother, he acknowledged. She was a woman with a heart as big as the sky. He didn't appear to have the same sized heart, because he didn't know if he ever wanted to forgive Myrtle for putting him in this position.

Tears streaming from Myrtle's eyes, she sniffled and dabbed at them with another tissue. She had a box tucked under one arm and was working her way through them as if the Nile was flooding. She looked to the detective as if he was her savior. "I won't have to go to prison?"

"No," he reassured her. "You won't."

Viggo wasn't so happy about that. "A few nights in jail might knock some sense into her overactive head.'

"It was an innocent love potion. I thought you needed a little help," Myrtle hiccupped between sentences. "A few drops in your water before you went on camera was all."

"A few? More like a bucket load," Viggo muttered. "You gave me an overdose."

"I didn't know it was going to knock you out. You need a woman in your life. You needed a nudge."

"A nudge to my grave you mean."

Myrtle burst into a fresh round of tears and looked to Detective Ranger as if he would solve all her problems and the world's as well.

Viggo's tone gentled. "You are my sister, Myrtle. You know I don't feel that way about you."

Myrtle looked completely gobsmacked. She battered her tears away with the base of one palm. "The potion wasn't for you and *me*, idiot. It was for you and Sally."

Sally blushed dramatically. "I appreciate your wanting to help me, Myrtle," she said. "But I'd prefer for you in the future not to interfere with my life."

"The question is, what do we tell the media?" George paced the kitchen floor.

"I don't care about the media," Charlotte said. "They'll write what they want to write, truth or not."

"I agree." Sally arched her neck to look up to Viggo. "What do you want?"

"What do I want?" He wanted to shake Myrtle until she rattled for her crazy foolishness. "I want this over. I want to go back to the way life was before I became more than a silent partner. I want for none of this to have happened."

He regretted his comment the second he saw a flash of hurt in Sally's eyes. He had no intention of hurting anyone, but right now, the past was reaching out and twisting his guts as painful memories surfaced, reminding him of another time he'd much rather forget.

George made a decision for them all. "The police are going to drop the charges as there was nothing in the food. All this fuss will all die away and the media will find something else to focus on."

"How do we explain Viggo's collapse?" Sally asked. "I've got another show coming up and people will want to hear something."

"You continue making your tarts and you say absolutely nothing."

Sally didn't hesitate. "But is it wise to ignore what happened?"

"We'll release a short media release, stating the results of our tests, and your innocence," Detective Ranger said. "That Viggo's collapse remains a mystery. There won't be any reason to say anything more."

Viggo fixed what he hoped was a steely-eyed glare on Myrtle. "That means you too. No talking about it to anyone."

Myrtle was miffed. "As if I would admit such an abject failure to another soul."

38

Two days later, Alice and Bill were ensconced in the lounge with Myrtle, the three of them huddled together, watching television, the sound up loud, as Bill had a slight issue with his hearing.

George had taken off to Charlotte's and Viggo doubted they'd see him again until tomorrow. Sally had gone home after Myrtle's confession the other night and he hadn't seen her since, and damn it, he found himself missing her.

Apart from the headache Myrtle had given him after her confession, Viggo was feeling good. He'd been given the all clear to fly to his conference in New York tomorrow, which meant that his term as temporary agreement with George on managing GVM was about to expire. Not that he'd had to do anything for the past few days anyway. George had pretty much taken back the reigns and there had been no complaints from either Sally or Charlotte.

He walked out onto the patio and investigated the horizon. There were too many clouds for a night of stargazing but he knew he needed to get away for a few hours by himself. Quietly, he headed through the kitchen, made his way down the hall, picked up a pen and wrote a short note. Leaving it on the hall table, he snatched up his car keys and snuck out the front door before anyone could ask him where he was going.

He drove straight to what used to be his grandfather's house. But it wasn't the house he'd come to see. Taking a blanket out of his boot he made his way into the park opposite and spread it out on the grass and lay down on his back. Despite the stars being blanketed by clouds, he stared up towards the heavens, just like he and his grandfather had done all those years ago when it was just the two of them. He missed him so much. The one stable influence in Viggo's early life, his grandfather's passion for sailing and the stars and his willingness to share it with Viggo was the reason he had not become another statistic on the streets of Seattle. Without his grandfather's influence, Viggo may have ended up in prison or high on drugs like both his parents and most likely, dead by now.

For a number of years, Viggo had returned to the park, trying to recapture the feelings of being with his grandfather while lying next to him. Sometimes, it had worked. Often it hadn't.

This time, he found he couldn't focus on the heavens. His mind kept returning to Sally. Instead of imagining his grandfather's presence next to him, he imagined Sally beside him, just as she had been when he'd taken her to his secret spot in Fall City.

So it wasn't a surprise to him that not long afterwards, he found himself back in the car and driving towards Sally's apartment.

He was commitment-phobic, but there was something about her that drew him in, and he owed it to himself to explore it a little more. The attraction between them was undeniable and he wasn't foolish enough to pretend otherwise.

Sally didn't seem surprised to see him at her door. Stepping back, she let him in and led him into the lounge. Snuggles was curled up sound asleep on one corner of the couch. An empty cocktail glass sat on the coffee table. Some girly chick thing was on the television but the sound had been muted, probably when he rang her doorbell.

She saw him look at the cocktail glass. "Do you want one? It's a Golden Dream. Charlotte introduced me to them. They're delicious."

He shook his head. "I'm more of a whiskey guy."

She batted her eyes and his heart did a funny squeeze thing in his chest. "Wouldn't you know it? I have some. Straight up? Ice? How do you like it?"

He damped down the urge to sweep her off her feet and show her just how much he liked *her* instead. "With ice if you have it. Thanks."

"I'll be back in a second," she said, and headed into her kitchen.

He walked over to the sliding doors leading out onto the patio where Sally had served him breakfast the other day. This time, the vista was completely different. It was night, and the city lights sparkled and winked. There was the faint hum of traffic, but the double-glazing kept most of the sound out.

He saw Sally's reflection behind him as she re-entered the room and walked up beside him and handed him his drink.

"So," she said. "What brings you here?"

"You do," he admitted. No point prevaricating. It was the truth.

"Have you come to continue what we almost started in George's kitchen?" she asked, referring to their near-kiss. She was staring at him via the reflection in the windows. He stared back.

"Maybe."

"You don't sound so sure. What the hell happened to you that has made you so afraid to accept there could be something good between us?"

He shouldn't have been surprised by the question, but he was. "Do you have magical powers?" he asked. "I find myself telling you things I never tell anyone else."

"Well, then," she said. "It's time to tell me a little bit more about yourself. Anything. A tidbit will do. Just tell me something."

Surprisingly, Viggo chuckled. Here was a woman who never gave up. She was determined as hell. But heck, so was he. "I'm not a forever guy." He shrugged. "You, on the other hand, are a forever woman. You need to find yourself someone who wants the same things you do."

That just seemed to make her mad.

"That's a bald-faced lie."

Several tendrils of her sleek hair had escaped her ponytail and he itched to push them out of the way.

She was such a bundle of righteousness. "I've seen you with George's family. You love them. Alice, Bill, George. Myrtle too, despite her interference. You can't stand there and tell me you don't."

No. He couldn't. "I don't intend to settle down. Ever." It was blunt. But it was the truth even if it didn't stop him wanting to kiss her until she was breathless?

Disappointment dulled her eyes. "Why not? What's so terrible about being with one person for the rest of your life? I have to tell you, although I guess you already know, that I've found my forever guy. And it's you."

She was so gutsy. Warmth unfurled a frond guarding his heart. If he was truly honest with himself, she meant something to him already. But the deeper he went, the more committed he would become, and the harder the fall would be when it all fell apart. "How can you say such a thing? We haven't even been on a real date."

"I knew the instant I saw you behind George's desk with that cat of yours. Nothing's going to change my mind. My middle name really should have been Persistence, because that's a character trait I possess, and I'm not giving up on you."

"My mother said the same thing, and yet, that's exactly what she did. She gave up on me." Why the hell had he even mentioned his mother? He cursed explicitly.

Sally's eyes widened, but she wasn't put off by his sudden outburst. Her voice gentled. "I assume you don't mean, Alice?"

He nodded, his lips pressed tightly together as pain lanced his heart. "My birth mother."

"So now we're getting somewhere."

He feared he would crumble. Memories of his early life spilled like an uncontrollable torrent into his mind. He squeezed his eyes shut tight-as-can-be in an attempt to will those unwelcome images away.

"I don't want to talk about it." An ache formed in his gut and he fought the urge to double-up in agony as an unexpected well of grief threatened to drown him.

Sally grabbed one of his hands and pressed it against her chest. "It's okay. You don't have to tell me anything else."

"I need another drink," he ground out, his voice shaky with grief. "Have you got any more whiskey?"

She nodded. Still holding his hand, she led him into the living room. "Sit," she commanded, and he did, gratefully, feeling weaker than he cared to admit. Seconds later she shoved a glass under his nose. "Drink up."

He took the golden liquid and slugged all of it in one gulp. "Damn," he coughed as the alcohol sped down his gullet, burning like liquid fire. He held out the glass, his hand trembling. "Another."

39

SALLY'S HEART SUNK THROUGH TO HER TOES. WHATEVER WAS holding him back, it was clear he had been and still was deeply traumatized by his childhood and she now began to get an inkling of why George, Charlotte and even Myrtle refused to tell her what had happened to him as a young boy.

"I'm sorry. You don't have to tell me anything." She rested a hand on his knee before getting up and to pour him another drink. She wanted to say something to cheer him up, but she realized he was too saddened, too shaken right now, so she remained quiet, waiting, hoping deep, deep down she hadn't ruined her chances of a relationship with this complicated man.

Her mind told her she was heading into dangerous territory. Her heart told her he was worth it. She sat back down beside him and handed him his drink.

Viggo shifted a fraction to face her on the couch. "I know my reaction isn't a normal one. Most people can talk about their childhood with ease. I'm not one of them. Mostly, it was full of darkness, disappointment..." He put the whiskey down on the coffee table, "...and death."

She felt her heart squeeze in her chest. "Death?" she whispered. Disappointment, everyone experienced that, but death? "Whose?"

"I guess you could start with my father. I never knew him, but I understand he was some random guy my mother spent time with in a drug-infused haze. From what I can gather, he died before I was born. Of a drug overdose of course. Mom moved in with my grandparents, and although she had a rocky relationship with them, she managed to quit drugs during her pregnancy and according to my grandfather, all was rosy for the first couple of years. But the lure of a high was too strong for her and she took to disappearing for a few hours at first, that then turned into days, sometimes weeks at a time."

He shrugged, as if it didn't matter, but Sally knew it did. She said nothing and waited.

Eventually, he said, "One day, she just never came back. My grandparents did their best, but the worry of wondering what had happened to mom took its toll. My grandmother died when I was four. I only have snatches of her in my memory and from what my grandfather told me of her. Afterwards, it was just him and me for a few years. I learned after his passing that he had developed Parkinson's disease. I remember people coming to the house, having discussions with him about me going into foster care. I didn't know what that meant, but I did know I didn't want to leave the only constant in my life. And if I left, how would my mom find me when she finally came home?"

Tears welled in Sally's eyes. Her nails dug sharply into her thigh and she welcomed the pain. "I'm so sorry," she gulped, and a single tear escaped one eye and ran down her cheek. It fell and dropped onto her knee.

Ever so gently, he wiped her tear away before placing a hand over hers as if to comfort her when it should be she comforting him.

"Before they could remove me to another home, my grandfather died."

He grew silent, a distant look in his eyes. Sally could tell he was lost in the past, remembering things she'd forced him to remember. She was so upset with herself right now. How dare she force this from him? She came from a happy, healthy home where everyone was still very much alive. Even her grandparents.

"So you went into foster care?" she nudged gently when he hesitated. There was conflict in every part of him. She felt it. She could see it. She knew that whatever was coming next would cost him dearly to say out loud.

"You've told me this much," she spoke softly. "Why not tell me the rest?"

"Because I've never told anyone the full story" he ground out. "Alice and Bill know the basics. I'm pretty sure George and Myrtle know, but it's not something we've ever talked about."

Sally swallowed. She waited quietly, wondering if he trusted her enough to confide in her. She jerked in surprise when he eventually broke the silence, his voice rough and unsteady. "I didn't tell anyone Grandad had died, peacefully, in his chair, while watching television. I left him there in the lounge for the next three days, and during that time I searched everywhere for my mom."

"But... how old were you then?"

"Barely eleven. I found a number for mom in his personal organizer he kept on his desk in his study. I rang her number a hundred times but she never answered. There was an address, so I took what cash he had in his wallet and made my way there."

He frowned, his focus returning to her. "I don't even know why I'm telling you this now."

Too afraid to love her in case she left him alone again. "My nan says it's always good to share your pain with another. That the pain will lessen over time if you accept your past and then let it go, so the hurt won't influence the choices you make for the rest of your life."

He shook his head. "It's best not to talk about it at all."

"And yet, here we are," she said softly, resting a hand over his. "Talking." Sally's heart ached for the boy who had never known his father, who had lost his mother to drugs, his grandmother and finally his grandfather. "Did you find your mother?"

"I did. She didn't recognize me. If it hadn't been for photographs in my grandparent's photo albums I wouldn't have recognized her either. She was a dishevelled mess, and when I told her grandad had gone to heaven and I needed her to come home, she laughed in my face and said I'd be better off without her. She told me to get lost." He shrugged. "So I did."

Sometimes life really was a bitch. More tears formed in her eyes and her voice quivered when she asked a question, even though she wasn't sure she wanted to know the answer. "What do you mean?"

"I didn't go home. I rang the social services number from a pay phone and told them about grandad. I lived on the streets. I slept in doorways. In bus stations. Anywhere I felt was reasonably safe. But eventually I did go home. Grandad was gone. They had taken him away and changed the locks on the doors.

He huffed as if amused, but there was nothing but gravity in his expression. "Nothing was going to keep me out of the only home I knew. I broke in and hid in the house for several weeks. There was a good stock of canned food which I eked out over those weeks, so I didn't go hungry. I spent most of my daylight hours in different libraries absorbing everything there was to know about astronomy because that kept me close to my memories of grandad. At night, I would creep outside and lie on the grass in the park across the road and look up at the stars

"But the neighbors must have been seen me sneaking in and out and eventually social services caught up with me and I was placed in a series of foster homes, all of which I ran away from until Alice and Bill took me in."

"What was so different about them that you decided to remain with them, then?"

"I don't know."

His reply was indifferent. She knew better. "Yes. You do."

"They're good people. George was happy to have a brother. Plus, they had already adopted Myrtle. They put up with my dark moments when I would retreat into myself. They didn't ask too many questions. And Alice and Bill were kinder than any other caregivers I'd had before."

"They love you. They might not be your birth family, but they are your family now. You love them too. Even Myrtle."

"I don't know if I can forgive her."

"Of course you can. Family knows the worst and the best about each other and still forgives. Besides, she had no idea what the end result would be. She was just trying to bring you and I together."

"Perhaps. But I can't trust her."

"She's mischievous, but her heart is in the right place." What Sally really wanted to know was whether Viggo's heart was in the right place too. Did he care for her, the way she knew she cared for him?

"Knowing the truth about you hasn't changed anything for me," she told him. "I care. I want you to care for me too."

"I'm a loner. I need my space. I'm not husband material."

A glimmer of hope warmed Sally right through to her hair follicles. He was thinking way deeper than she'd expected him to.

"I'm not asking you to marry me." Although she definitely wouldn't say no if he did. "I'm asking you to sleep with me and see where this attraction of ours goes." She held up a hand when it looked like he would protest. "Don't you dare deny there's something special between us when, clearly, there is. So there's no misunderstanding here, there's nothing sweeter in life, for me, than you."

40

VIGGO HAD NEVER MET ANYONE LIKE SALLY. HE'D SURE AS heck, had never divulged so much about his early life to any one person either. Bits and pieces here and there, but never the hard unvarnished facts. What was it about her that made him want to spill all his dark secrets? Secrets he'd buried deep with the intention of never divulging them to a single soul until he met his maker in Heaven.

Bizarrely, unburdening his heart, a heart which had been heavy for so long, somehow grew lighter. "You are...," he paused, trying to figure out just exactly what she was, "... amazing. I've never met anyone like you." Or likely to again.

Moved by his revelations, it was clear Sally was attempting to hide her shock. Her smile wavered, as she said, "Flattery will get you everywhere."

She had bounded her way in with an abundance of delicious sweet joy, but could it be sustained for a lifetime of togetherness? "I've been on my own too long. I like things my way."

She batted her beautiful long lashes at him. "I'd love it if you had your way with me right now."

He stood up. He should leave. Now. Before he was in too deep. "You make it hard for a man to say no."

"Don't then." She reached up to cup his cheeks in her small hands before he could put any distance between them. "You think too much. I believe we should just do. It's a cliché, but actions speak far louder than words and I'm all for action right now."

She waited, her body as close to him as it could be with clothes on. There was no use prevaricating on his part. It was evident to her, from the flicker of her eyes down to his groin, that despite all his protestations, his body was willing. It was no use denying he wanted her as much as she wanted him.

Gripping her under her arms he hoisted her upwards until she was nose to nose with him, her feet dangling a few inches off the floor. "You are incorrigible."

Lickety-split, she wound her legs around his hips and crossed her ankles, locking herself in place. "Keep talking sexy to me. I'm liking it a lot."

His head rocked back, and he groaned. "You're turning my world upside-down."

"You can turn me upside-down too."

His head rocked forward and he stared into eyes that glittered with a keen, open and frank desire. "There's no doubt about it. You're a delectable minx."

"Keep the compliments coming." She indicated the hallway with her head. "My bedroom's down there. Last door at the end. Let's whip up something delicious in there."

"Are you sure about this?" He felt like his voice belonged to someone else. It had dropped to a husky urgency that had him pressing her butt against him, his body hard and ready. "There's no denying I want you. But I need to be clear, that you understand this doesn't mean we're beginning a long-term anything."

"I get that." Her grinned dropped a fraction and he pretended not to notice when she added, "Although I feel a fraction guilty about this when you're feeling so low."

He huffed out a sudden burst of amusement. "Only a fraction, huh." Sally was proving to be balm for his battered heart. "I'm already feeling better."

"Well then. Let's bake a batch of lust in the bedroom. Or here. In the lounge. Or the kitchen, perhaps? How about the bathroom? I really don't care where. Let's make some happy memories to keep you smiling when you find yourself all alone in your hotel room in New York."

"Well, hell," he growled, and caved to her will, which was, clearly, far mightier than his. He dipped his head and kissed her like the starving man he was. Apparently she was extremely hungry as well because they dined on each other in the bedroom, devoured each other in the shower and finally in the kitchen, while serving mouthfuls of decadent chocolate tart in various interesting ways before collapsing in an exhausted, satiated heap back in the bedroom.

Propping his head on one hand, he gazed at her as she lay beside him, boneless, her skin glowing with a rosy hue. He didn't believe she could get any more beautiful. He pushed a wayward strand off her cheek. "I don't think I've got the strength to stand."

She walked her fingers up his bare chest. "Stay."

"I have to pack."

"What time's your flight?"

He looked over at the digital clock on the bedside table. "I'm taking the red-eye. Six hours from now."

He witnessed the flicker of disappointment in her eyes, but she covered it up quickly.

"When will you be back?"

"Four days from now."

"Well then," she said, as she leaned in and stole a kiss. "We've got just enough time to bake something else." Her palm swooped down under the sheets, reaching for him.

"You're insatiable," he said.

He sucked in a breath when she reached her target. She looked him in the eyes and he realized he was doomed when she said, "Yes. I am. For you."

41

Attending an astronomy conference in New York was Viggo's idea of a good time. It was what rocked his world. Doing the accounts for GVM was, as far as he was concerned, a sideline. A successful one, enabling him financially to concentrate on what he loved most. Stargazing.

This was the first time he'd arrived for a conference ill-prepared. He still had notes to make for his talk. Although he knew his subject well, and had already spent an extraordinary amount of time researching and documenting everything for his presentation, the time spent in hospital and convalescing at George's had put a huge dent in his plans to complete a final draft and rehearse it before leaving Seattle. This presentation was supposed to be one of the defining moments of his life as an amateur astronomer.

But another defining moment, make that defining person, had wheedled her way into his life. No matter how much he attempted to corral his mind into some kind of order, his thoughts broke free, returning always, to Sally. His mind was consumed by images of a heavenly body, and it wasn't any of the ones residing in the sky.

He was more at ease talking about black holes and heavenly particles than he was making small talk with anyone in general. In this environment though, he could relax, be himself, talk with other like-minded individuals, discuss theories into the small hours, so he did his best to put aside the events of the past few weeks and concentrate on the present.

Physically tired from inner emotional turmoil and lack of sleep, despite being intellectually recharged from the first day of the conference, he headed back to his room early with the intent of going through his notes and rehearsing his speech one more time. He was presenting, first thing the next morning.

But Sally struck again, the sneaky woman! A chiller box rested on the desk in his room, with his name scrawled in large letters across it. He paused, half expecting someone – Sally – to jump out of a wardrobe and shout surprise. He wouldn't have put it past her to turn up unannounced. He tossed the thought around for a second, and found it didn't bother him as much as it should have. He studied the box again. It was wrapped up tight with URGENT stickers all over it and FRAGILE tape sealing the sides.

"What the hell?" he muttered, and dug in the drawers for a knife, but in the end had to phone reception for one. When it arrived, he cut through the tape and carefully eased the top off. Inside was another chiller style box and a large ice pack. An envelope was taped to the chiller, with his name on it.

He tore the envelope open and pulled out a small note.

Dearest Viggo,

In case you've forgotten about me, here's a little something to remind you.

Enjoy.

Sally.

He eased the box open, already knowing what it would be. Yep. A tart. And not just any tart, but a singularly spectacular triple-layered chocolate tart. All for him. He considered taking it downstairs to share with his buddies, but as he cut himself an enormous slice he knew he wasn't going to do anything of the sort. This was Sally on a plate. All her layers of deliciousness right there for him to devour. His head rocked back as he recalled the other night, when he'd eaten tart straight off her belly, and he nearly came right then and there.

"God help me," he muttered, cut another slice and collapsed into a chair, ignoring the fact he had work to do, because somehow in the last five minutes he'd lost the inclination to do anything except revisit his adventures in Sally's arms before falling into a carbo-loaded slumber.

His talk was a huge success. Nobody noticed his slight case of the sugar jitters, and when it came to the Q&A at the end of the presentation, he knew he'd intrigued many. Buoyed by his success, he spent the remainder of the day and most of the evening fielding questions from friends and colleagues and didn't get back to his room until close to midnight.

And yep. Another tart waited for him. This one was labeled Sally's Dreamy Peanut Butter and Salted Caramel Tart. It was sweet, delicious and incredibly decadent. Just like Sally. He moaned as he licked the sticky gooeyness from his fingers. His eyes nearly rolled back into his head, and he muttered, "What the hell are you doing to me, Sally?"

He really should be jotting down notes into his iPad on the talk from that day, but the sugar – he could blame the sugar – made him want to call her and tell her to hop on the first plane to New York so they could get sticky together as soon as possible.

Could it possibly be that he cared more than he'd expected? Being reminded by the delivery of a Frangipani Tart on the third day didn't help. He tugged the note out from the first tart delivery and read it for the ninth or tenth time.

A little something to remind you of me.

He admired her tenacity. He looked at the tart and then at his watch. Surely this was the last one. Tomorrow was the final day and he would be taking the red-eye home tomorrow night. Knowing he couldn't eat another bite, and not wanting to spend another night in a sugar-induced haze, he hiked the box under one arm and went in search of a few friends to share it with.

42

GEORGE ERUPTED FROM HIS CHAIR. "YES!" HE YELLED AT THE top of his lungs. "Myrtle! Get in here."

Myrtle raced in seconds later and he wondered if she'd been hovering by the door.

He waggled the email he'd printed off in front of her face. "Look at this."

"If you hold your hand still long enough I will," she muttered as she attempted to snatch the piece of paper from his fingertips and failed.

"Sally is going to be ecstatic." He grabbed one of her hands and smacked the email into her palm. "Read it. Who would have thought? It turns out you did us a huge favor by poisoning Viggo."

"I did not poison him on purpose." Myrtle's eyes flashed with a flicker of guilt but then her eyes squinted and she gave him what he termed, her evil-eyed glare. "Viggo is well. The television studio loves the ratings. The police have *not* charged me with anything. The substance wasn't illegal. Yes, I was stupid. I hope you're not going to bring this up for the rest of our lives."

"Don't get your knickers in a knot. I'm not angry. Well, I

was. Momentarily. Not anymore." He stabbed at the email with his index finger. "Not after reading this piece of news. It will improve your day. Maybe your entire life."

Myrtle blinked, took a good measure of George's excitement, and read the email. Slowly a smile stretched her mouth into the widest grin, and when she looked up, she and the rest of her jiggled with excitement. "Eureka! We've made the big time."

George decided to tell Charlotte the good news in person. He figured she would need persuading as well as time to mull the deal on offer over. He also accepted she would want to speak to Sally first. They'd become fast friends. Go figure! He couldn't contain his grin on his drive over to her house. Who would have thought such a disaster could turn into an amazing opportunity for them both?

He let himself in, she'd given him a key now that they were back together, and strode down the hall into her office where she was typing up a new recipe.

As he expected, Charlotte wasn't as excited as Myrtle.

"The entire country. Nationwide. Possibly worldwide." Grasping her stomach, she doubled over, and rested her forehead on her knees. She looked up, her beautiful green eyes wide with genuine fear. "I'm going to throw up."

He hunkered down in front of her and grasped her hand. Cupcake wriggled in next to him and placed his chin on her knees. "Are you okay?"

"No!" And then she poleaxed him by declaring, "What on earth will I wear?"

Only a woman would think that. "That's what you're worried about?"

"Pretty much. Although, I'm not *that* keen on all the notoriety now everyone knows I'm Madam Delicious."

George could hardly believe how easily she'd accepted the

notion of going mainstream. "They want to call it Tart vs. Short-cake again. The same format as the last one where you work together, old-fashioned versus modern. Myrtle has given me her word that she will not be putting love potions in anything. Ever again."

"Get it in writing first. She's a pushover for a piece of tart or shortcake."

George couldn't believe how well this was going. "If it makes you happy, I'll draw up something as soon as I'm back in the office."

"Show me the signed document and we have a deal."

"What do you think?" Charlotte asked Sally who visited her later that day.

"I'm ecstatic. Aren't you?"

"Driving Men Wild want to do a revealing article about me and my alter ego, Madam Delicious, and now a major network wants us to do a nationwide bake-off. I'm scared beyond belief but I've said yes. Because it's with you."

Sally hugged Snuggles under her chin and danced a mini jig on the spot. "It will be fabulous. The sales of your books will go through the roof. We're going to be megastars."

Charlotte couldn't think of anything worse.

"And you know what else?"

"What?" Inside she was feeling petrified.

"We could do a cookbook together. We are going to be so famous."

"Oh crackers. Don't. You're freaking me out, even if I love the idea of doing a book with you." It appeared there she wasn't going to be able to wriggle out of this one. She sighed. Heavily. "I guess you're going to have to help me buy a whole new wardrobe for the magazine photo shoot. I can't wear the same dress every time. And I'm going to need something extremely sexylicious for the bake-off too."

Sally high fived Charlotte. "With pleasure. You know how I love to shop."

Charlotte opened the fridge and took out a bottle of champagne. She'd been saving it for a special occasion and this looked like the time.

"Ooh. Goodie." Sally put Snuggles on the floor and he tiptapped his way to Cupcake who was lying stretched out on the cool tiles. Snuggles sniffed the larger dog, turned around three times and then "snuggled" in, between Cupcakes head and front paws. Cupcake licked Snuggles. Snuggles licked Cupcake, then both, amazingly, fell asleep.

"Best buds for ever," Charlotte declared. "Let's toast not only our good news, but to Cupcake and Snuggles."

"Yes let's," Sally said and sat down on one of the bar stools on the other side of the kitchen bench.

Charlotte paused. Did she see a cloud of despair forming over Sally's perfectly put together head? "What's going on with you and Viggo?"

"Nothing, it seems."

Charlotte unscrewed the wire keeping the cork in check. "What do you mean, nothing. There's clearly something."

Sally blinked and a film of moisture brimmed in her eyes. Uh oh! "Nothing."

Charlotte wiggled the cork. It popped and flew across the room and bounced off a window. Bubbles spilled out the top of the bottle and down the sides. "Well, he is in New York?"

Silence. Charlotte stopped what she was doing and witnessed true despair in her friend's eyes. "He'll be back soon."

Sally took the glass of bubbles Charlotte held out to her. "He hasn't even called once. Not even a single text to thank me for the tarts I've sent him."

"You sent tarts to New York? And he didn't even text you a

thank you? He's an ungrateful so-and-so. When he get's back I'm going to kick him in the butt."

"Thanks. But I want that pleasure. But I still want him. I can't help myself. I'm crazy for him."

"If Myrtle were here she'd call you a woman with no backbone. What's wrong with your texting finger? Text him yourself. Get on a plane and go to him."

"No. He has to come to me. Besides, he's due back tomorrow. I've chased him enough. He knows exactly how I feel. I can't force him to care for me."

"You do know he has commitment issues?"

"Tell me about it."

"I can't."

"No. I mean I know all bout his past. He told me everything before he went to New York."

Charlotte reared back in total surprise. "What? Everything?"

"I think so."

"Wow! That's... well... he must *really* like you."

Sally perked up a fraction. "I hope so."

Charlotte refilled Sally's glass. "I'll say. Don't you know he keeps everything close to his chest? In all the years I've known him, I've never seen him in a relationship. He's brought dates to events, yes. Usually, we never see that particular date again. The fact he's told you about his past speaks volumes."

"What if I'm a one-night stand and that was all there was to it?"

"You've slept together." Charlotte grinned. "This story just keeps getting more and more juicy."

Charlotte clinked her glass with Sally's. "Here's to hot sex."

"I never said it was hot."

"You're blushing like a scarlet rose. It was hot. I can tell."

Sally raised her glass. "Yes it was hot. But I don't want to talk about him anymore. It's too depressing. Let's toast our new joint venture instead. You and me."

Charlotte clinked her glass with Sally's. "I'm only agreeing to do this because it's you. Otherwise I'd be running a mile in the opposite direction. I had plans to run away to New Zealand if George and I didn't resolve our issues."

"I think that's what Viggo has done by putting distance between us. I know he cares about me, and I thought we were getting somewhere. But now I'm not so sure."

Charlotte ran a soothing palm down Sally's arm. "One of the things I've learned since George and I hooked back up is to never give up. If you doubt how Viggo feels about you, then ask him. Put it on the line. It's the only way."

"I want him to come to me."

"Let's hope he does then. And if he does, don't try to change him. I learned that little gem the hard way. It was me who needed to change. Not George. I needed to learn to love myself." She giggled. "George loves himself enough already."

Sally chuckled. "That conjures up all kinds of images I have no wish to see."

Charlotte grinned. "And you know what else?"

Sally held out her glass for a refill. "What?"

"I'm so glad we're friends."

Sally's eyes brimmed. "Me too. Here's to friendship."

"Friends forever."

Their glasses clinked. "Forever."

43

SINCE BILL AND ALICE HAD RETURNED HOME AND VIGGO HAD taken himself off to New York, Charlotte pretty much moved in to George's house, and was spending most nights of the week at his side. She was also making good use of the kitchen, baking up a bevy of delicious treats and using her cottage as her office in the daytime.

The magazine interview had gone better than either of them could have hoped for. George had just about rolled on the floor with laughter upon hearing the journalist had asked for Charlotte to pose with a mostly naked male cover model. They had tried their utmost and failed, to get her to slather the extremely buffed guy with extra creamy chocolate sauce. She'd refused point blank. Instead she'd posed fully clothed, hanging on to one of those luscious biceps, with one foot raised in the air as she gazed up at him. Dressed in a retro sexy dress Sally had helped her find, the article would be out in a couple of weeks' time. They'd already viewed a mock-up and thankfully, there were no surprises and the article was tasteful, yet playful.

Charlotte was icing an enormous chocolate cake. He walked over and nuzzled the back of her neck. She dipped a spoon into the mixture, turned in his arms and smeared icing on his lips and then took her time kissing it off. "I'm so happy we made up."

"Not as happy as I am." He grabbed the spoon off her and smeared what was left in the center of her clavicle. He dipped his head and nibbled.

"My, you're awfully hungry," she said. "Anybody would think you've had nothing to eat for a very long time."

"Some real food would be good," he admitted. "I mean, food without sugar in it," he added, when she frowned at him. "But what I'd like more is to sample that new recipe you've written for Drive Men Wild."

She pursed her mouth and took the spoon back off him and tapped the back of it against her lips, leaving traces of chocolate on them. "It will cost you."

"What? Anything."

She grinned. "Anything?"

He paused and narrowed his eyes. "What's going on in that deliciously devious mind of yours?"

"Do you think you could get Sally and me a book contract? We want to produce a cookbook together."

"What? Easy. Anything else?"

"How do you feel about very, very, cold ice cream? I've a hankering for something a little bit hot and whole lot cold."

"So what's the hot?"

Charlotte gave him, her *are you kidding me* look. "Why, me of course."

"I love you hot," he told her. "But before we explore your new idea, there's something I've been meaning to ask."

She scraped the wooden spoon around the edges of the bowl for more icing and then licked it off. "Oh, what's that?"

He felt his heart go hop-skippity-jump against his rib-cage.

She frowned at him. "Why are you trembling?"

"I'm nervous." An understatement! He was petrified.

"Why?"

"Because…" He leaned in and kissed a smudge of chocolate

off her lips. "I'm crazy for you. And, well, here's the thing." He dug in his pocket and pulled out something square.

A box. A small turquoise box. It was small and perfectly formed. Charlotte told herself not to get excited. It could be anything. She'd made too many incorrect assumptions in the past. She wasn't going to assume anything now. All the same, a well of emotion rose in her chest and her eyes brimmed with sudden moisture.

"I'm crazy for you too." She was finding it hard to breathe. "What's in the box?"

He held it out to her. "Open it and see."

Her skin was tingling. She felt weird and wonderful all at once and wondered if she was going to faint from the sheer surprise of what was happening. "No. You open it."

George choked up. He cleared his throat. His eyes looked all dreamy and determined and yet his hands shook so much she wanted grab that gorgeous little box out of his hands. But she wanted him to do it. And fast, before they both passed out from lack of oxygen.

"Get on with it, so I can say yes."

He opened the box, holding it out for her to see. It was a single empress cut, pink diamond, and it sparkled and winked invitingly at her under the kitchen lights. Oh sweet heaven! He'd been paying attention when she'd drooled over this exact ring in a magazine a few days ago.

"You better love me as much as I love you," he said. "And you better love this ring just as much," he growled. "It nearly cost more than this house."

She screamed and jogged on the spot, vibrating with sheer exhilaration. "Ohmygod. Ohmygod. Ohmygod."

He bent down on one knee and looked up at her and she saw just how true his love was. "I can't imagine life without you in it," he told her. "I want you in my life. I want to grow old with you. I want to make babies with you, and have fun trying."

His voice shook as he said, "Let's not waste any more time.

Let's get down and dirty in every room of this house every day for the rest of our lives. Charlotte Meyer. Will you marry me?"

Collapsing to her knees , she screamed again and held out her hand, her ring finger at the ready. "Oh my sweet shortcake. Yes to everything. Yes. Yes."

He tugged the ring out of the box and slid the ring onto her finger. Charlotte looked at it for a second and then threw herself at him and they collapsed onto the floor. "We should start getting down and dirty now to seal the deal," he said as their limbs tangled.

And that's what they did, until the deal was well and truly done.

44

SALLY HAD SPENT THE BETTER PART OF LAST WEEK CREATING A new shortcake for Viggo. This would be the last one she made him, unless he was willing to commit to some kind of relationship between them. She was calling it Sally's Constellation T'Heart.

It looked amazing, even if she thought so herself. It tasted even better. Oozing with a filling of decadent dark chocolate mousse and topped with a thin, perfectly tempered sheet of white chocolate, she drizzled freeze-dried blueberry powder over the surface to resemble an inky midnight-blue sky and then piped twinkling golden stars on top.

It was the most awesome creation she'd ever made. She should know, as she'd made about ten already in an effort to achieve the texture and flavor she wanted. This tart represented the love she had for Viggo, and whether he accepted that love or not, he would know, without a doubt that her love for him was as big as the inky night sky and the Milky Way combined.

She ran her hands over her hips. Her skirt was feeling tight and she knew it was from consuming way too much sugar over the past few days. She didn't mind the extra inches. What she did mind was not having heard from Viggo. Surely he was back by now.

She'd done enough chasing in the verbal sense. And the tarts, well, she couldn't help herself. They were her way of reminding him of her existence. They'd done the deed in her bedroom, the kitchen and everywhere else in her apartment. If she meant anything to him at all, he would come to her. So she was just going to have to wait it out and see what happened next – after she'd sent him her final masterpiece.

She'd told Charlotte he would have to come to her. But because Persistence really was her middle name, she had decided to give it one last go. Ever so carefully, she put the tart into a box, then tucked it securely in a labelled chiller box that held a FRAGILE sticker on it. Feeling somewhat fragile herself, she called a courier to send it to his apartment across town. After that she hunkered down in her apartment with Snuggles and consoled herself with Gilmore Girl reruns and one too many Golden Dreams while she waited.

Surely he would come. Either to tell her it was all off, or that they would continue on with their relationship. It was make or break time, and she had never felt so anxious in her life.

She swallowed back her fear and kissed Snuggles' head as he rested his little paws on her chest and looked adoringly up at her. The TV played in the background, but finding it difficult to concentrate, she ended up wandering aimlessly from room to room, cuddling Snuggles and waited.

And waited. And waited some more.

Viggo's red-eye flight had been delayed due to mechanical diffi-culties. Having just landed after being up all night, he decided to pick up Osiris from George's later and headed straight home to shower before heading to see Sally.

He couldn't shake the warm tingle of anticipation every time he thought of Sally. She'd bewitched and bamboozled him. It turned out that the only star in the universe to brighten his life wasn't in the sky above, but living in a small apartment twenty minutes' drive away. His world had been catapulted into a new orbit with Sally at its center. He'd meant it when he'd said he didn't want a relationship. The biggest loss in his life had been caused by a woman.

But when he'd taken a long hard look at his adopted family and the life Alice, Bill, George and yes, even Myrtle, had given him, he realized the only way forward was to put himself out there. One day at a time. That was all he could offer Sally.

He hoped the offer would be good enough to satisfy her.

Despite the shower and putting on fresh clothes, he was exhausted. He sat down on the edge of the bed and lay back, intending to rest for five minutes.

His door bell went and jolted him awake. Cursing explicitly, he bolted from the bed feeling disoriented and his eyes blurry with sleep. "What the hell?" He glanced at the clock and charged down the hall. He'd been asleep for two hours.

He looked out the spy-hole. Nothing. Whoever it was had gone. He opened the door anyway. At his feet was a box. He couldn't help it. He huffed his amusement, leaned down and picked it up.

He took it into the kitchen, found a knife, cut the seals, and opened it. Then he stood staring at the most amazing creation he'd ever laid eyes on. There was no way to discern what the flavor was, but the tart's top was an inky sky blue, interspersed with swirl of tiny yellow stars. It looked like the Milky Way and damn it, it must have taken her hours to do.

He stood transfixed, taking it all in before leaning over to sniff, his nose nearly touching the masterpiece. He straightened up and he knew what he needed to do. What he was looking at wasn't just a tart. This incredible concoction was Sally's heart on a plate.

The doorbell chimed and Sally's heart skipped a beat. Snuggles barked and raced rings around her legs.

"Sit," she instructed. Miraculously, Snuggles sat. She bent down and patted his head. "Good boy."

The doorbell went again. She walked down the hall. She was reluctant to answer it and be disappointed if it wasn't Viggo. "Shall I answer it?" she asked Snuggles.

Snuggles barked.

It sounded like a yes to Sally. She looked through the peephole and her stomach flipped. She didn't know whether to be happy or just plain scared. It was him. Holding the tart she'd sent him.

"Sally," he called. "I know you're in there. Answer the door."

"Do you come bearing good or bad news?" she called back. "If the news is good, I'll open the door. If it's bad, go away."

He had the gall to laugh. She whipped the door open, feeling furious with him for laughing at her. "I'm not chasing you anymore," she said. "You didn't call or text me once."

His eyebrow arched. "You didn't call me either."

"I sent you tarts."

"They were delicious."

"You didn't even text me a simple thank you."

"I wanted to thank you in person."

"I don't need your thanks. I need something else from you."

His expression gentled and he stepped forward, forcing her to step back. He walked in and shoved the door closed with his foot. "That's why I'm here. We need to talk."

"I'm done talking," she said. "You know how I feel. It's how you feel I'm interested in."

He leaned over, the boxed tart between them, and kissed the top of her head. Walking past her, as if he owned the place, he went into her kitchen, placed the tart on the bench and opened the box.

She felt a mix of hope and dejection at the same time. Despite the fact he'd kissed her head, his action was as if she were a schoolgirl and not the woman he desired. Where had all her positivity gone?

He hadn't even cut a single slice of her precious concoction. Her hope sunk. "You haven't even touched it." She'd spent more hours than she cared to count making it perfect and he hadn't so much as swiped a finger over it.

He searched in the drawers for a knife and laid it on the countertop. "It's the most magnificent thing I've ever seen. And you made it for me. I'm honored and humbled." He pulled his phone from his back pocket and took a snapshot of it. "For posterity," he said, and tucked the phone away again.

She hesitated. Was that warmth in his voice? Did her eyes deceive her or was she witnessing a transformation of trust in her that hadn't been there before? Her eyes filmed over, but she held back, not wanting to be wrong. She knew he cared for her. What she didn't know, was whether he was strong enough to let go of his past so he could explore a brighter future.

With her. Together.

He reached out and gripped her waist and tugged her to him. She didn't say anything. Didn't reach up to run her fingers through his hair like she wanted. Her heart was doing an erratic dance in her chest. For someone never short of something to say, she seemed to have lost her vocabulary altogether.

She stared into his eyes and saw a vulnerability that she'd not seen before. Being this close to him, and pretty much holding her breath, she felt him tremble. Finding her voice she asked, "Why haven't you even tasted the tart?"

"I'm tired of doing everything alone." His voice was husky with emotion. His pupils dilated and she saw for the first time, when he didn't look away, that he was allowing her to see his heart through his eyes and not just his stomach. "I want to cut into this tart with you at my side."

A crazy warmth stole into her heart and her voice trembled. "You do?"

He nodded. "I'm crazy about you. But then you already know that. It's just that, I don't know how to do relationships."

"Yes, you do," she said, and reached up to cup his jaw. Was it possible. He was letting her in. This was such a big deal. All his hopes and dreams and fears were there, in his eyes, for her to see. She brushed her thumbs backward and forward over his cheeks as if to reassure herself. "Are you sure?"

He wavered between sounding vulnerable and determined. "It's early days and I'm not sure how all this will play out, but I want to be in your life. I'm here if you'll have me. I can't say what the future will bring. I've never loved anyone like this before. Except for my adopted family, but that's a different kind of love. And here's the thing. While in New York I learned something about myself. Can you guess what it is?"

She held on to her excitement even though on the inside she was jumping insanely for joy. She wasn't going to second-guess. He would have to tell her. "What?"

"That I hated not having you at my side. I deliberately didn't call because I needed to know for certain that these feelings I have for you are not going to go away. I've never felt like this before. You win over an astronomy conference any day. The only thing that kept me from cutting the entire trip short were the tarts you sent me every night. You have no idea how much I looked forward to them."

He indicated the tart on the bench. "I was already on my way over here when this arrived."

Her eyes remained focused on him. "It's a one-off special. Never to be repeated."

"Then we better make sure we enjoy it to the fullest," he told her. "You sent me your heart in the form of a tart. Well, I'm here to tell you, you can have my heart if you want it. It turns out, I can't run away from love."

She jumped and he caught her, his hands moving to cup her

bottom as she wrapped her legs around his hips. "Your words are music to my ears. But don't get carried away now. I have high expectations. I'm going to be famous. How do you feel about having a famous lover that's always in the news?"

"As long as you don't listen to Myrtle and act upon any of her suggestions we should be just fine," he rumbled. Turning, he rested her butt on the bench, leaned over, grabbed the knife and cut a huge slice of tart. "I'm not promising that this relationship will be easy and straightforward. There might be the odd day where I have to disappear, to be by myself. Can you deal with that?"

She looked deep into his eyes, knowing he was taking a huge leap of faith all because of her. "It's a cliché, but we'll deal with what life throws at us one day at a time." She leaned into him as he bent his head and their lips met. "Together."

He rested his head on her forehead and inhaled. "George is going to fall off his perch when he hears about this."

"Who cares about George right now. Let's eat this tart. I called it Sally's Constellation T'Heart, but I'm changing it right now to Sally and Viggo's Constellation T'Heart." She reached out and picked up the slice he had cut and lifted it to his lips. "Eat up," she said. "And then you can have me for dessert whenever and wherever you want."

A FEW WEEKS LATER

Balloons festooned the blooming roses rambling in and around the arched entranceway to George's house – now Charlotte's home too. She walked down the path in her bare feet, back to the house, through the front door and down the hall into the kitchen.

She could barely believe her luck at living in such a beautiful home. Her dream home. But it wasn't the house that caused joy to bubble in her veins and fill her heart to overflowing. It was the knowledge George loved her. Moisture rimmed the edges of her lower lids and she blinked it away. A small smile played on her lips as she accepted that with her new outlook on life, trust had entered her heart, and with that trust came George with a heart wide open. It had always been wide open. It had just taken her a long time to figure that one out.

George walked through the open doors that led out into the wide expanse of garden. He had been grinning since waking, well before the birds had left their nests. He walked up to her, grabbed her waist with his strong, ever so capable hands, and swung her round in a circle before deliberately sliding her down the length of his body until her feet touched the floor.

"Today's the day," he said.

"Today's the day."

Cupcake bounded in, a garland of thornless roses roped around his collar. He jumped up, his large paws landing on both Charlotte and George. "Woof!"

"Exactly," said George. "Woof." He grinned. "Are you ready to get hitched?"

"I'm ready." She kissed him soundly. "All we need are the guests and the celebrant and we're good to go. Sally's bringing the cake she made for us. And Viggo of course."

George nuzzled her neck. "I can't believe she managed to knock through that wall he'd built around himself."

"I know. But she's nowhere near as happy as me. No-one is."

He huffed his amusement. "I wouldn't be so sure. Every time I see her looking at Viggo, I think about a cat who's managed to lick all the cream."

Charlotte laughed. "I happen to know she and Viggo have been experimenting with some of the Madam Delicious recipes."

George erupted into an uncontrollable fit of laughter. "Don't tell me anything else. The only sex life I'm interested in is ours."

There was the sound of feet on the upstairs floorboards and voices calling out to each other as his parents and Myrtle moved about getting ready for the afternoon's celebration. He grinned. "Later, you and I are going to try out some of those recipes ourselves."

"There's no way we're doing the deed anywhere in this house until everyone has gone home. I've booked us into a boutique hotel about twenty minutes' drive from here for tonight We can get down and dirty there. I have cream, I have strawberries and I have you. I need nothing else."

Except perhaps the pitter patter of a baby shortcake. But that dream could wait for now.

There was a wedding to get ready for.

The End

Thank you for taking time to read Tart vs. Shortcake. If you enjoyed it, please consider telling your friends or posting a short review. Reviews help my visibility on Amazon. Word of mouth is an author's best friend and much appreciated.

ALSO BY ROWENA MAY O'SULLIVAN

The Greenwood Witches Series

(magical romance with a dash of humor)

The Silver Rose

The Jade Dragon

The Spell Weaver

The Greenwood Witches Trilogy Bundle (3 books in 1)

An Oaktree Falls Paranormal Romantic Comedy

Footloose & Faerie Free

THE SILVER ROSE

READ CHAPTER ONE NOW

ADEN DRAGUNIS ARRIVED IN Raven's Creek late one Sunday in September in the wake of a southerly squall fresh from the Antarctic. His early arrival sent a flurry of whispers out on the wind and before the sun had set, nearly everyone who was anyone in the small town knew he had arrived and was booked into Room 22 at Raven's Creek's Inn.

Aden wasted no time. He lifted the window latch with the flick of a wrist, pushed it open, and stared out and down the main street into the epicenter of Raven's Creek. Crisp, cool air assailed and grounded him. Focused, he cast a locating spell and found his target within seconds. Magic fairly sparkled down the short lane where the sisters resided. All was as it should be, he acknowledged, so he paused to inspect the quality and luminosity of their skills. A protection spell like no other deserved his grudging appreciation. Closing his eyes, he went inward, connecting with his inner sight before tracing the intricate network of ley lines threading the entire street. With stealth, his magical nature and superior ability helped him evade the security network protecting their homes.

Ah, yes. Magnificent.

Three cottages.

Three witches.

Although Aden's physical body remained stationary at the window, he could see clearly, as if his eyes remained open. He moved on through the town, following the ley lines as they merged and branched out into the neighborhood. This time he searched for others with magic. With senses honed from centuries of practice, he investigated the side streets and alleyways with the speed of a hawk seeking its prey. He went deeper; opening his mind's eye to utilize his ability to soar freely outside his body, he extended his vision into the surrounding countryside. Through Great Kauri Park, past a sentinel eight-hundred-year-old native Kauri tree, then deeper into the countryside where lifestyle blocks blurred one into the other. He hunted for others of his kind until he reached the ocean; the tang of salt from the sea spray dusting windows of homes built precariously close to the sea. Waves crashed and rolled on shores.

Nothing. Not a trace of warlock essence. Anywhere!

His eyes snapped open, and he was back in his dismal hotel room. "Dragons' Blood!" It was going to be a tougher assignment than anticipated. He could not piggyback upon the magic of another warlock in order to hide his own if there were none like him living nearby. Caution was imperative. Living within the circle of the Greenwood witches would entail the strongest shielding spell he could cast. Magic of an intricate blend only few could successfully weave would be essential. Only those who attained immortal status were capable of such skill. One such as he. Aden Dragunis: Warlock, immortal and Dragon of Marylebone Coven.

Unable to stand another second in the close confines of his room, he hooked his ankle-length coat over two fingers, flung it across his shoulder, and headed out into the waning light. The coat flapped like wings behind him, and he felt neither the cold nor the sting of the biting wind swirling debris in his wake as he strode purposefully down the street until he reached the infamous Greenwood Gallery.

It was closed.

A renowned showcase for New Zealand talent, the gallery was owned and operated by Rosa and her two younger sisters. Rosa's work as a silversmith and jeweler was rumored to be as good as his. He huffed and amusement tugged at the corners of his mouth. This he found ludicrous. Witch she may be, but immortal she was not. Taught by the greatest Master Warlock in Witchdom, and with several hundred years to perfect his craft, Aden was confident her work would not be equal to his.

But what he saw next had him unwillingly reassessing his opinion. Squinting against the reflection of the setting sun in the windows, he inspected the protective spell encasing the building. Three layers of color, one for each sister melded into each other, twisted into a complex protection spell like none he'd seen before and yet he knew instinctively to whom each color belonged. All reflections of their innate magical abilities. Vibrant purple for the volatile middle sister Alanna and a radiant azure for the younger, peaceful Beth. Rich magenta for Rosa, his current assignment, haloed by the most brilliant band of gold light, a color only for those whose time has come. Aden sucked in a breath. He did not need to meet the person this magical spell and glorious aura belonged to in order to recognize just how close she was to achieving mastership. What a complete waste it would be if her life were snuffed out by his charges, the small but lethal dragons of Marylebone.

But there was another thread woven into their magic. Something he had never encountered. Something new that both intrigued and aggravated him. He'd thought this assignment an easy one. He was beginning to get an inkling it was anything but. A Maori blessing had been braided into the spell, ensuring the old Kauri gallery remained impenetrable. Even he, one of only a handful powerful enough to meld his magic into the network surrounding the gallery, felt the prickle of warning and resistance as he pushed against it, testing, judging, and finally admiring. He might not have met Rosa yet, but he could not fault the perfection of this magnificent spell. It was masterful in its inception and creation. It was better than any he'd ever created.

Rosa was worthy of the Bells.

They all were.

Ominous and powerful, the encroaching mist blinded Rosa Greenwood as it swirled about her ankles, ensuring she could see nothing. Expectation whispered secrets across her skin. Fear, unexpected and unwanted, curled through her. Her life was forever changed. She knew it as clearly as she breathed. A metallic presence on her tongue caused a tremble of apprehension in her heart. Acid pooled in her mouth, and she licked dry, burning lips.

No. Surely not...

Suppressing a growing unease, she felt blindly ahead with her hands knowing the ornamental pond she habitually sat by to mull over the day's events was close but the cold surface chilled her right through to her soul. Her skin prickled with warning. She circled quickly, certain she was being watched. But how? And by whom? Pressing her palms together, she entwined her fingers, twisting them into white knuckles of anxiousness.

Then she heard them. They tolled, heavy with portent. Echoes reverberated through the vapor, jangling her nerves. No mist could hide what they signified.

"No! It's too soon. I'm not ready!" Her heart beat an erratic staccato against her breastbone. Fear pricked her skin like a thousand sharp needles.

It should have come as no surprise. It came to all wielders of enormous, powerful magic. She should be prepared...but she was not.

It was futile to block her ears with the palms of her hands.

She tried anyway, but the sound resonated within and without, leaving her with no choice but to accept the inevitable.

The Bells of Marylebone tolled for her.

A gust of wind corkscrewed through the branches of the trees in the yard, causing them to sway to a force greater than their own. Leaves danced in spirals of never-ending motion, teasing the ground before soaring off again and taking all traces of mist with them.

The Bells of Marylebone tolled for Rosa Greenwood, mortal witch with too much power and not enough strength to control it on her own.

Rosa's mind churned with the implication such a momentous event brought with it. Her life was forever changed. Her dreams, her hopes and wishes hung in the balance. She had thirty days to bind her magic with a mate—someone with powerful magic or potential. It was the only way she would survive. Either that, or surrender her magic forever. But that would be like surrendering her soul. She wanted to live to see her sisters happily married with children. She dreamed of achieving Mastership, of ascending Marylebone and taking on the mantle of immortality. Her dream to preside at Marylebone Coven, the worldwide ruling body for all witches, was in danger of never being realized.

Failure would bring Witches' Ruin.

She should have been more prepared. She should have taken more notice of her mother's warning before her untimely demise all those years ago. *Remember the bells, Rosa, my love. Remember the bells. The more power a witch has, the more likely they will toll.*

Well, she had power by the bucketful. More than she'd thought. So much it seemed that she now understood why she was experiencing uncontrollable surges of magic at the most inopportune moments. She'd thought it a lack of skill as she worked on more intricate and complicated spells. She blanched, realizing now that those flare-ups had been a precursor to a more dangerous power. One that could hurt her, her family, and everyone else in her small community.

What fool she. Rosa didn't deserve to attain immortal status. She was an unprepared witch.

A foolish, unprepared witch.

To continue reading The Silver Rose

ABOUT THE AUTHOR

When she was young she dreamed of becoming a writer and devoured books and magazines like they were food. Rowena also dreamed of becoming a ballerina, performing in musical theatre, a hairdresser, an adventurer. You get the picture. She was pretty good at day-dreaming.

Despite falling down a manhole while reading Joan of Arc on the way home from school, reading is still her passion.

She loves to write, creating characters she likes to read herself and hopes you loves them too.

To learn more about what's next you in the world of Rowena, you can subscribe to her newsletter on her website or follow her on social media.

See you there.

For more information:
www.rowenamayosullivan.com
rowenamayo@rowenamayosullivan.com

www.ingramcontent.com/pod-product-compliance
Lightning Source LLC
Chambersburg PA
CBHW060907250626
47159CB00008B/2905